The Flaming Rebellion

Kiera A. Reynolds

Contents

Chapter One
Reflection

Ryn

Threy stands in the doorway of the bathing chamber, water dripping down the hard lines of his chest. Licking my lips, I follow the next drop as it pools in the hollow of his throat and overflows. It follows the crease in the middle of his chest and continues over the bulging muscles of his abdomen. The drop disappears in the white towel that hides the bottom of the V leading below his waist.

"Sertran to Ryn."

Blinking, I look up at the dragon staring at me with a knowing smirk. What can I say? It's only been a few days since certain death turned into destiny. The storm and dragon fire that transformed me from a weak human into the strong dragon that's meant to take down a tyrant. It's a lot to take in.

What makes it all worth it is this delicious man standing in front of me, grinning and making sure he twists in ways that draw my eyes. Two can play this game.

"Sorry, I say," stretching my arms into the air and arching my back until I'm sure my hard nipples are visible.

Threy grunts and deflates, which makes me giggle. "You win," he says.

"I know."

Standing, I walk over and run my hands through his long blond hair. He hums with pleasure. As much as I'd like to make other sounds issue forth from his hard chest, I know that's not possible. I braid his hair for him, assuming no one would care that my scent is here. Threy often needs help to be presentable.

This distance makes me want to groan. I thought that once we figured out how to keep me from being murdered for the time we share in the sheets—and on his desk, in the steaming pool, the couch, etc.—that we wouldn't need to hide. If anything, things are so much more complicated now that my true form has been revealed.

My fingers long to run down his spine and make him squirm. How we came to this, I'll never know. I lost the family I knew to be enslaved in the stables and gifted to Ildracan. The heir to the clan ripped me from the comfort of horses to gift me to his younger brother in a cruel scheme to force him to submit. We fought our attraction for so long, only giving into it when things became too heated.

I reveled in that love. For once, life was more than darkness. We kept our secret for a while, but in the end, we made too many mistakes. I was taken to make room for the dragon female Threy's parents wanted him to mate with. They underestimated their third son. He fought with everything he had to save me. It was my own destiny that kept me from burning to death when it was all said and done.

I've yet to fully accept the fact that I'm a dragon. It leaves me with so many questions. Who were my real parents? All I know is that one was a drake and one was a fairy dragon. Why did they hide me with humans? Why did those humans take me in as one of their own, putting their real daughter in danger? What do I do now?

Warm hands engulf mine. "Ryn?"

I refocus my vision to see Threy standing as close as possible without saturating either of us in the other's scent. "I hate this. How do I go back to being your servant after everything that's happened?"

Threy raises a hand but stops before he can cup my cheek. "I'm so sorry. I wish there was another way. We have more time now."

"Do we? What if your parents decide to tell the king? Your mother would give me up in a heartbeat to get Iara back."

He sighs and walks into his room for a pair of pants. When he returns, he says, "She won't disobey Father's wishes."

"It's not that easy. Iara is held hostage because I exist and the king doesn't know. I truly think you are underestimating a mother's love. Delto knows the truth about our feelings. You know he won't let it go that easily. He tore us apart once. He's the heir. What if your father tells him?"

The thought of the heir to the Ildracan clan makes me shiver. Those cold blue eyes scanning my body from head to toe in the dungeon haunt my dreams. He thought giving me to Threy and him falling in love with me was nothing but a method of control. The vile man used me as a pawn to hurt his brother in the worst way possible.

"We have to hope father won't confide in him. He's not stupid. Delto only knows that you weren't sacrificed. He doesn't know why," Threy says. "Just keep acting like a quiet human."

"I don't smell like a dragon now?"

"You always did."

I furrow my brows. "I did?"

My dragon nods. "Yes. No one knew it because we thought you just smelled odd for a human, and it isn't typical of any type of dragon I've smelled. We saw what we thought you were and what you acted as. Keep your mind on being my servant. No one will know you're a dragon."

I walk over to the couch and plop down. "A powerful dragon meant to take on a cruel king with a powerful artifact but can barely light a candle."

Reaching for the small flame on the table, I run my fingers through it. Once, Delto's women tried to drown me in water hot enough to make me feel as if I'd melt. The heat terrified and burned me. Now, I feel nothing when I touch it. Even Threy is amazed at how easily I can touch fire. He can control it, but it still burns his human form.

"You lit that?" he asks.

Flinching, I nod. Threy can make heat and fire without thought. He can control the magic lamps hanging throughout the room. As a dragon, he spews flames over enemies. I can light a candle without any accuracy. Why does he sound impressed?

"Don't get discouraged," he says, reading my thoughts. "It's a great start. Your dragon was suppressed for a long time. It'll take time to become one with her. Still no idea on your whole name?"

Tears threaten. "No. I don't even know how to go about finding it out. It's not like she talks to me."

Threy kneels down in front of me. I can tell by the look in his green eyes that he wishes to wrap me in his arms. Since he already bathed, he can't. We're to resume our life as normal until things are figured out.

What if figuring it out means we're torn apart again? What if we don't come back together this time?

Losing him scares me worse than being executed by a king who used to own me but never met me. That's not an option for me. Death would be kinder. I can't let him go again.

Threy rubs the back of his neck. "I promise we'll figure this out. I'd go to war against the king for you."

I laugh, but my heart's not in it. "Only I can withstand the Jeweled Dracon. I won't risk you like that."

The dangerous artifact held by the king. That's how he holds his power over the other dragons. A gift from the dragon god himself, it creates a fire so hot that no other dragons can withstand it. Threy explained that his fire can injure another dragon if he puts enough force in it, but it can't destroy one. These flames can burn down any obstacle.

Any obstacle but me.

I can withstand the heat that no others can. Me, the woman who had nightmares about the heat of Delto's bathing chamber pool. It destroyed an entire dragon race full of potent magic, but it can't hurt me. Fairy dragons had the most magic of any dragon clan. The fire ripped through them and destroyed them all. Fairy dragons are no more.

"I will do what it takes to keep you safe, in case you haven't noticed that yet," Threy says.

This time, my laugh is true. "You showed that quite well, and that's what scares me."

"I would do it all over again if I needed to."

There's no doubt in my mind that's true. Hunter jumps onto my lap for a scratch. Even as a dragon, my orange cat trusts me. Threy has only recently become tolerable to him. He told me about the guilt trip

Hunter laid on him to come find me. An amusing tale of sentient cats that makes me laugh.

It was right before Delto...

No, I won't think about that. Us falling in love and being torn apart was all part of his evil plan. "How are you going to be able to face him after what he did?"

I don't have to say his name for Threy to understand. He grimaces and stands. "It's going to be hard. I tried to kill him. We both know how that ended. I'll do it for you though. Anything to keep your secret safe."

My secret. Such a small word for a hidden dragon of prophecy. It feels inadequate. Sighing, I look out the window. "Guess I better clean you off of me."

Threy nods and walks away. His fists clench and unclench. I can't blame him; I wouldn't want to face everyone after what happened. They don't know what truly happened, but they do know something did. Threy hurt others to get to me. Those men won't be happy with him.

I walk into the bathing chamber and strip. The hot water caresses my soft skin. Curious, I try to focus on my inner heat. Threy can do it, so I should be able to as well. Taking a deep breath, I keep my hands in the water. I imagine my inner heat flowing down my arms and into the pool. Nothing happens.

With a loud growl, I slam my fist into the yielding surface of the pool over and over until my frustration cools. What kind of red dragon can't make heat? How can I defeat a king when I can't even warm an already hot bath?

What's my name?

Silence greets me. I can't use my magic. I don't know my dragon name. It's not safe for me to shift, even if I knew how. Can I really call myself a dragon? This is ridiculous. Maybe we dreamed everything. I wish that was true.

Once clean, I stand and throw on a robe. My room isn't used often, so it's beginning to feel a little stale. With a few grunts, I open the window by my bed. Hunter jumps on the table with my mirror as I settle down to run my brush through my long red hair. Too annoyed for any further effort, I leave it down and get dressed.

When I exit, Threy is strapping on his sword. His strong back faces me. Every time his arms move to position and tie, the muscles flex. I bite my bottom lip, not hard enough to damage the soft skin. His ass flexes and tenses with each movement. I could watch this all day. Too bad our voluntary exile from public ends today.

"Ready?" Threy asks.

Taking a deep breath, I nod. That's a lie. I'm not at all ready. Threy has to face those he fought in his attempt to save me from being sacrificed to Drakyth. I need to look like a properly disciplined servant once accused of stealing. Word was supposed to be put out that it was false accusations that led to that, but how many will believe it? I hope these few days in solitude helped more than hindered the reduction of the rumors.

Threy looks at me without moving. I scrunch my brows with thought. What is he waiting for? Oh, yeah. I forgot. Servant. I'm the servant. These last couple of days have spoiled me.

Walking forward, I open the door and let my master through. Dragons serving dragons. This'll be interesting. No, I can't think like that. I'm a human. Nothing more than a weak, submissive human. This will definitely be interesting.

Chapter Two
Retribution

THREY

Walking through the hall is difficult. All eyes turn our way, and so does the whispered conversation that can't escape the enhanced hearing of a dragon. I smell the slight scent of uncertainty and annoyance before Ryn covers it back up. It's hard for her to learn how to control her emotions after not having control for so long. We can only hope they don't get her into trouble.

Not that I blame her. If I can hear the questions and accusations, so can she. Her dragon is newly awakened, but she has all the abilities except the emotional and magical control. Oh, and the freedom to shift and learn who her dragon is. There's no way she can feel whole this way. How can I help her?

"She stole from Lady Iara."

"No, that's not right. I heard it was from the lord and lady themselves."

"They say she was falsely accused."

"Please. Dragons don't make that kind of mistake. I wonder if she has some bad gossip and used it for them to let her live."

By the time we get past that group, I can almost feel the tension flowing from Ryn. I sidestep from the main hall and into the garden. As usual, the beauty and colors are enough to calm some of her wayward anger. I don't miss the fact that the closest magic lantern blares brightly before returning to normal.

I'm thankful the garden is empty. "Breathe, Ryn."

"I can't help it."

"I know it's difficult, but they don't know the truth; they *can't* know the truth."

"But I am not a thief. I'm paying for your parents' unwillingness to admit they were executing me because you fell in love with me. It's not fair, and I hate them for putting me in this situation."

Looking at the bright blue sky, I take a deep breath. "Me too."

That makes her giggle, easing my own feelings of guilt for my part in what's happening. My love is the fated red dragon, who is meant to save us all from the evil tyrant that has his claws around our necks. The thought that Ryn has such a dangerous destiny stops my heart when I think about it. He won't go down easily, fighting with claw and fang. What if defeating him kills her?

And my parents... The thought that they attempted to kill her makes my blood boil. I now know how little my happiness means to my family. It's all about what use I can be to them; position, alliances, reputation. If I'm not useful, I'm expendable. Now, I don't just love the wrong woman; I love the dragon that will set the eyes of King Darac down on us. Those claws will tighten fast if he finds out we're hiding his destruction.

"Threy?"

Blinking, I turn to look at the woman I love but can't touch out in public. Even the slightest touch makes the next more irresistible. It's not worth the risk. What I wouldn't do to be able to follow the mating ritual and declare her as mine. Ever since the time we spent together when we returned, I feel so connected to her. Even without her scent, I'd be able to find her in a crowded room. What would it be like to have the whole connection with her?

"Are you alright?" Ryn asks, reaching for me but stopping before she can initiate anything intimate.

Why does life have to be so cruel? I'm finally given the love I crave, risk my life and station to keep her in my life, and I have to keep her in a box. Ryn's true self must remain out of sight. Maybe we don't have to follow the prophecy. I want her to be safe.

"Threy, talk to me."

I shake myself from my thoughts and look at the woman watching me with worried gray eyes. Longing to take her into my arms is overwhelming. She needs comfort. I hate this.

"I'm fine," I say. "I just want to stay in my room longer to keep you all to myself."

Her eyes turn watery. "I'd love that, but you know we can't. In fact, aren't we going to be late?"

With a start, I realize I'm forgetting the need to get to the training grounds. Something about this woman is the biggest distraction I've ever come across. Hurrying, I walk from the garden and rush through the halls, Ryn keeping pace behind me. This is my first day back to training, so I can't be late.

Outside, warm air blasts me in the face with a forceful gust. The desire to take flight makes my muscles ache. Threysoryth hasn't been able to soar since the rescue of Ryn. He wants freedom. I wish I could fly through the clouds with my red dragon at my side. With a promise to my scaled half, I turn and almost run for the training area.

My uncle waits with his arms crossed over his broad chest. He watches me with cold eyes, unlike the warm ones with our previous sessions. A few of the men in the group readying for practice glance at me. I recognize the two I knocked out in the dungeon by their glares. Other angry stares make me wonder which ones were involved in my sky battle.

"General," I mutter.

He lifts a corner of his lip to reveal a sharp fang, showing me he's angry enough that his dragon is right under his skin. One quick glance looks behind me to see Ryn, and they darken. My scales ruffle, ready to defend her if he tries anything. Nothing that happened is on her. If I have to fight the general again to prove that point, I will.

A wooden sword flies my way. I catch it while Ryn gasps in shock behind me. My uncle steps to the side and signals for me to enter the training circle. Looks like it's swords today. I hand my real one to my servant and step inside.

I stop by the general when I notice his eyes are still focused on her. "Touch her, and I won't hesitate to do worse."

"She's safe from me because of my brother's orders. I don't follow yours, boy. You tricked me, and I will see that you pay for that in the training ring today. I suggest you don't push me."

His tone stiffens my muscles. "I don't care what my father says. Do not harm her."

"She is the downfall of our family. Hiding her is a mistake. She's safe because your father ordered it... for now."

Threysoryth threatens to come forth. Neither of us will let anyone hurt Ryn. It takes everything I have to hold him inside because I can't let him out in violence. Maybe after practice I can drop Ryn off at the room and go for a fly. At this point, I don't trust anyone around her. Only those of us that were there that night know who she is. The current conversation is low enough for just us to hear.

I send one last warning look at my uncle before entering the practice area with my wooden sword. The fact I'm paired with the two heads I knocked against the wall doesn't shock me in the least. He meant what he said; he's going to make me pay for beating him on the cliff that night.

My opponents don't wait. They split to keep on either side of me, making it difficult for me to watch them both. At least they're trained well enough to understand that two against one is an advantage to be utilized. They move together.

I catch one practice sword on my own and duck beneath the other. I'm thankful for the hours I've been drilled in the use of a weapon. We don't need them often, but we need to be equipped for any threat in an area where we don't have the room to shift. These two will have practiced just as much. My only advantage is my birth and the strength it brings me.

Might be the only thing I'll be grateful to my parents for.

The next block jars my wrist because I catch both swords at the same time. I counter, catching one on the ribs while the other jumps back. My uncle swears at the one hit about watching a stronger opponent better. After a few wheezing breaths, he's back on me. Both hit me with furious attacks that I need to parry and dodge, unable to strike in return.

It's not until a foot trips me that I realize how close I am to the edge of the training area. My stumble leaves an opening that results in a wack to my knee. I yell and hop, turning to keep my attackers in sight. From the corner of my eyes, I notice both Ryn's hand over her mouth and a man smirking to the side. He probably tripped me on purpose.

While I don't regret what I did to save Ryn, I know I'll need to earn regard all over again. I've made some of my future men unhappy with me. Maybe letting them beat on me like this is a good way to cool their anger. Not that I'm not going to fight back.

My sword hits one in the head. That one is really not going to like me with all the cracks to the skull I'm giving him. The other makes contact with my shoulder hard enough to draw blood. Since the one is still dazed, I focus my attacks on the other. By the time I sweep his legs out from under him, I'm turning quickly to avoid my own knock to the skull.

As the training comes to a close, I find myself panting and covered in bruises with spots of blood. I'm going to feel that until Threysoryth heals me. Ryn is careful to keep her expression calm, but I can still see the lines around her eyes that speak of concern. I make sure not to draw attention to her by pretending to look past her. As soon as the warriors are away, I plop down onto the dirt.

"That was harsh," Ryn says quiet enough to not be heard by only me.

"It's payback. Even the lord's son isn't immune to anger at being attacked. This is a good way to heal that rift."

"They beat the crap out of you."

"It's how it is."

She lets out a deep breath. "Stupid, arrogant dragons."

"Watch what you call yourself."

Her gray-eyed glare almost makes me laugh, but I have to avoid showing that kind of emotion right now. Anything that might say that there's more to us than master and servant needs to be done behind closed doors. All we need are rumors that give my parents a reason to send news to the king. To keep her safe, I have to keep my distance in public.

I stand and get ready to tell Ryn I need to take a fly. A messenger runs up to stop me from doing so. "My lord, your father wishes to speak to you now."

Holding back my frustrated growl, I push the dragon within me down. His frustration at not getting airtime is strong, but my father hates to be kept waiting. For now, I need to play the loyal third son.

Ryn watches me stand with a wince. The pain will recede as Threysoryth heals me. The bruises will be yellow by the time the meeting is over and gone by tonight. Scratches are already bleeding less. I'll be fine in no time.

I try to ignore my limp as I walk into the castle. Dragons pop their heads out of large doors to startle human servants. Others in human form call out orders and yell at slaves making mistakes. Once, this all seemed normal to me. Now, I cringe inside, remembering that Ryn used to put up with this all her life. She's right.

Stupid, arrogant dragons.

As I reach for the doorknob, a voice makes me bite my tongue. "Brother! Little Rabbit!"

Chapter Three
Perfect

RYN

I cringe at the sound of the voice hailing us, careful to keep my head down. Goosebumps litter my flesh, and my heart skips a beat. I take deep, calming breaths. For some reason, despite my right to anger, I still feel fear around Delto.

He orchestrated my near death to prove a point to Threy and lord his power over him. He's hurt the man I love many times over. I should feel rage and anger. I should be imagining myself ripping his throat out. Instead, I picture his dragon devouring my human body. Now that the imminent danger is passed, my defiance is gone. I'm once again the scared little slave girl under the gaze of a predator.

I hate him with every fiber of my being.

Threy pushes me behind him with a growl. I feel his claws grow out on my arm, but he's as careful as possible not to pierce skin. Not that I can't heal quicker now. It shows his love and care for me, which is what I need right now. I'm sure my fear is impossible to miss with their strong sense of smell.

It's amazing how every strong emotion has a scent of its own. Threy's anger smells hot. Delto's arrogance smells like rotten meat. I wonder what fear smells like. Delto seems to enjoy it. I wish his mate was better at keeping his attention. Although, she'd probably approve of his treatment of us. Two dragons carved from the same block of stone.

"Now, brother, is that any way to treat your future lord? Best keep your temper in check," Delto's voice says, raising bile.

"Delto, enough." So focused on Delto, I didn't realize their mother was with them. What is it about that man that ties me in trembling knots like this?

"Mother, he needs to learn his place."

"I'm pretty sure Rakurn is awaiting your presence in the library."

Delto groans. "Mother, I don't wish to spend my afternoon on history."

"Well, you should have paid better attention in lessons, instead of wasting your brother's time like this."

He scoffs. "My time is loads more important than the hours he spends poring over books."

"Now, or I'll mention this insolence to your father."

The heir grumbles but does as commanded. I'm amazed that Lady Belra is able to control the arrogant dragon as she can. If it wasn't for the fact I hate her so much, I'd be impressed. As it is, I glance around to see no one close and level a scowl at her. Her rotten treatment and near frying of me will not be forgotten. Since she is one of the three that know of my true identity, I don't need to hide behind the mask of a slave for her.

"If you have nothing of importance to speak with me about, Mother," Threy says with a cool voice, "Father is expecting me."

She's careful to avoid even glancing at me, as if to say I am nothing worth paying attention to. "I am well aware. Your servant will need to remain out here of course."

"I'm not stupid," he growls.

"I didn't say you were, third son. You may hate me for the part I played now, but you'll understand when you have children of your own."

I glance up to see him pull his lip up to bare a fang. "I will never use my children as nothing more than game pieces."

She laughs. "You're still young. You'll understand."

With a snarl, Threy opens the door and enters his meeting with his father. Even with him gone, I don't look away from her hard blue eyes. I wonder if there's any love for her children in there. I think I saw a spark of it when Iara was escorted to the capital. Lady Belra tries to walk around me.

"He's never going to understand your cruelty," I say, unable to keep my mouth shut.

Her blonde hair whirls as she turns. "You little tramp. Do you have any idea what you have done to this family?"

"I didn't do a thing. It was all you and Archon."

"That's Lord Archon to you. I don't care how important you think you are because you are nothing. Threy will come to his senses and toss you aside."

"How has that hope worked out for you in the past?"

Belra crosses her arms over her chest. If anything, the look in her eyes turns even colder, enough to freeze the water in the sun on a hot day. Too bad for her, I'm made of fire that can't be frozen. I return her gaze, glare for glare.

My verbal sparring partner scoffs. "If you think I'm going to allow you to get my only daughter killed, you have another thing coming. Your time will come, and I'll laugh as the execution ends your wretched life. Mark my words; your time is limited."

When she walks past me, she knocks my shoulder. Unwilling to show weakness, I don't rub the instant throb like my hand twitches to do. While her exit leaves me annoyed, her words chill me to the bone. Will my arch enemy do something stupid to get me killed? If anyone can, it's her. She has the power to make my life more miserable than it has ever been, which is saying a lot.

The door swings inward, and I jump. Threy looks angry, but his eyes soften when he sees my fright. He sniffs. "Is everything alright?"

Am I scared enough to let her words affect me? My trembling hands tell me yes. I open my mouth, but I'm not sure how to bring it out here in the open. Threy notices my predicament, shakes his head, mutters something about not flying now, and leads me to his room.

On the other side of our privacy barrier, he drops his sword on the table and turns to me. "What's wrong? If it's Delto, I give you my word that he won't hurt you."

"Your mother is the one worrying me at the moment. She seems sure I'm going to be executed. How can she?"

He lets out a deep breath. "Don't worry about her. Father still hasn't made a decision. He called me in to ask how my first training session went since the attempted sacrifice. You're safe."

"Would he tell you if I wasn't?"

Threy opens his mouth to speak but closes it without a word. We both know his parents know he'd do whatever he had to if my life was on the line. If something were to happen, there would be no warning.

"As much as I want to say he wouldn't do that," Threy says with a sigh, "I don't trust my parents anymore. I have no idea of the deception they're capable of. I do know that he hasn't sent any word to the king. My father likes to think things of this magnitude through before acting. He specifically told me he hasn't made a decision yet. If he was lying, he wouldn't have brought it up."

I take a deep breath and look away. Why don't I feel reassured? After all, Threy knows his family better than I do. Then again, he was sure Iara wouldn't tell her parents that he loves me, but she did. We all know where that got us.

You think I'd be happy that my secret identity being hidden got her taken by the enemy, but I don't. At the time, she thought she was doing the best thing for Threy. She didn't know who I really am. None of us did.

Threy mutters about asking for food to be delivered to us and walks to the door to flag down a human. Pushing my worries down, I walk over to the table and run my fingers over the hilt of his sword. It's a little big for my hands, but I manage to wrap my fingers around it and pull it from its scabbard. It shines in the magic globes lighting the space.

The man I love walks over to me. He steps behind me, bringing his hands around my front. Taking my other hand in his, Threy places it on the hilt, then moves both until positioned properly. The feeling of his hard muscles against my back dries my mouth out. I inhale deep. That only fills my nose with his delicious scent.

As he makes a few cutting motions with the blade, his flexing muscles cause warmth to grow within me. My nipples tingle as desire courses through me. That's when I smell the scent of his arousal. It's enough to undo me.

Letting the sword fall onto the carpet, I turn in his arms. Threy pulls me tight, leaning down to devour my mouth with his. I moan and grab his hair to squish his lips tighter on mine. Strong fingers slip under my shirt, and I gasp as they glide up. His thumbs run along the underside of my breast, bringing an ache to the pebbled nipples begging for his attention.

My shirt comes off under practiced hands. His fingers squeeze my breasts while I trace lines over his chest with mine. When he lowers his mouth to encircle one perky nipple, I whimper and feel heat pool between my legs. Can this man feel any better than this? As if I don't know the answer to that.

Threy lets his tongue roam back up until he's nibbling at my throat. Reaching down, I undo the laces of his leather pants. He shimmies his way out of them while doing the same with mine. Calloused hands run down my back until they cup my ass and give it a squeeze. I groan.

Spying the couch behind him, I grin and jump to throw my legs around his waist. The sudden weight makes him stumble backward until the piece of furniture hits his calves and makes him fall back. Before I know it, he's sitting on the couch and moving his hot mouth back to my neck while pinching my hard nipples.

Throwing my head back to give him better access to my neck, I reach down and grasp his hard shaft in both hands. He growls into my neck, the sound sending pleasurable shivers down over my entire body. I growl in return, letting the dragon in me surface. I may not know the beast inside of me, but she loves whenever we do this.

I lift up and settle his tip at my entrance before letting myself slide down his length. Fangs scrape over my throat as hands squeeze my breasts until it almost hurts. The little pain there is only makes me moan. He fills me as if meant to be mine. This man is perfect.

Lifting my hips, I ride my copper dragon, feeling my own fangs poking because of the sensation of him sliding in and out of me. Our mouths meet in a tangle of tongue and pants for air. I can taste his breath, and I long for more. Up and down, I move with increasing speed while the ache builds and heat rises. Threy grips my back, giving me the feel of his claws on my skin.

This man is worth all the pain and fear I've had in my life. The feel of him. The taste of him. His smell. It's all enough to chase away the darkest of my thoughts. Sure, getting here was hard, but this is worth more than I can ever say.

The ache becomes too much, and my body tenses and shudders. Threy growls as my release triggers his. His eyes squeeze shut with the euphoria as he spurts hot liquid inside of me. I once worried about making little dragons because I now know I'm one, but he told me that the female dragon chooses when to conceive. So, instead of worrying, I let any concern fly away with the pleasure of him finishing inside. It fills me with warmth, hot like the fire that comes from a dragon's belly.

Once spent, I lay my head in the crook of his neck and take deep breaths. Threy remains silent, running his fingers up and down my back. Both of us keep words down and revel in the feeling of being together this way. This is perfect. The past and future don't exist when we're one like this. I'd do it all again to end up here. Wars mean nothing. Tyrant kings are so far away. I don't want to destroy King Darac.

This is what I want, and I'm not willing to give it up.

Chapter Four
Where I Belong

RYN

I brush my wet hair back behind my ear before I flip the page. Threy washes in the bath now. Any time we need to bathe this late, we usually do it together. We didn't tonight after the mess we made. I washed up first, then returned the spilled tray back to the kitchen. Now, I enjoy one of the dirty books I've found myself addicted to. Dragons have such sick minds, and I'm finding that I enjoy this part of my new species.

As I read about the characters tasting each other behind the royal assembly curtains, I find my attention straining for the closed door that hides Threy's naked body from my eyes. Neither of us are planning on being out in public for the rest of the night, so it wouldn't hurt if I joined him. A knock at the door interrupts my contemplation of surprising Threy with a little fun in the bath. With a sigh, I stand and make my way to the door, wondering who would be knocking at this hour. Most dragons and humans should be in bed for the night.

A messenger waits on the other side of the door. "Lord Threy is requested behind the keep. Some of the horses broke free, and Lord Archon wants to make sure it's not the actions of rebels."

"I will tell him. He will be there shortly."

He nods and trots further down the hall, probably to wake Threy's brothers. When I turn, my copper dragon is exiting the bathing chamber with a question in his green eyes. My gaze travels across his naked chest, disappointed to find a towel around his waist.

I clear my throat. "I guess there's a disturbance behind the keep. Your illustrious father requests your presence."

Threy groans. "Alright. I'll throw pants on and head out. Stay in and finish your reading because one of us might as well be comfortable. Besides, I could smell you through the door. I'd like you to continue getting ideas."

I laugh as he walks for the door and exits. Just as I'm settled in, another knock sounds. Grunting with frustration, I stand at the further interruption. Can't a girl read a dirty novel in peace? I want to be ready for Threy when he returns.

At the door, I find Elda with a tray. My brows scrunch together. "We didn't ask for anything."

"You didn't?"

"No, Elda. Why are you delivering anyway?"

The kind woman in charge of the kitchen grunts. "Everyone else is already in bed, and I don't want to wake them for this. There's a note that goes with it. Can I bring this in, so I can sit it down and double check?"

"Of course."

When I step away from the door, she rushes in with thanks. As soon as the tray is down on the table, she looks around the room, including peeking into the master bedroom. My jaw drops to the floor at the lack of decorum from this experienced servant. Nothing in her actions is appropriate.

"Is there something else, Elda?"

"Is Lord Threy in here?"

"No, he was called away to help with horses. Why?"

Some of the tension falls from her shoulders, bringing my attention to the fact that she was tense to begin with. "Good. It worked."

Alarms go off in my head. "What did? What did you do? Elda, please."

"I don't want to scare you, but there's no help for it. I know who you are."

I force a laugh, but even to my own ears, it sounds fake. "Of course you do. You were the first person that was nice to me after Delto dragged me from the stables and gifted me to Lord Threy."

Her warm eyes find me, telling me she doesn't believe my deflection. I swallow and look away to hide my discomfort. It's not like I haven't overly displayed it already. What does she know? How can I fix this? Maybe she wants a bribe.

Elda decides to put me out of my misery. "I know you're the dragon of prophecy, Ryn. Please stop acting like I'm stupid."

Her voice turns cold. I stutter a little before my tongue works properly. "I don't know what you're talking about. Are you sure you're alright?"

That doesn't sound the least bit convincing. I bite my tongue to keep from making it worse. No one can know. If the king finds out... No, I can't let him find out, but how do I stop her? There's no way I'm going to hurt the first person to show me kindness in this keep. Not even my fellow humans did when they almost drowned me in scalding water.

Don't make me hurt you.

"I suspected from the beginning," she says. "There were rumors amongst the rebels."

I gasp. "I thought you weren't a rebel."

"I'm not. I'm a sympathizer who feeds information to them as needed."

"There's a difference?"

"There is. I'm not actively attacking the dragons. The more I got to know you, the more I was sure of it. Then when they took you for execution and brought you back alive, I knew I was right."

I swallow. "I wasn't killed because I was proven innocent."

Elda laughs. "Of the false charges? Ryn, I know you well enough to know that no one could even suspect you of thieving. Stop stalling. We have little time."

"Little time for what?"

The kitchen manager rushes to the bathing chamber to return and throw a robe at me. "Put this on. You can't go out in your nightgown."

"I can't go out at all," I reply, looking at the robe in my hands.

"There is no time for this!"

"For what?!"

Confusion and fear are eclipsed by the anger growing in me. Why can't she just speak plainly, so I know what actions need to be taken? When I notice her looking at my fingers, I retract my claws. Well, there's no bluffing my way out of this now.

Not like you were doing a good job to begin with.

I push the annoyed thought away. Elda growls. "Lady Belra sent a message to the king without Lord Archon knowing. The rebels intercepted the reply. She's exchanging you for the return of her daughter. I swear that's the only child she truly loves."

"Threy said she wouldn't go against her mate's wishes. The lord rules the keep."

"A mother's love is a difficult thing to predict. Did you know that dragon females choose when to conceive? Good. The Ildracan lord didn't want more children after Threy because he felt three sons were enough. She did it anyway and hasn't had another since. It looks like she really wanted a daughter. Her sons never enjoyed the same attention Iara did, doted on at every turn. She went against his wishes to have the daughter. You can bet she'll do it again to keep that same daughter alive, which is why we have to leave."

I want to argue, but her words ring true in my ears. Lady Belra's words today come back to my mind, and I gasp at the truth they bring home. She was expecting me to be gone soon because she put it into motion. All her threats and disgust point to that.

My arms are in the robe before I can say, "But what about Threy? I have to talk to him."

"There is no time, and we can't trust the dragons."

"I'm a dragon, Elda."

"Not like them. We can't trust him."

"Threy fought against his parents to save my life. I need to at least leave a note to say goodbye."

Elda grabs my hand when I turn to do so. "Now! The distraction won't hold for long. We need to get you out of the city. I will talk to him if it makes you move faster."

Indecision wars within me. I can't leave the man I love like this. Thoughts of what the king will do to me fights against the desire to say goodbye. In the end, I decide that me alive will hurt him less than risking my death to say goodbye. Tears sting my eyes, but I follow the woman out of the room into the unknown.

The halls are almost completely empty as we rush through them. A few humans on late errands glance at us but look down quickly. I'm not sure if they know what's going on, don't care, or just don't want to be seen. Not being seen is the best way for a human to remain alive in a dragon's world. I should know because I used to be one of them, and being seen is what put me in Threy's hands—in care of Delto's cruelty.

She takes me out of a side exit, never letting my hand free from her tight grip. Cool night air blasts my face, bringing the scent of dirt and grass with it. My enhanced hearing picks up the sounds of hooves on the opposite side of the keep, along with dying shouts of annoyance. Elda stops and flattens against the stone, so I follow her action.

A couple of dragons talk as they walk past our hiding place. The smell of fire and smoke is enough to identify what they are. As much as my identity turns my life upside down, I must say my super senses are useful. As soon as the two men are past us, we move again.

We duck around a few buildings and move toward the wall. I look at her, confused as to why we aren't heading out the gates. Are we going to climb the wall? That might be difficult in nothing but a nightgown and a robe. When Elda drops to her knees and moves a large stone, I realize I'm going under, not over.

Beneath the wall is a hole dug just big enough for one person. I look up, remembering how thick this wall is. A tiny tunnel is not somewhere I want to be climbing through, particularly with tons of stone over top of me. She can't be serious.

"Go, Ryn."

Blinking, I shake my head and take a step back. "I can't crawl through that."

"You must. It's safe. Your escort already crawled through it while we smuggled the horses out. There's no time. I need to retrieve the tray and be back in the kitchen before anyone suspects anything. Please, go."

I don't want to get her in trouble. I look back, wondering if I can just sneak back in, tell Threy, and come up with another idea. Anything has to be better than crawling through a dark hole under crushing rock.

"Ryn!"

Groaning, I kneel and crawl into the hole. When the stone covers the entrance, I find myself in pitch blackness that makes my heart race. There's no going back now, so I feel ahead and use my elbows and knees to push myself through the tunnel while trying to ignore the fact the heavy wall is right above me. Breathing becomes more labored the further I go, and I worry I'm going to be trapped in here until I slowly run out of air or starve to death.

By the time I feel like giving up, the scent of fresh air penetrates the smell of disturbed soil. My efforts pick up, hurrying to get me out of this black hole. When my hands feel the cool breeze, it takes everything I have not to yell in triumph. That would certainly give me away, so I settle for a few deep gasps to fill my lungs with fresh air. I take a few moments to calm my racing heart and stabilize my breathing.

Calmer, I brace my palms against the dewy grass and push. Being free fills me with elation, and I roll over to look up at the night sky. After a few more deep breaths, I stand and look at the hole I climbed out of, shocked that I fit through. I find another large rock and lift it to hide the tunnel. Two horses wait on the other side of the bushes I find myself in, so I cautiously step forward.

My mouth drops open when I recognize the form perched on top of one of the horses. "Atan?"

"About time, Ryn."

"What are you doing here?"

"Elda stopped by today and asked if I'd be willing to help you. She told me everything, and there's no way I'm going to let some stuffy dragon king execute my best friend. Get on Beland. We have limited time."

The scar on the horse's flanks tells me that it is indeed Beland. The animal neighs as if happy to see me. "Where are we going?"

"Elda gave me directions to the nearest rebel base and a note to get us in if you're not recognized. Hurry before the distraction wears down."

Sighing, I place my foot in Beland's stirrup. I take one last glance in the direction I know Threy is. It's strange that I can feel him as I do. He told me he thinks it's part of the mating connection; it would get stronger with the ritual. That's if we'll ever be allowed to do it.

My heart aches with the need to speak with him, but I know I can't go back now. Ever since I lost my family to a jealous dragon, I feel like I never found a new home. Until I found Threy. Threy is my home, one I'm leaving for supposed safety. I didn't want to leave him to fight a tyrant, but destiny is forcing my hand.

It seems my wishes don't matter. Fate will do with me what it wants to. I can only hope I'll find my way back into his arms. It's where I belong.

Chapter Five
Homecoming

RYN

I feel overwhelming joy with each step Beland takes beneath me. I'm not sure where the emotion comes from because I don't have any reason to feel it. Not even my favorite horse and stable friend can dull the pain of the distance we are putting between me and Threy. How is he going to take my absence? Will he hate me for leaving? I know I hate myself.

My lower lip bleeds with the newest bite. I've done great at not biting it. Threy loves my lips, so I try to keep them in perfect condition. What does it matter now? Tears threaten, but I angrily blink them away.

Beland looks back at me, and I feel the strange joy lessen. I stare at the horse through blurry, moisture-filled eyes, wondering what those big brown pools are telling me. He looks saddened by something, but I can't figure out why. Beland is free from the cruel dragons that left him scarred from the terrible hunting 'accident.'

I will only give this horse peace from here on out—as much as I can. Looking up at the dark sky, I trust Beland to keep pace with Atan while I gaze at the bright stars above. The night sky is even more beautiful than the daytime blue. What would it be like to soar beneath those stars? I snort lightly. What would it be like to soar at all? I've never had the chance to use my wings. A red dragon is something that needs to be hidden from the view of all the dangerous people out here.

Atan casts a glance my way. The concern in his eyes makes me throw a fake smile at him. Does he know what I am? Atan has never tried to hide his hatred of our overlords. Will he hate me on principle now? They wouldn't have him escort me if he didn't know, right?

He looks back in front of him, and I make my lip bleed more. Even with the ravages of my pink skin, I would give anything for Threy to see them. I'll take any scolding if it would give me his presence back. How does one survive without half of their heart?

Chirping bugs fill the night air and break the silence. Wind picks up, swaying the long grasses of Ildracan hard enough to sound like the crashing waves of the ocean. I close my eyes to the memories of the night I saw the ocean, the night Threy's parents almost sacrificed me to their god, Drakyth. Well, I guess he's my god too now, or has always been. I don't know if I'll ever get used to being someone different, someone who feels foreign and uncomfortable in her own skin.

The next gust brings the scent of bison, and I turn my face into it. Threy's favorite meat has always been buffalo, both in human and dragon form. His copper-colored dragon could take out an adult without any problems whatsoever. Can I do that? I never went on a hunt before, but I'm a predator now.

I suck the metallic flavor from my lip and find it's already healing. Well, there's that at least. Faster healing has to mean something, doesn't it? Along with my improved night vision, enhanced sense of smell and sight, and newfound strength and speed. I've always been faster and stronger than the other humans I worked with. That's nothing compared to now.

Still, all this newfound strength means nothing without the man who I want at my side. I sigh. Beland sways to the side with his next concerned look in my direction. All the strange joy is gone from me. My emotions no longer conflict.

Atan looks at me once again. "Is everything alright?"

I give him a dark chuckle and look up at the dark sky again. "You mean besides fleeing in the dark from the man I love?"

Atan remains silent, so I look at him. He's facing forward with his jaw set tight. My eyes narrow as I wonder why he suddenly seems upset. My friend that I tried to keep at arm's length was happy to see me not long ago. What changed?

I shake my head. "How long have you been a rebel?"

"Since tonight."

My mouth opens and closes a few times before I can speak. "Why?"

"Well, I've never known how to become one, let alone how to escape those vicious beasts until Elda showed up. As I already said, I'd jump without notice if it means helping you."

"Do you know who I am?"

His brown eyes find mine before examining the landscape again. "I do. Who would have thought it? Did you know you were a dragon?"

I laugh, keeping it soft to keep it from carrying. "No. I was expecting to die in the flames. It felt like it too, but that heat was coming from my inner self it seems. I grew up with humans and had no reason to doubt I was one of them."

"No hints at all."

Shaking my head, I take a deep, shaky breath. "Only that my hair was a different color than the rest of my human family. They always treated me like one of their own. No one ever questioned it. I'm not sure how they managed it."

We continue on in silence, both taking in what we've learned just now. Atan knows I'm a dragon and still wants to help me, so he doesn't hate me. That's a relief. I don't think I could handle being hated by my escort right now. Not with how raw I feel.

The shadowy grass stretches on forever. Nothing breaks the scenery but the occasional stack of boulders or small groups of trees. After a while continuing in this landscape, I can't hold back my curiosity. "Where are we going?"

"Elda gave me directions to a manned rebel base. She says we'll move once we get you there to keep anyone from finding us. The objective is to get you as far away from any settlements as possible and train you."

"Train me?"

Atan shrugs. "I'm not sure. Elda wouldn't elaborate. If you want to help, we need a group of boulders surrounded by a ring of trees."

Nodding, I keep my eyes out for anything strange like that. "Did she say how far?"

"Nope. She told me to keep that bright star in front of us, and we'll find it."

My eyes look up to see one star standing out from the others. We are indeed following it. I trust Elda, even though I've learned that she was never who I thought she was to begin with. That may not be true. I saw her as a kind human who only wanted to help. That seems to be her true nature, so it's not fair of me to think otherwise. This night has me questioning everything.

I begin to wonder if Atan chose the right star when I see something ahead and to the right. "Is that it?"

His gaze follows my pointing fingers, squinting hard in the darkness. "I can't see anything."

"Sorry. I'm still getting used to better vision."

"If you see something, lead the way. We'll check it out."

I turn Beland to face the trees I see in the distance. As we get closer, I notice rocks behind the ones I see. Butterflies fill my stomach to bursting. What kind of training? There's no doubt I have a lot to learn because nothing seems to work right. It still feels like there's some kind of block inside me. Would I even be able to shift at will?

Beland snorts and falters, sidestepping as if nervous. I search for any threat and feel his muscles tense. Nothing can be seen, heard, or smelled in the grasses around us. Nothing moves or makes any noise. Atan looks back at me, the question clear in his eyes. I can only shrug in answer. My horse seems fine now, so we move on, leaving the strangeness behind us.

When we draw near, heads pop up over the grass. An arrow lands between our horses, and we pull to a stop. "Who are you?"

Atan glances at me, then turns to the people threatening us with bows. Most smell human, but a few scents I'm not used to filter back to me. Not that I've had time to practice sniffing people and things. I've been a bit sheltered.

"I was told to bring Ryn to you," Atan says.

"Prove it."

"I have a note from Elda."

"Notes can be forged. She needs to show us her dragon."

My mouth falls open. "I'm not sure I know how. I shifted once due to the dragon fire that should have melted me and was coached into changing back."

"You lie."

"She does not lie," a calm voice comes from the stand of trees behind the people with weapons.

A small magic light globe appears in the air above a man and woman stepping from the trees. The man has bright red hair and blue eyes. The woman has brown hair and light brown eyes. They walk forward with confidence.

The man threatening us looks back. "How can we be sure, Dyne?"

The woman laughs. "Do you think he wouldn't know who she is, Trev? Besides, open your nose. She smells like a dragon."

"It's been a long time. Scents can be changed, and not all dragons are friends."

"Not that long, and scents can only be changed by one such as you. Do you think that's even possible?"

Atan looks at me with wide eyes, but I'm sure mine are just as big and round as his. I have never seen this man before in my life. Wait, that's not right. Something is familiar in his features. Although, I can't point out why it triggers memory. I don't know a Dyne.

Sniffing, I pick up a strong scent of dirt and trees coming from the man. The smell of stale air comes to me from the woman. Neither are human, so they have to be dragons. I'm not sure which kind though. I've met other types, but that was before my super smell developed.

Trev and Dyne talk in hushed tones while the woman moves forward. "My name is Nova. Please forgive the rude welcome. We need to take care not to let the wrong ones through. Come, Ryn. We can easily house you and your horses. It's best to get inside before someone notices."

She looks over at my friend, who nods and says, "Atan."

"Atan, welcome to the rebellion. You will find you will be much better respected within our numbers."

As they speak, I slide off Beland's back. The horse nudges me with his nose as I move toward his head. I give him an absent-minded scratch. "Atan said Elda told him we will move on."

Nova looks apologetic. "I'm sorry; I'm sure you're tired. But we need to move. I'm assuming a distraction was provided. As soon as they realize you are missing, they'll mobilize. We have someone following your trail back to mask it, but we can't take any chances. Staying isn't really an option. We won't go far though, and you'll get to rest before our destination."

I do feel weary, but her reasoning is sound. "Okay. I understand. There is still a little adrenaline left in me to push on."

"Good. Keep your horses in check. We do have hay to keep them fed, so no worries there. They might not like the closeness of the cave though."

Beland shifts as if he understands the words. My hand on his nose calms him. "I've always been good with animals, especially horses. We'll be fine."

"Great. Let's go."

We walk past the men with their bows strung over their shoulders now. Trev and Dyne are in a heated argument, but I press on. I'm not sure who this man is or how he knows me, but I'm determined to find out. Right now isn't the time.

It takes a little coaxing to get both horses between the tight rocks behind a tree. Somehow, I manage to get them both into the cave. It takes a lot of touching and calming words.

"How long are we walking tonight?" I ask Nova.

"A few hours. Don't worry. It will give you time to catch up with Dyne a bit. I'm sure the time will pass quickly."

"Who is Dyne, and why do I need to catch up with him?"

"I'm your father," comes the voice from behind.

Atan starts coughing while I turn to look at the man with the red hair. Trev stands behind him, trying to glare holes into me with his striking light blue eyes. I ignore the angry man that looks not much older than me.

"My father?" I say, feeling breathless.

"It's nice to see you again, Ryn. I've missed you all these years."

Chapter Six
Shattered Heart

THREY

Weary from a night spent chasing horses, all I want to do is snuggle up next to my love and fall asleep. Enjoying her delicious body is also on my mind, but I don't think I have the energy. Maybe after a little rest if she's up to it. I just need my bed and the warmness of Ryn telling me she loves me as she cuddles against me.

Threysoryth still begs for me to let him out, and I will need to soon. Just not tonight. I can't because exhaustion weighs too heavily on me. Right now, all I need is peace. I'll make time to let him out tomorrow, maybe before training. The last thing I need is for him to force himself out during a mock battle. My future men are already upset with me after the pain caused by my rampage to find the person they consider to be only human.

If only they knew...

They can't know. No one can, or I'll lose her. I need Ryn by my side to be the best that I can be. Distance makes our budding connection weaken until I can only tell she's alive. It's no longer a beacon that would lead me to her. Once again, I wonder what it will be like to be fully mated to her. This is a new experience for me, one I want to revel in for as long as possible.

At my door, I push away my excitement to be back and enter. Inhaling deep, I take in the ashy scent that I connect to Ryn. It is soaked into every piece of my belongings. When I realize it's not strong enough to indicate her current presence, my brows furrow while I let out my breath. Where is she? The door was locked, and there's no way she'd wander the halls alone.

The first place I look is our bedroom. Scents in here are old, telling me no one has entered. Maybe without me here, she didn't want to sleep in our bed. She has before, so that doesn't really make sense, but she has to be somewhere. In the servant's room, the air is even more stale. My heart skips a beat, ready to panic. She has to be here.

But she's not. No matter where I look, my search comes up empty.

I frown and take another deep breath. A third scent that's neither mine nor hers is mixed in. Closing my eyes, I sniff specifically for the unknown signature. I realize who it is, and my eyes snap open. Why was she here? Her scent has the same strength as Ryn's, so they were here at the same time. The woman better have answers for me.

My feet carry me back out the door and into the hall. Trying not to look like I'm the mess I am, I hurry along without running. Few are up at this hour, and most are humans who won't question a dragon running through the halls. That doesn't mean I can throw caution to the wind. I need answers, but I need to make sure the truth remains secret.

Caution is difficult when half my soul is missing. Panic continues to grow until I can't help but run. Who cares who sees me? I need to find her. Ryn needs to be in my arms again. If Elda did anything to her, she will regret it deeply. I swear it with everything I have.

Entering the kitchen, I bypass the table of late-night snacks and move to the door at the back of the empty room. My fist pounds loud enough that I worry I'll wake the entire keep. That doesn't stop me from banging until the knob turns. More important things are on my mind.

A sleepy Elda opens the door with a yawn. Apprehension causes her eyes to become alert. "My lord?"

"You know why I'm here."

Wincing, the kitchen manager peeks around me to ensure the open room is empty, then opens the door wider to allow me entrance. I don't hesitate. As soon as the door closes, I growl, "Where is she?"

"My lord, I don't know what you're talking about."

She squeaks when I angrily stomp in her direction until she backs up against the wall. "Don't you dare lie to me. Your scent is all over my room and mingled with hers. Where is Ryn?"

"I know what she is."

Elda flinches when I slam my hand on the wall next to her head. "What did you do?"

"She wasn't safe here, Lord Threy. I meant to save her, not harm her."

I feel fury rise from deep within, the heat almost unbearable. Threysoryth fights for control, which is made harder to fight after his long absence from the sky. This woman took Ryn. She took the only person we've ever loved this deeply. My dragon wants to tear her limb from limb. Fighting him down is difficult because I want to as well. We need answers first.

Fear tells me Elda sees my barely contained rage. "Your mother betrayed your father. I received word that the king's men are on their way to take possession of the red dragon of prophecy. If I didn't get her out, she'd be taken and executed."

"You lie."

"I do not. A message was intercepted by a rebel faction. They sent me word that I had to get her out. I sent her with the stableboy to the closest occupied base."

"Tell me where it is."

Her eyes harden. "I won't. Even if I would, it wouldn't do you any good. They have moved on by now. Be assured that she's safe."

Claws grow over my nails, digging deep gouges into the stone beside Elda's head. She tenses but makes no other move. "Ryn is dear to me and my dragon. I'm losing control over him. Tell me where I can find her before he does something unpleasant."

"I couldn't even if I wanted to," she says. "I'm only a sympathizer. They know of me, but I'm not in direct communication with them unless there is deep need. I have no idea where they would have gone. I'm willing to speak more of this when you're calm and in control, my lord. Kill me now, and you'll lose the last chance of gathering information."

Despite her fear, she speaks calmly. I grit my teeth at the pain that comes with Threysoryth battering at my mind and body. With a snarl, I stomp from her room and rush outside. As much as I want to let my rage take over, she's right. She's the best chance I have of finding Ryn. I need her alive.

I dash out into the cool night air as my control fades away. I'm not even halfway across the yard before my dragon takes over. Copper-colored scales form on my skin. My body grows while bones snap and muscles twist. I fall to my hands and knees.

Within moments, I take to the air, flying as high as possible to hide the roar of anger and anguish that erupts from my chest. Fire bursts from my throat, launching high into the air. Reminding myself that I need to keep my tantrum secret, I fly on with a determination to find her. If Elda won't help me, I'll find her myself.

Only... I don't even know where to start.

Frantic, I fly in every direction, searching for any hint of the woman with fiery red hair. Nothing breaks the swaying waves of grass below me. This weak connection we have is no help either. It only tells me that she still lives, which is a blessing. How long will it stay that way? Why can't people trust me to take care of her myself? I would have kept her safe.

My search leaves my claws empty, but I can't return like this, so I let Threysoryth have the lead and fly wherever he wishes. I need to calm myself, then return to request Elda's presence by ordering food that I want only her to deliver. Not that I can eat with my stomach in my throat. I need answers. I need to know where my Ryn is.

After a fly to the ocean, the rage turns to grief. I cry out my pain into the sky, feeling my heart break into a million pieces. Attempting to pick up the jagged shards does no good because they slip through my fingers, slicing deep into my soul as they fall. I've lost the one person I care about most; the only person who makes my heart race and my soul feel whole.

The sun is starting to brighten the sky when I give in to the need for rest. Turning toward the keep is hard, but I don't have any choice. She's gone. Elda promised to give me more answers. I need to know what's going on if I want to protect her from whatever is happening. My mother wouldn't have gone over my father's head.

Would she?

My claws clench. Mother just might; she's defiant enough. When I land in the yard and see the stable slaves handling a bunch of unfamiliar horses, my heart stops. I shift and run over to the stable to find the human in charge.

"What's going on?" I ask.

The man turns to me. "King's men showed up not long ago. I have a bunch of horses to take care of, and I'm short people."

"Short people?"

"The woman your brother took was invaluable to the stable. No one could take care of the horses half as efficiently as she did. Besides that, one of the stable boys is missing, along with two of my horses."

I rub my hand over my face and run for the keep. Please don't mean that Ryn is with the man who kept flirting with her. That can't be right. He was meek and subservient. There's no way he is a rebel. Then again, I thought that of Elda too, and she mentioned a stable boy. The thought of the two of them riding away together makes me snarl so loud that multiple humans jump and cry out in fear.

A messenger blocks my path, wringing his hands at my temper. "Your father wishes for your presence in the meeting room, my lord."

"Should I go naked?"

The young woman squeaks. "Of course not, my lord."

I brush past her and move quickly to my room. As I'm tying my pants on, my door bursts open. Mother walks in with a group of men wearing king's colors and smelling of wyvern. I scowl at the woman who shows no ounce of love for me.

"That was locked for a reason," I growl.

My mother sends me a glare as the men search my rooms. "Where is she?"

"Who?"

"Your servant?"

"I don't know. She was gone when I came back from taking care of the sabotage we had. I've been searching for her and can't find her, so I was about to let people know I have a runaway and to find her before I got the message that father wishes to speak to me."

"Where's the red dragon?" one of the men says.

Acting innocent, I let my eyes go wide. "I can assure you if I knew, I would let the king know to get my sister back."

My mother's jaw ticks. The man turns to her. "If this was a ruse to manipulate King Darac, we promise you will pay the price."

"She was here. No one else knew of her presence but me and my husband, so my children know nothing. I sent word as soon as we figured out her trickery," she says back to him. I wish I could find it in myself to be shocked at how good the lie is. Her recent behavior makes me believe lying is something she's used to.

"We will be reporting back to the king."

"I swear we will find her again. She must have figured out you were coming and made a run for it."

"See that you do."

They leave with one last annoyed look our way. As soon as they're out of range of hearing, Mother slaps me across the face. "What did you do?"

"I didn't do anything. She wasn't here when I returned, and I've been searching for her. It was probably your words in the hall yesterday that frightened her into running."

While I want to go after the rebels, I won't release the information I have. No one but me can find her because anyone else would mean her death. I'm furious at Elda for stealing Ryn away from me and hiding her, but I won't give her up. I need answers if I'm to find my heart.

My mother calls me a liar and rushes from the room. It's ironic that she'd call me a liar after what I just witnessed. I follow and close my door, stopping a human to let him know I need my lock replaced. By the time I make it to the meeting room, everyone is already there.

"Imagine this, brother," Delto says from the seat across from the one I fall into. "You hid the red dragon right under my nose."

Crossing my arms over my chest, I say nothing. All he gets from me is a glare. Rakurn looks curious, for once not in a hurry to bury his nose in his books. Seems this is one thing that can grab his attention.

"Enough, Delto," my father says. "It was kept secret to decide how best to proceed. Too bad that decision was taken out of my hands."

Mother glares from her seat. "I'm not sitting on my hands while my daughter is stuck in the capital."

"Glad to see you love one of us," I tell her.

She opens her mouth to argue, but Father slams his hands on the table and stands. "Enough! We need to think of how best to go about this. Now that he knows, we have no choice but to hand her over. Where is she, Threy?"

"I have no idea. She wasn't in my room when I returned. I tried to find her, but the trail was already cold."

Delto scoffs, but I catch a hint of glee under it. "It seems we can't trust your word. I am relieving you from your position as my general until I can find it in myself to trust you again."

"Fine with me."

"We need to keep this as quiet as possible," Rakurn says. "If people know, we will face ridicule after demanding our nobles hand her over."

"There's no help for that now. The king's men weren't discreet, so we need to move on to damage control and find her," Father says.

Talk moves to the next steps, but I stop listening. My mind goes over everything that I can do. Our guards can't find her because my uncle will be happy to do whatever it takes to use her for vengeance against my earlier actions. She needs to be found, but it needs to be me to do it. I'm sure I'll be watched closely. None of that matters. I have to find Ryn first.

Chapter Seven
A New Bond

RYN

After dropping his identity on me, my father walks beside me without speaking. I can only assume he's trying to give me peace to process this revelation. It's not everyday you meet the father you didn't even know you lost.

No. He's not my father. It doesn't matter if I'm part of him; I barely know the man. My real father is the man that protected me and raised me all my life. He's the one that was slaughtered by a jealous dragon over the quality of his wooden furniture.

Dyne is simply Dyne. There is relation only by blood, not by anything important. My memories are still full of my human parents, and they always will be. He can't just come into my life, say something like that, and expect me to run into his arms. I don't even know the man.

"My father was a human woodworker," I say after my long silence.

I notice Nova glance at me with sympathy in her eyes that I don't want or need. My life has changed so much recently, but this isn't the direction I'm going down. My parents are the ones that shaped me into the woman I am now. It doesn't matter if they're human and I'm a dragon. All that matters is the love and care they gave me. Blood doesn't mean family.

Dyne sighs. "And I don't expect you to see me as such after a life of absence."

"Then why bring it up?"

"As much as you loved those that raised you—and they raised you well—you need to know where you come from to come to terms with the new direction your life is going in. You're not human. I know you know this, but to understand who you truly are, you need to understand where you came from. I'm not making excuses and never will. It won't make a difference, and I don't expect you to act like my daughter. I did what I did because it was the only way to keep you safe, even at the expense of losing my only offspring."

Trev scoffs behind us. "You may only be my uncle, but you were more a father to me than anyone you talk about."

"I raised you after your mother—my sister—was burned alive by King Darac. I treat you as my own because I see you that way. That doesn't make you mine in the sense I'm discussing right now."

"But the one who doesn't want you is?"

I flinch at both their words. Trev is a cousin, so that's something... I guess. So far, my real life family doesn't impress me much. I prefer the ones that live only in my mind, memories both good and bad.

Dyne sighs. "Trev, I consider you my son as much as is possible, but in this instance, I'm not talking in the way you are. Ryn needs to know her bloodlines if she's to truly accept who she is."

"Whatever," Trev mumbles.

Dyne squeezes between his eyes, and I ignore his distress. I now know why he seems familiar; we share a few similar features. He isn't familiar because I've met him before. He's familiar because parts of him have stared back at me from the mirror my entire life. My red hair. My nose and chin. Those are his, which means everything else must come from...

"Is a woman going to jump out of the crowd and tell me she's my mother?" I ask.

Guilt overrides my annoyance when the look of grief passes over Dyne's blue eyes. Trev calls me heartless and swears for a few seconds, something about her being more his mother than mine. I won't refute that. I don't even know who she is.

My heart hardens and pushes away the guilt. What do I have to feel guilty about? It's not like I knew. I was given to a human family and hidden away. Neither of them wanted to keep me close enough to fight for me. I know who my real parents are.

"Raya, your mother, died protecting you," Dyne says when he recovers from my unintentional barb.

I bite my lip, the guilt threatening me again. "I'm sorry."

"We were just attacked by the king's men while topside. I was on a mission to the south of camp and was separated from the two of you. The mating bond told me she fled to the capital and was in danger. I tried to get to her as fast as I could, but the mating bond snapped before I could sneak into the city. She never made it out.

"I was sure you were dead too, so I went into the city to drown my grief and maybe get caught. Life without Raya wasn't worth living.

Morill, your proper father, found me when he was on errands and dragged me back to his shop. That's where I saw Lenyr holding you."

We walk in silence for a few more minutes. Beland nudges the back of my head, so I reach back to pat him absently. I don't need to lead him because he hasn't left my side since I coaxed him into the cave.

"You didn't take me with you," I say.

It's not a question, and he doesn't treat it as one. "Right. Lenyr told me that Raya promised she'd come back to you, but they heard the news about a rebel being caught and executed. I was able to confirm it was her. Morill said that after she dropped you off, he watched from the shop as she distracted the city guard from searching for you. They chased her instead. That was the last anyone saw of her except those that took her from me.

"I wanted to take you with me, but after discussing it, we realized the king knew about you. The rebels would be the first ones they hit in search of you, which they did. It was safest for you to be raised under his nose and thought of as a human child. It was my magic that blocked your dragon until the first part of the prophecy was fulfilled. Then I walked away. Anyone seeing us together would see the resemblance."

Tears threaten, but I push them away. I don't know these people, so I shouldn't have to mourn them. They mean nothing to me as it is. How can I mourn what I never knew? None of these thoughts stop the overwhelming sadness.

"And you never even checked on me?" I ask, despite my inner thoughts.

"I did, but I did it from afar. I didn't walk away from you because I didn't love you. I wanted you to be safe."

"You wanted me to finish the rebellion for you." I can't keep the bitterness out of my voice.

Dyne lets out a deep breath. "I'm hoping that's how this ends, but you were always more than a means to an end, Ryn. You are my daughter. Even if I no longer have the right to claim you as such, my heart feels it."

Atan walks a little ahead, and I can't take the pity in his eyes when he looks back. I wipe the traitorous tears from my face. This man isn't my father. I don't care what he says.

"And you think you can just randomly come into my life after twenty-five years, and what?" I ask.

"Nothing. I know you don't owe me anything. I know I don't have the right to ask for a relationship. All I ask is that you help me train you. Not many can handle someone with the magical strength you have."

I laugh. "I can't even access my magic in any reliable manner. The best I've done is light a candle."

Trev snorts. "I don't think she's the one, uncle."

"Her rebirth happened as the prophecy stated it would," Dyne says.

"I still don't believe it. Our savior is supposed to be strong. This Ryn seems pretty weak."

Having enough of his mouth when I'm already on edge, I turn and punch my cousin in the face. "I've survived more than you will ever understand and came out on top. Use the word weak to describe me again, and I'll show you just how strong I am."

The line stops around us, most people watching with shock. When I see the blood on Trev's lip, I fight back my apologies. Violence has never been part of me. I've always been the meek slave focused only on survival.

I'm tired of being underestimated.

Turning, I walk on, the people in front of me hurrying ahead of my fury-filled gaze. Dyne joins me, and I'm happy to see Trev hold back a little longer to be lost in the crowd. The prick doesn't deserve the right to judge me. Who does he think he is?

"Don't mind him, please. He's used to having me to himself," Dyne says.

"He can have you," I mutter, ignoring the disconcerted look in his blue eyes. "If you are the only one that can help me with magic, I'll let you train me. Don't expect me to call you Daddy and run into your arms."

"I don't expect that and never will."

"What makes you so strong that you can help?"

"I'm a fairy dragon."

I blink. "Threy told me fairy dragons are extinct because they tried to overthrow the kings."

Dyne chuckles. "And so does the majority of the dragon population believe. We weren't eradicated because not every member of my people were in the forest when he burnt it down with the Jeweled Dracon. It happened before I was born."

"Did they really try to usurp him?"

"No. Darac feared fairy dragons because of our magic and the fact that we are needed to make a red dragon. It was the last human seer that made the prophecy. Fairy dragons had no investment in politics. It wasn't enough for him because only a drake and a fairy dragon can make a red one. Here you are."

"Here I am," I echo in a whispered breath. "I'm not sure how you can help. My magic doesn't work. I don't even think I can shift."

"It may just take some nudging. When I suppressed your true nature, I buried it deep. To everyone, you were a human raised by a wood craftsman and a jewelry maker. You were the daughter of a human couple. It may take time to uncover both your dragon and your magic."

"What if we can't?"

"We have to believe we can."

My laughter sounds dark, even to my ears. "Really? I'm sorry if I'm not that optimistic."

Dyne falls into silence, and I don't try to start the conversation again. Instead, I move closer to Atan, the one person here that knows who I truly am. I shake my head when he gets ready to speak. By the time we stop, my legs are like jelly. I find a place off to the side to settle down.

"We only have a few hours before we need to be up because we have to put a lot of distance between us before they start looking for you," Dyne says from in front of me.

I open my eyes. "I'll fall asleep quickly."

"Let me check the magic block first to make sure it's completely gone, then I'll walk away and leave you to sleep."

"Fine."

Dyne puts his hands on my head. Tingling washes over me, making me shiver. Atan mutters about finding some water while I focus on the sensation running over me. After a minute, my supposed-father sits back on his heels.

"The block is gone, but like I thought, you're still buried deep. Without the block, we will be able to release both your dragon and magic."

"What's my dragon's name? Threy told me the parents know."

He nods and looks around to make sure no one is close. "You are Rynmoriath, the red dragon of prophecy. Keep your full name to yourself because it's dangerous in the wrong hands."

"Threy already told me."

"This Threy is the third son of Ildracan?"

"Yes."

"How long have you been mated to each other?"

Startled by the question, I jerk hard enough to smack the back of my head on the wall behind me. "What? We've never gone through the ceremony. I can feel him sometimes, but I figured it was just from the intent to mate like he told me."

"Red dragons don't need the ceremony."

"What does that mean in this situation?"

Dyne rubs the back of his neck. "Red dragons are so powerful that the magic within them is enough to mate without the ceremony. All you need is to declare your love, match your hearts, and mate. Did you have a time where it felt like fire from both of you was rising to meet?"

My mouth falls open. "Yeah. The first time we gave into our desires and every time after that. Shouldn't we both feel more?"

"While normal dragons do feel some sort of connection if they try to mate without the ceremony, it's really a small thing. When a red dragon realized others couldn't feel the same bond, they came up with the ceremony to help others bond. Only certain types of magic can perform it. Certain fairy dragons or someone holding an artifact with the power within it. What you feel is the mate bond. My guess is your stunted magic is keeping it from flowing freely. It's possible that releasing your magic will strengthen the bond. This isn't good."

"Why not?"

"If they find out about the bond, they can use his name to force him to follow it."

My heart skips a beat. "He wouldn't do it."

"Names are powerful things. He won't have a choice. I'll need to think if there's a way to keep him from finding you."

Dyne stands and walks away. I stare after him in shock. Atan settles next to me with a cup of water and a handful of concern for me. I brush away the concern, grateful for the water. He wouldn't understand. It's clear to me that Atan hates Threy. Letting him know I'm mated might not be the best idea at this point.

Threy is my mate, and I left him.

Chapter Eight
The Logical Thing

THREY

The sun glistens off Mother's blue scales as we all stand around in a show of fake solidarity. Rumors abound over the visit from the king's men and the red dragon. Father ordered us to act like a united front and threatened to disown anyone who went against his wishes in this. No contacting Darac to tell him I knew all along. No fighting with each other in public.

The only thing that is supposed to change is my position as future general. Delto is adamant that someone like me can't be left in such an important position of authority. That's fine with me. Less responsibility. Less having my own people wanting to knock me down a peg for the damage done saving Ryn. I'm okay with all of it.

Maybe this means I'll be left to my own devices. After everything that has happened—all the betrayal and lack of care—I'd rather travel the kingdom than stay in Ildracan. I'd rather do that with a certain redhead at my side.

That thought sours my already bleak disposition, hidden behind a fake smile and wave as the lady of Ildracan lifts into the air and flies east. Mother is determined to make King Darac see reason and give Iara back to us. She has her work cut out for her because our king isn't very reasonable. I still almost feel sorry for him when he has to deal with a determined Lady Belra. If my mother is anything, it's infuriatingly stubborn. This will be an impressive battle of wills I don't mind missing.

I'm the first to turn and leave the steps of the keep. Traveling the halls affords me many speculative glances. A mighty lord of Ildracan didn't know his personal servant was the red dragon of prophecy. If they only knew the truth. They never will though. It's a secret I'll always keep to myself until I can be reunited with the woman I love away from this den of vipers.

I'm glad to see my new lock is installed as I open the door and lock it behind me. Her scent is so dim in the air that I feel my heart break all over again. Walking into the servant's room, I pick up her brush and sniff it. The grooming tool holds the smell of my little dragon more than anything else. I put it down once I get my fill, not wanting to deplete it of its ability to remind me.

I look up at the painted landscape of Ildracan I bought Ryn. With my lips pressed into a thin line, I remove it from the wall, carry it into my bedroom, and hang it there. The memories it brings belong where she last slept. I return to her room, tripping over Hunter on my way in. He also seems to miss Ryn.

The orange cat jumps onto the bed, then her table. In front of the mirror is the carved cat that reminded Ryn of the cat sitting next to it. I walk over and pick up the crudely carved and painted animal. Despite the more amateur curves and lines, she had to have it. I carry it into my room as well to place it on the table next to the bed.

After staring at the two pieces that hold the most memory for a few minutes, I plop facedown on my pillow. I feel Hunter climb onto the pillow next to me, and I sigh. It wasn't until he helped me realize I needed to save Ryn from my parents that he stopped growling and hissing at me. I've finally earned his trust. Even now, I don't lift my head, smothering myself in my pillow until sleep takes over.

The brightness of the sun tells me it's after lunchtime when I wake again. The orange cat snores lightly on the pillow next to me and doesn't stir as I climb out of bed. I'm not even hungry. A knock sounds at my door.

Sighing, I glance once more at the painting and head to answer the annoyance. I'm surprised to find Elda standing on the other side with a tray. "May I come in and serve you, my lord?"

I'm about to tell her I'm neither an invalid nor hungry but remember we need to talk. Instead of pushing her away, I step aside and let her in. Like the perfect servant, she walks over to the table and places the tray down gently.

"I'm not hungry," I mutter.

"If you want me to answer your questions, you are going to eat."

"I seem to remember that I'm the dragon and you're the human in this situation."

"I know. Master and slave. Believe me when I tell you it's not something I can forget, but I'm not going to let you waste away pining for Ryn. As much as I know that you're a dragon, I always considered you one of the good ones. Besides, Ryn will be upset if I let you starve yourself. I'm assuming that will mean something to you, Lord Threy."

With a grunt, I sit down in the chair. Elda reveals a bison steak sandwich and roasted potatoes. The bowl of fruit makes me grimace.

She notices. "I figured you'd like some."

Would I? In the end, I nod. Any reminder of her is welcome. I start with the fruit, spearing each piece with my fork and enjoying the sweetness that brings more memory.

"She wanted to say goodbye, by the way."

The fruit turns sour in my mouth. "You didn't let her."

"I couldn't bring her to you, then take her away. We didn't have time for her to leave the note she kept begging for either. We had to get her out and on her way before our distraction was taken care of."

"You released the horses?"

Elda chuckles. "Not at all. That was a few others that helped. I spoke to Atan beforehand, and he was able to smuggle out two horses in the confusion."

I wince and look up from the empty fruit bowl. "He loves her. You know that?"

The woman raises an eyebrow, refusing to talk again until I continue eating. She watches me like a mother with a child who complains that he doesn't like what she made to eat. I take a few bites.

After a few more, she relents. "I suspected when I saw how ready he was to jump to help. You don't need to worry though. That girl is smitten with you. No one will ever make her eyes stray. Thank you for saving her."

"I didn't do it for you."

"I know, but I still am thankful, whether you want to accept it or not. This isn't what either of you wanted; I know that. The prophecy needs to be fulfilled. All you can do is support that."

"I'd rather support her."

"You can still do that from afar."

That makes me laugh. How can I support Ryn and protect her when I don't even know where she is? She needs me, and I'm held back where I don't want to be. "I would have gone with her."

"Can you truthfully say you wouldn't tell them where she is if you were found? Family is binding."

I laugh, but she's partly right. I am bound to my father. He can use my name to call me back and force me to his will. Betraying her would kill me, but I wouldn't be able to resist.

"I see you get the point," Elda says.

"Not in the way you're thinking, but you're right. Will I ever see her again?"

"Ryn is glued to you, Lord Threy. Once this is all over, you two will be in each other's arms again. You just need to be patient."

"Do you have any idea what you're saying? I have no patience when it comes to her."

Elda collects my empty dishes in a neat stack on the tray. Years of experience make her a professional at the delivery and return of food. "You had patience with her before. You'll need to find it again."

"I was dying inside until we finally gave in to our desires."

"But you survived. Listen, I know you worry about her. Remember how strong she is and how much she survived. She will get through this, and so will you. You can't escape fate."

Without another word, she walks toward the door. I want to interrogate her about Ryn's location, but I believe her now when she says she doesn't know. Even if she did, telling me wouldn't be a good idea. Father didn't want to tell the king yet. Mother forced his hand. He will do what is needed to keep our family alive and in place. That includes finding Ryn and handing her over to a tyrant for execution. Me not knowing her location is for the best; no matter how much being apart from her breaks my heart.

Unable to stand the silence of my room, I leave and make my way through the halls. As I pass the library, Rakurn calls for me. I grimace and consider pretending I don't hear him, but I'm a dragon, so that would be an unbelievable lie. Too many people are watching from the halls. We have to act like we're united, so I enter the library.

Before my butt is settled in the chair across from my brother, he starts talking quietly. No one is in the library, but people are still traversing the halls. They'd hear if we spoke normally.

"How long did you know about your servant?" Rakurn whispers.

"Since her almost-execution. How long did you know of Delto's plans for me?"

"Since before he took her from the stable. If it's any consolation, I advised against it. We both know how well our older brother listens to the advice given to him."

A growl rumbles in my chest. "Did it ever occur to you to warn me?"

Rakurn sighs and closes the book his nose is buried in. I notice it's a book about the prophecy and human magic. His green eyes find me. "Did it occur to me? Yes, it did. I'm Delto's advisor. Anything he says to me needs to be in confidence, so it was only a passing thought. I did warn you to be careful with him, but you didn't heed my warning."

"Not like it was clear."

"Not like I could break my oath and make it clear. Use your head, Threy. I know Iara and I got the brains in this family, but you can at least try."

"Forget it."

As I stand, Rakurn says, "We need to follow the law on this. You know that?"

"I'm not giving her up, if that's what you're saying."

"Look at this logically; she's a criminal. I can only assume that the rebels have her now. Don't look at me like that. It's a logical conclusion. The rebels rely on the prophecy, so it's the intelligent thing to think. It is our duty to follow the king's orders. It's also our duty to make sure our only sister is kept safe. The solution for both is clear."

My answer is nothing but a snarl before I stomp out. If everyone thinks I'll just let them have her, they better think again. Ryn is mine to love and protect. They can't have her. The rage on my face must be clear because people jump out of my way without more than a glance from me. I turn into the garden.

The fresh air brings a little calm. Not near enough. My body thrums with the need to take out anyone who wishes to harm Ryn, even my family. I will do whatever it takes to keep her safe. It doesn't matter if I'm close or far. If that means feeding Elda information for the rebels, so be it. Ryn won't be murdered by a fearful king.

Stripping, I place my clothes on the nearest bench and shift. I flap my wings to lift into the air. Once high enough, I fly over the grassy plains. After passing a few herds of buffalo, I realize I'm not out here to hunt. My eyes strain for the slightest hint of red in the sea of green and yellow.

Chapter Nine
Origins

RYN

Dogs that I didn't notice at first bark and mill around as everyone settles in. Nova told me they keep them ahead and behind to warn of any intruders. It's one of the few things that has kept this group alive as long as they have been. The king apparently likes to use moles to find the rebel groups and attack. It became worse after I was born and abandoned. Once that conversation ended, I had too much quiet to think through. My mind kept turning to Dyne.

Yes, I agree it was probably necessary, but I haven't gotten over the hurt of my father simply walking away from me. My mother planned on coming back, but he ran in the other direction. His reasoning doesn't matter. It doesn't make him my real father.

Okay. I may still be a little bitter about what was dropped on me the other day. After three days of traveling through caves, I've had plenty of time to stew. The information hasn't aged well.

For some reason, my red dragon status affords me my own space. Most people without mates bunk together. The only members that get their own rooms—or round caves in this instance—are the ones with mates. They need their privacy.

And red dragons apparently.

"Suitable?" Nova calls from the makeshift doorway.

My eyes scan the plain walls of rock. The only thing that breaks it is the cot that was added before I 'moved in.' I guess training will keep me busy, so the boring that is this hole in the rock won't matter. It's still disappointing after living in light.

"It's a little dark," I say.

"Make light."

I flinch and look away. "I would if I could."

"Sorry. I didn't realize what I was saying. You'll learn soon." Nova settles a light globe by the door.

I stare at the brightness of the ball. Another reminder of my failure. "An all powerful, magical red dragon that can barely light a candle."

"You'll get there. I trust Dyne will pull it out of you."

"You've known him long?"

"Since before you were conceived. Him, your mother, and Trev joined us after Dyne's original group was destroyed. I became quite close to your mother."

My mother... I've met the dragon that helped conceive me, but I know nothing of the mother that gave her life to keep me safe. Do I want to know? The decision isn't hard to make. "What was she like?"

"Raya? She was strong and fierce. She and Dyne didn't think they'd conceive since crossbreeds are extremely rare, particularly red dragons. The woman loved your father so much that it didn't matter to her. When she became pregnant, both were overjoyed. They loved you very much."

"How old was I?"

"Just under three months. As Dyne said, we were attacked, and they were separated further while he was on a mission. Raya ran to the city to seek refuge with friends. Some followed her because they realized what you were."

I sit on my cot. "How did no one realize I wasn't human?"

"Dyne's magic is quite powerful. He's stronger than any other surviving fairy dragon. No red dragon of course. That and you were small enough to pass off as newly born. Lenyr didn't go out much. She was a pretty thing, and you know how dragons value pretty."

That I do. They can even find the prettiness under a few layers of stable grime too. That's how I ended up gifted to Threy. Feels like so long ago.

"Listen," Nova says, cutting into my thoughts, "I know you aren't happy with Dyne right now, and I can't say I blame you. Try not to be too hard on him. He did what he thought was safest and best for you at the time. Not just because of what you are. This is a hard life. Yes, he left you, but he's a good man."

"I'm not going to treat him like my father."

"I'm not asking you to. Just don't be too harsh please. He's lost a lot, and losing you almost did him in. Cut him however much slack you feel you can."

"Are you two?"

Nova laughs. "Not at all. We're good friends. There is nothing in my heart that looks at that man like anything other than a brother in arms, maybe a non-related brother for real. Besides, no woman could ever get close to him after your mother died. She was the only woman for him."

"I know what that's like."

"If he's as loyal as you say, which I believe since he didn't turn you in, you two will come back together when the time is right." Nova walks into my room and drops a sack at my feet. "We can't offer much more than water and rags to wash until everything is settled, but they're in here, along with some clothes that I think might fit you. Once set up, we have an underground stream."

Nodding, I remain silent. She squeezes my shoulder and walks away. I'm no longer in my nightgown, but these clothes feel musty. I find the inadequate washing materials and strip. When the new clothes are over me, I step into the hall in search of food. Someone directs me in the direction we came from, and my nose does the rest.

A bowl of stew makes its way into my hands. Finding an empty spot in a corner, I walk over and poke around at the dried meat in the broth. This is better than what I had before Threy, but I've gotten used to the luxuries of being a beloved personal servant. It's going to be hard to revert back to enjoying food like this. Sustenance is sustenance.

After my third bite, Dyne slides into the chair beside me. I glance at him and try not to be rude. He surprises me by saying, "I think I know how to block Threy from being able to find you."

The spoon stops halfway to my mouth. I forgot all about that. My heart squeezes when I think of losing the connection we have. It's not much, but I at least know he's alive.

"You'll still feel each other. He just won't be able to follow the connection to you," Dyne says.

"Are you reading my thoughts?"

"Your facial expressions and scent gave me a reason to believe the news upset you. I figured that would be the reason why."

I look out over the people entering the dining area. Little children hop around their mothers' legs. These people aren't just rebels; they're family. My stubbornness can't be allowed to put them in danger, so I sigh. "Fine."

"It'll just take a second."

Dyne touches my forehead with his fingers. A tingling runs over me. Threy becomes muffled, but he doesn't go away. Not that I could feel more than his presence to begin with. I still miss the little bit of closeness that I lost. It's not worth being the reason people die.

"Done," Dyne says, turning to his stew to begin eating it.

Atan takes a place on my other side. "Both horses are taken care of. They have more than our two."

I look at Dyne. "How do you keep them fed?"

"We're rarely far from an exit. Long grass is in abundance here in Ildracan."

He's not wrong. "What's the next step?"

He takes the time to swallow before answering. "Train you in magic and connecting with your dragon. Security is tightened, so you will be safe. I'll show you the marks that mean tunnels that can withstand the Jeweled Dracon."

I drop my spoon into the stew. "I thought nothing could."

"Red dragons can. So can their magic. The wards are fading but still offer enough safety to make it toward an exit if you're quick."

"How quick?"

A haunted look crosses his face. "Really quick."

Part of me wants to ask him what memory casts that sort of darkness over his blue eyes. I don't because that might mean bonding. Nova wants me not to be too harsh, but that doesn't mean I'm going to bond with the man. He hasn't earned that yet.

"When does training start?" I ask to change the subject.

"Tomorrow. After the escape and days of walking, I feel you need a night of freedom and rest."

Trev walks in and glares at me with his light eyes when he sees Dyne sitting next to me. I sigh, which makes the man in question follow my gaze with a grunt. "I'll go sit with him to give you peace and give him the closeness he needs. Thanks for trusting me enough to cover the bond."

He walks away. Atan asks, "What bond?"

This is not something I feel like arguing with Atan over, so I laugh it off. "A stupid dragon thing. Nothing important." My friend looks like he's about to ask something else, but I don't let him. "Do you miss the stables at all?"

"No."

"Not even a little? I missed them when I was taken."

He looks at me as if shocked, somehow hopeful. "Really?"

"Yeah. The horses always brought me peace."

"Oh." Hope in his eyes dims. It's his turn to cut me off before I can ask questions. "I suppose I miss it a little bit. The horses were nice, so I understand why you miss them. I hated shoveling shit, but I at least got some fresh air. There's none to be had underground."

"It is a bit dim down here."

Atan laughs. "Wish I could see their faces after I left. We were already short-handed."

Memories of the look of indifference from the stable master come to my mind. He didn't care that they were dragging me off in the middle of the night. His only concern was probably rearranging tasks to be covered properly with one less person. I can't find it in myself to care about the predicament losing Atan would give him.

"Does it bother you that I'm a dragon?" Despite his seeming acceptance, this thought has been nagging me. I just never had the guts to ask. It would be better to know than always wonder.

"Nope, which I already told you in a way. I mean, I was in shock at first when Elda told me. In the end, I figured you are still you."

"Am I?"

"Seem to be."

We let the conversation drop and eat the rest of our meal in companionable silence. Nova walks in shortly after and sits next to Trev and Dyne. The former lights up with her presence while Dyne offers a small smile. As I watch them, I realize she's right. There are no romantic feelings there, only strong friendship. I don't know why I feel relieved.

My mind drifts back to my mother. I wonder what it would have been like to know her. If Dyne is the fairy dragon, she would have had to be a drake. At least, that's what Threy told me. I have no reason to believe he's wrong. Would she be proud of who I am or be disappointed in my earlier weakness as a stable slave?

I wish I knew more about the woman. Despite my attachment to my adopted parents, I still wonder what it would have been like to grow up knowing my heritage. I'm not a slave. I'm a dragon. A powerful one at that.

Would I be better with magic and my dragon if I grew up with them? I'm assuming Dyne wouldn't have blocked me if I did, so I would have to be a lot more powerful then. Things would have been so much easier to be raised as a dragon, even a rebel one.

And I wouldn't change it for the world. Without my upbringing and less than ideal situations, I would never have met Threy. My entire life led me to him and to who I am. I can wonder all I want; it won't change anything. While the past would be different, I would lose out on those that I grew to love.

According to what I've learned and overheard, I'd probably still know the people I look at as my mother and father. They seemed to have been an integral part of the rebellion, which still surprises me. At no point in my life did I ever expect them to be anyone other than who they appeared to be. Maybe I didn't know them as much as I thought I did. They raised me, but they were still strangers.

Standing, I brush off Atan's concern and feign exhaustion. It's not a complete lie. The desire to be alone is more important than sleep though, so I say my goodbyes and head back to my stone cavern of privacy.

Once alone, I go through the bag that Nova gave me. Under all the clothes, I find a couple of books, including a journal. That makes me laugh. I've never kept a journal before because who would want to know the life of a lonely slave?

My mind goes over that thought, and I shake my head. That's not who I am anymore. A human slave is below notice, but the red dragon of prophecy is not. After some thinking, I open the book and find a pencil.

I write a summary of my life and all recent events. I record my feelings, both good and bad. At the end, I write a description of Threy to keep his handsome face and hard body in my mind. I do this until sleep takes over.

Chapter Ten
Doubts

RYN

"It's not working," I say with a whine.

Dyne sighs and looks back at Nova, who is supervising this session because she says she has nothing better to do. Over the last couple of days, she's been a constant, offering encouragement and suggestions. As much as I don't want to admit it, I'm starting to look at her a bit as a mother figure.

My father is still kept at arm's length, but I don't act hurtful or accusing toward him anymore. In the end, he's trying to help me, which is something I feel grateful for. He's patient and calm always, traits that Nova assures me have always been him. He never loses his patience. He never yells or growls. Dyne simply tries to find a new way to explain or attempt things. So far, none of it has worked. I find myself liking him, no matter how much I want not to.

"I warned you that this might not come easy. You need to have patience with yourself, Ryn," he says.

"But how can I picture my dragon when I haven't seen myself as one? Threy was able to use this tactic to get me to change from a dragon because I know what my human side looks like. All I know about my dragon side is that I have red scales and wings. That's not helpful."

Nova drops her arms from her knees before folding her legs under her and leaning forward. "What are you picturing?"

"A red drake. Threy told me I look like a drake, so I picture him, except red instead of copper."

"That might be part of the problem," Dyne says. "Red dragons are not drakes. They are a mix of that and fairy dragon."

"But he told me that's what I look like. What am I supposed to look like?"

"That's the problem. We don't know. All of them looked like a mix of fairy and drake, but none of them looked the same."

Growling, I let myself fall back onto the stone floor. This is impossible. How can I picture my dragon if no one here can tell me what I look like? I need Threy, for more reasons than one. Every day finds me missing him more and more. It's an ache that never goes away. He would be able to tell me what I look like as a dragon too.

"Can we maybe ask Elda to ask Threy?" I say.

"We can't risk it."

I groan while looking up at the stone ceiling above me. "Then what do you suggest, oh illustrious instructor?"

"I'm going to assume you have characteristics of both types in some way. You're going to need to experiment."

"And how am I going to do that?"

"Show her your dragon, Dyne," Nova says.

I watch the man who sired me flinch, which only makes me curious. One, I've never even imagined what a fairy dragon looks like. Two, there's something that makes him apprehensive about showing me. What is it?

In the end, whatever objections he must have mean nothing. Dyne doesn't argue or deny; he simply stands and strips. As his shirt comes off, I notice a bunch of scars on his back. I gasp, and he turns to see me with my hand over my mouth.

"Very old injury," he explains.

"I thought dragons don't scar."

"They do when they barely escape the devastating power of the Jeweled Dracon."

"The thing the king has?"

"Yeah. The same fire that almost drove my people into extinction scarred me for life."

Horrified, I stare at his back as he turns to remove his pants. I can't take my eyes off the raised lines of old burn marks. The skin is rough, and I can see it stretch and pull as he moves.

My curiosity gets the better of me. "Does it still hurt?"

"From time to time, but it's not as bad as when it first happened. The agony of it was less than what I was left with when I was forced to abandon my sister to save Trev when she ordered me to," he answers without looking back at me.

Such destruction to a being that isn't easily hurt. If I didn't have a reason to hate Darac before, I do now. It's not just the treatment of humans that can be laid at the king's feet. His fear and paranoia have caused so much pain. I feel my heart soften toward Dyne a little.

Orange scales push their way out of his skin. His fingers shrink, replaced by paws as he drops to all fours. I watch in wonder as the bright orange takes over. Two fluffy antennas sprout on top of his head, right above his blue eyes. Wings, so thin they are almost see-through, sprout from his back. They're a pale gold color at the base, growing into orange and red the further out they grow. Almost like fire.

I jump to my feet. At the end of his wings, black edges that look almost melted end abruptly. His wings are damaged to the point that they aren't nearly big enough for him to fly. He's the size of a horse, much smaller than the dragons I'm used to seeing. The coloring is magnificent, but his scarred wings pale the beauty of his scales.

"The Jeweled Dracon did this?" I say with a gasp.

"This is what a tyrant is capable of. Dyne will never fly again. He hasn't been able to since right before he met your mother. Look at all his features though. He's much smaller than any other dragon. He has paws instead of claws and rounded teeth instead of fangs."

I look over the fairy dragon before me. He's definitely smaller. He's also more colorful, but I'm not sure that will help me. I'm red. Everything she said is different goes in and right back out because I can't keep my eyes off his wings.

What has it been like for him for all these years without the ability to fly? All my life, I've wanted to soar through the sky. What would it be like to have that, then lose it? I know I haven't had a chance to fly yet, but it still hurts my heart to think about it. I want the freedom of flight and have never had it. My longing is enough to give me a sense of what Dyne has lost. It's enough to break my heart.

Never in my life have I known such freedom. I can only imagine what it's like to feel the wind under my wings and leave the world behind. No more war. No more threat of execution. Only me and the clouds. The rush of the wind over my scales. I want that more than anything in this world.

Dyne changing startles me from my thoughts. It starts with absorbing his strange antennas, then his ruined freedom. The transformation continues until he's dressed and sitting in front of me again.

"You're going to want to experiment with the differences you saw in my dragon from what you know a drake looks like," Dyne says, hurrying to continue when I grimace. "I know it's not the best and will take time, but please have patience. We don't have much of a choice right now without a way to know exactly what your dragon looks like."

"Why can't there be more information on hybrids?"

"Because they're all different, which is a good thing. Breeding between species is hard, but it's what has shaped our kind."

My brows furrow. "Do you mean wyverns?"

He nods. "But that's only the biggest change, and I believe not being part of one of the original dragons weighs heavily on wyverns."

"Not me. I couldn't care less," Nova cuts in because she's a wyvern.

"We all know you're much better than the king and his lackeys, Nova."

"Wanted to make sure you didn't forget."

Dyne chuckles. "Anyway, the only dragon type that hasn't changed over the generations is the fairy dragons. Drakyth designed us differently, but He gave us room to grow. For instance, the drakes that you know so well? They used to be smaller and wingless. Breeding made them larger and gave them the ability to fly. Wyrms basically look like giant snakes with fins and legs. They didn't have legs to start."

"But they don't have wings?"

"They're water based, so they don't need to fly. Their strength resides in swimming. Enough history. Let's work on calling your dragon forth."

I want to argue about how hopeless this feels but bite my tongue. Pessimism won't help here, no matter how much it drags my thoughts down. Closing my eyes, I take a deep breath. The red drake I've been using pops into my head immediately. I shrink it in my head, then play with what it looks like. I'm pretty sure I remember feeling fangs, so I leave those the same. I'm unsure about the claws. Maybe I'll adjust those. When I'm semi-happy but still unsure, I call to her.

Rynmoriath, please come to me. I want to be you again.

A bestial sense appears within me. As it grows, I feel more powerful. Heat builds in my veins, searing to levels a human wouldn't be able to take. I revel in it, breathing in the scent of ash that comes with it. I feel my dragon at the edge of my consciousness, and she seems happy to feel me in return. She molds into my consciousness, stopping there and waiting. I push her toward the image in my head.

She balks and retreats. Panicked, I reach for her and yell her name in my mind. The heat cools. The power weakens. I sob.

Come back!

Rynmoriath fades back into me, leaving me feeling empty and alone. She's still there, only hidden away in the recesses of my soul. Our closeness is one I crave. I've seen how easy it is for others to transform. They are one with their dragon, and I'm a stranger to mine. I want to be close to her. I want to feel her. I want to soar.

Opening my eyes, I feel myself deflate. My shoulders slump, and my head hangs low. "I feel her, but she won't stay."

"I'm sorry, Ryn. Patience is necessary here. I know I keep saying it, but it's the most important part to remember. The first shift is always difficult. It's worse for you because you don't know what you're supposed to look like and your dragon has been locked away for so long. Think of it as any skill. Did you think the man who raised you was born with exceptional skills working wood?"

"No."

"Right. It took practice. You'll get it. Keep trying."

And I do until it brings tears to my eyes.

I push more stew around in my bowl. Another failure of a day behind me. Dyne changed lessons to magic when the repeated loss of my dragon left me a bawling mess. He says that we should try to focus on my magic for a while because maybe being more powerful that way will make it easier.

That didn't work well either. I'm tired of hearing about patience and calm. So much hinges on me becoming the powerful red dragon everyone tells me I am. Without it, I can't defeat the king. Without it, I will never know who I am. Without it, I'll be separated from Threy for too long.

Atan makes me jump when he sits down next to me. "Looks like another rough day?"

"You can say that again, I grumble."

"Want to take a walk after supper? It might make you feel better."

I consider the offer, rubbing my temples to try to soothe the incoming headache. It doesn't work. "No. I'm too tired. I think I'm going to go back to my room and get some sleep. Tomorrow is another day of hopelessness."

"I'm sure you'll get it."

"At least one of us is."

"And I'll always have that faith in you."

I laugh and finish my stew. He's putting his faith in the wrong person. On the way out, I run into Trev. He glares at me and pushes past without a word. I sigh. Maybe Trev is right. Maybe I'm not the one. I don't feel special.

Chapter Eleven
New Blood

THREY

Reaching over, I rub the empty side of my bed. After sweet dreams, I tend to forget the only woman I'll ever love is not beside me. This is the reason I wake up in a sour mood every single day. Emptiness only leaves room for foulness.

Taking a deep breath, I roll over and look at the ceiling with a groan. I don't wish to get up. It's not like I have duties anymore. It's not like I want them anyway. I wonder if the rebels will let me join. Probably not since the naming magic is still an issue. There's no way they'd trust me not to be pulled back and forced to give away their location.

A blind hand reaches over to grab Ryn's pillow. I shove it over my face and take a deep breath. Despair overwhelms me when I remember her scent is already gone from it. Little is left to remind me of her, and it only breaks my already shattered heart further. She's alive; that much I know.

"Where are you, Ryn?"

As expected, silence answers the question spoken into loneliness. No loving giggle or passionate sigh. No questions about what we need to do today. It's all gone, hidden away from me in a way that can't be found. Not for the first time, I wish that we had been able to complete the mating ceremony. I'd feel her more.

A meow pulls my attention to the empty side of my bed. Green and yellow swirl in Hunter's eyes as he watches me from his perch at the end of her side. He gives me a slow and accusing blink while curling his orange tail around his front paws. The end of it twitches up and down.

"Don't start with me," I say.

Hunter shakes his head with a sneeze that I can feel all the way over here. By the brown paw prints on my sheets, I can tell he was in dusty sections of the personal servant's room again. The cat spends most of his time in there, waiting for the return of the woman he befriended in the stable. At least he no longer hates me. Small consolation.

When the tail twitches higher, I roll my eyes. "What do you expect me to do? I have no idea where she is. It's not like I can simply find my way to her. I go out every night, looking for any sign of Ryn. She's nowhere to be found."

When Hunter only stares, I threaten him with her pillow. The only reaction I get in return is another blink. My eyes narrow into a glare, but the infuriating cat shows no reaction. How can one animal upset me this way?

"She's not safe here anyway. The king knows who she is. If she returns, my father will turn her over to save Iara."

He yawns with a strained meow. With a sigh, I return Ryn's pillow to its spot. Hunter wastes no time, curling up where her head used to lie. He buries his face under his tail and purrs loudly. I roll onto my back again, determined to spend my day in this position, lost in memory of bright red hair and gray eyes. It's the perfect place to be.

As if the world is against all my plans, I hear a knock at my door. Maybe if I ignore it, whoever it is will go away. The louder knock tells me I'm an idiot for actually thinking that will work. Growling, I drag myself out of bed. I'll yell at whoever disturbs me, then return. I will spend the day in self-pity, and no one can stop me.

I yank the door open. "What?!"

The human on the other side jumps before he starts to tremble. At one point, I would have pitied the man. Not today. I'm all out of pity, besides what I plan to shower myself with when the annoyance goes away.

"Your father requests your presence, my lord," the trembling human says.

"Of course he does." I'm about to tell the man to go away and tell my father I'm in no mood for one of his meetings, but I bite my tongue. He'll only send someone else with a threat until he lets himself into my room. It's happened before. "Fine. Go away."

The servant yelps and scurries down the hall. Without bothering to clean myself up—if he wants to interrupt my day of doing nothing, he doesn't deserve me smelling like roses—I walk out of my room and slam my door hard enough to startle everyone in the hall. I used to be the reasonable dragon in the keep, but lately, everyone jumps out of my way in the corridors.

My fury has only fanned the flames of the rumors. I don't care. Let them talk. Nothing is more painful than the truth.

I don't bother to knock on my father's door, which earns a grunt of frustration. Something else I don't care about. He's tried everything to remove my heart, and he's succeeded. All respect is gone. He can be as angry as he wants to be because it doesn't match my frustration.

"I'm still the Lord of Ildracan," he says after I sit in a chair.

"And you're still the man that took the love of my life away from me."

"What happened with our united front as a family?"

"I got bored with it after waking up repeatedly without her."

Lord Archon rubs his eyes and sits back. The pinching of his nose is a clue that his patience with me is wearing thin. As proven at the cliffs, I can't defeat a lord in battle, but I'd welcome the fight. Threysoryth has been itching to bite someone for a while. He doesn't care who he takes a chunk out of.

"This isn't about her. I'd like to speak about Lorsa and Sule," Father says.

I grimace, remembering the sisters who tried to force a mating. "What a way to make my mood even worse."

"Their father offers money as recompense."

"At this point, I don't care. I never want to hear of them again."

Father slams his hand on his desk. I don't even twitch, letting my head fall back to look at the ceiling again. It's a better view than an angry lord that I don't care about. My whole family sucks.

"I don't care what you want."

"That's apparent." Drakyth, I sound like a moody teenager. Too bad I couldn't care less.

"You will knock off this sulking and remember who you are. You are the third son of Ildracan and will act as needed for respect, which is why I plan on not letting it go with this paltry sum. It must be known that our authority and laws are not to be trifled with."

I sneer at the ceiling. If he can't even hold the respect of his own son, how is he going to make the rest of the clan bow down to him? Lord Archon can bluster all he wants because I will never bow down to him again, even if it means my death. He took my world from me, and I'll never forgive him for it.

Wiping the unattractive look from my face, I blank my expression and drop my gaze back to the man demanding underserved respect. "And what do you plan to demand from the noble and his ambitious daughters?"

"One will remain with us to be made a servant for your sister when she returns. While he's here, I expect a formal and public apology from his entire family, along with a larger amount than he's offering."

I flinch. "While it'll help for his daughters to learn a little humility, I really don't relish seeing them again. Have you heard from Mother yet?"

"Yes. She was able to wear down the king. They will return in time for your brother's mating ceremony. We have agreed to hunt down the traitor and take care of her for him with proof. If we do this, he will forget that we didn't turn her over right away. If we don't, Iara will return to the capital as proof of our loyalty, and we will give him our third son for imprisonment and questioning."

"You sold me."

"It's your doing. It's not like Delto plans to use you in a respectable way anymore. Besides, this will give you an incentive to be more understanding with what's going on."

I scoff. "You mean the attempted execution of the only woman I want by my side."

"I mean the rebel red dragon that will keep you from inquisition. It's for the best that you give up these ill-thought feelings and fall in line. As soon as everything is taken care of, Tiera will be returned to us."

"I won't mate with her."

"You will do as you're told, or you'll be forced to."

"I'm sure using the naming artifact on me to mate with your cherished noble's daughter won't be insulting at all."

"They won't know about it." I open my mouth to argue, but he slams his fist on the desk again, hard enough to crack the hard wood this time. "Don't you dare think to defy me. You will either mate Tiera or be given to the king. Those are the two options with preexisting conditions. Deal with it."

A knock interrupts my scathing reply. A human enters when told to. "Lady Saysa is approaching the keep, my lords."

He ducks out at my father's signal. We follow, me a little less happy about it. My mating with Tiera was scheduled for a month after Rakurn's. Lord Archon probably has orders that the red dragon is to be destroyed by then. I can't let that happen. Ryn must be kept safe.

Too bad I don't know how.

We reach the steps after my brothers, and our father slips past Delto. Rakurn waits to greet his soon-to-be mate while I hang back behind the heir of Ildracan. The carriage carries the woman we await. Rakurn gives her his hand as she steps gracefully from her ride.

At the steps, they stop for my father to apologize for the missing parts of our family. Lady Saysa gives us a radiant smile, her brown eyes twinkling beneath a head full of coiled brown hair. She's small and polite, curtseying for my father and brother.

"It's no matter, my lord. I take no offense. A mother must defend her daughter," the new woman says.

I bite my lip to keep my sarcastic reply to myself. As they pass, Rakurn's mate looks at me with curiosity. I can't blame her for that. There's no doubt in my mind that all the rumors are being spread in all towns. I'm sure she's heard of my personal servant turning out to be the prophesied red dragon. I doubt she knows the truth; there's more to us than master and servant.

After a long supper with the new member of our family, I find myself in the courtyard again. Deep down, I want to return to my room to sulk. Threysoryth is restless and in need of our nightly search. There is no denying him.

Even if there was, would I want to? Not at all. What if the one night I don't search for her, she appears? It's not likely, but it's also not something I wish to risk. If she's out there, I must find her. I can't take losing Ryn longer than I can help. I want her in my arms again.

Letting my dragon take control, I change in the courtyard. Crickets chirp from the grassy areas not trampled down between buildings. I can smell them in my scaled form as I take in the fresh scents of the night and the nearby stable. Even blood and sweat remain in the air from training that I'm no longer welcome at. I bunch my legs and thrust myself into the sky.

The air is cool on my scales, bringing a slight dampness that leaves us uncomfortable. Eyes strain for a flash of red that will make the discomfort of every night worth it. When it doesn't come, I let Threysoryth rage and throw his fire into the sky. She has to be out here. We have to find her. No other result is acceptable. The search will continue until she's found.

Chapter Twelve
Return

THREY

I stand in front of the mirror, braiding my blond hair with difficulty. As much as I can handle things on my own, this is so much easier for another set of hands to achieve, particularly when those hands were Ryn's. Her deft fingers can weave a braid in seconds. Just one more way my life has been inconvenienced by her absence, one of the smaller ones. The list is endless.

A knock startles me enough to make me drop my hair. The tightness of the braid becomes loose, and I sigh my annoyance. I used to do this every day, sometimes multiple times a day. I can take care of my own hair. Not having Ryn makes everything seem like a much harder chore than it should be.

When I open the door, a familiar pair of blue eyes looks back at me. Joy threatens to edge into my tumultuous emotions, but I squash it down. Maybe she didn't know she was Delto's accomplice. Knowing or not didn't change the outcome. She ratted me out to my parents and started the landslide Delto was trying to nudge along.

Instead of acting on the moment of relief, I flatten my lips. "I see you're back, Iara."

"I am. You weren't waiting in the courtyard. Rakurn said you knew I was on my way."

"I didn't feel like it."

"Can I come in?"

My first reaction is to send her on her way. I catch myself at the last moment and stand clear to let her in. As much as I don't want to see her right now, she used to be my favorite sibling. She's helped me enough in the past to deserve some consideration. What she says will determine how long her presence will remain.

Iara perches on the edge of my couch, looking around my room in thought. My fists clench when I remember what's missing. My sister sits as if it's a normal day and the last time she was here didn't end with her leaving a gash on my face.

"You haven't gotten a new servant," she says, making my muscles tense.

"I never wanted one to begin with. I definitely don't want someone other than the last one."

My sister flinches and looks down at her hands. "I'm sorry."

The easy and sincere apology knocks the wind out of me. Iara has always been elegant and gracious, but she's also as stubborn as Mother.

Admitting fault is easier for her than the lady or the keep. That doesn't mean it's usual or expected.

I look over my sister that spent so long at the royal court. Once, I thought of her as beautiful, with her blue eyes and sandy-colored hair. She still has the same grace as before and looks unharmed. It's hard for me to think of her as beautiful any longer after what happened.

When I don't answer, she looks up at me. "I didn't mean to hurt you so severely, brother. I've had a lot of time to think over everything as I left it. At the time, I thought I was doing you a favor. I figured the longer you were left with her, the harder it would be to break what was forming between the two of you. Mother and Father would never let that go. I didn't want to see what her death would mean to you when you were too in love."

Crossing my arms over my chest, I walk over to my desk chair, turn it to face her, and sit. I'm not ready to forgive her or share the couch with the woman that almost got Ryn executed.

"As it turns out," she continues, "I was only playing into destiny's hands."

I stiffen. "Don't use the prophecy as an excuse for what you did."

"I'm not. I'm still in shock over what Mother told me. It's hard to believe that Ryn wasn't a human after all."

"Would it have changed how you felt?"

Iara shrugs. "Slightly. At least she's a dragon. The issue still would have been going against our parents' wishes. That never ends well."

"I was willing to face the consequences."

"And you did. Even when you thought you won, you still lost. Listen, Threy, I really am sorry. It took me time in a very dangerous place to learn that you can't help who you love. Forbidden doesn't mean easy to resist. It's hard to go against your heart, and it was wrong of me to force yours into events that I knew would break it, even if fate was involved. I thought I was protecting you, but I hurt you instead."

Something in her voice softens the tension in my shoulders. "It sounds like you know what I'm going through right now."

Iara offers me a sad smile. "Maybe I do, but that's a story for another time. Have you found her yet?"

"What?"

"Please, brother, I know better than to think you haven't been looking."

My fists clench again. "I'm not sure if I'd tell you if I did."

"I deserve that. Broken trust is hard to repair, but I'd like to try. I hope you do find her though."

It's my turn to look away while my fingers pluck at the leather of my pants. Not that I'll admit it right now, but I do wish to have my sister back. That desire won't blind me to the danger of trusting wrong again. As if I have any secrets to hide from her right now.

I run my hand over my face. "Me finding her instead of Father will put the two of us in danger."

"I don't wish to return to court, believe me. Maybe it would be retribution for what I did to you."

Ignoring the retribution part, I let the subject change. "What was it like?"

"Challenging. It's a pit of snakes there. Everyone has their own agenda, so it was best to keep to myself and not take sides on anything. Even giving an opinion on which horse is prettier would make enemies. It's crazy."

"So, no allies or friends?"

"There was one. Other than that, not really. Not even the wyrm hostage was friendly."

Iara stands and walks over to me. Graceful fingers undo my loose braid before reweaving it tightly. While she works, I ask, "Who was the friend?"

My sister ties off my hair without speaking. She remains quiet for a while before finally answering. "Again, a story for later. We need to get ready for Rakurn's ceremony."

"Why does it feel like you're keeping secrets?"

"Because I am. It's not a trust thing right now, Threy. I don't have the right to mistrust *you*. The issue is that I simply don't want to speak of it right now. Too fresh."

I want to ask more. In the end, I decide it's not my business to pry into. She'll either tell me or she won't. If she does, it'll be on her time.

"Besides," she says as she walks to the door, "none of my secrets are nearly big enough to compete with the hiding of the red dragon."

"I didn't know until Mother tried to kill her."

"It was a joke, Threy. Don't be a stranger, please. I want to be your sister again, even if I need to prove that I'm not still an enemy first."

Once she's gone, I allow myself the thought that I'd like her to be my sister again too. The past won't let me trust her yet. Iara betrayed me. What she did led to where I am now; alone and heartbroken. Wishes aren't enough to erase betrayal.

It would be nice to have an ally though.

Groaning, I stand to dress. An annoying shirt goes on first, followed by the itchy robe meant only to torture. The formality of the mating ceremony makes me want to skip it. It's not like my family cares enough. Although, my defiance stops when royal representatives are involved. If I make the king's people suspicious, it may become harder to keep Ryn safe. I can't find her while I'm in prison.

The time has come, so I exit my room and make my way toward the throne room. I walk through the large double doors, barely noticing the speculative looks coming from the bowing guards. The blue and silver decorations, along with the representation of the Jeweled Dragon, don't hold my gaze or thoughts. I don't need further reminders of royalty when I'm currently hating the king more than ever.

Taking my place next to my father, I'm happy to have him between me and the heir. The more distance between the two of us, the better. Not a day goes by that I don't envision tearing my oldest brother to shreds after what he plotted and almost succeeded in. I'd rather he keep away from me as much as possible.

Glancing over at the woman's side shows me Mother's hand on Iara's arm. I clench my teeth at the show of favoritism. I can't help but wonder if my mother would have fought as hard to have me back as she did her daughter. Something deep inside tells me she wouldn't. I'm surprised to find myself not caring as much as I feel I should.

The sting of rejection pales in comparison to the other emotional agony I'm in. I stopped caring when I realized how little they consider my happiness and welfare; how much they're willing to hurt me to get what they want. I mean nothing to them but what can be gained from me. If only I would have learned it sooner.

The doors open to reveal Saysa. She walks in with a smile on her face, her blue and silver robes matching tones with my brother's. I'm sure she let him know which shades to wear, unlike Delto's mate, who sits on the other side of my mother. I'm glad I can't see her. She's the mirror image of the cruelty Delto flaunts.

Saysa stops at the steps, and the royal clerk enters to perform the ceremony; another reminder that the king knows everything. Rakurn descends the steps and they climb together to meet the official. Here's where I stop paying attention. I know the responses that are needed enough to mutter them with others, so this isn't important.

My mind strays to imagine me in Rakurn's place and Ryn in Saysa's. What would it be like to be joined like this with the woman I love? I would love to find out someday, but if I save her like I want, I'll be imprisoned instead. Small price to pay to know she's alive and will remain that way. Even if my life becomes forfeit, I will make sure Ryn will live a long and happy one.

Drakyth help anyone who gets in my way of that goal.

The only thing I need to figure out is everything. How do I find her? How do I keep her safe from my father and the king? How do I avoid being forced to betray her?

I almost snort. Such an easy task to do what I want. I only need to go against a king and a lord, who happens to be my father. Naming magic isn't easy to circumvent. There's so much to consider. That doesn't mean I'm not going to put my everything into achieving it. I will keep my love safe.

The couple in front turn into dragons. At least neither of them has human collections to kill. Screams and the scent of burning flesh and blood are not things I can handle in this mood. That's what Iara was trying to protect me from; watching Tiera kill Ryn. Dragons give any humans that might cause jealousy to their mate. I couldn't stand by and watch that.

And Iara knew it.

I press my lips tight, refusing to give in to my sister's logic. I don't care what the reason is; I can't forgive that easily. Even Iara doesn't deserve the regard that comes with easy forgiveness. We used to be very close, but she lost that privilege. She isn't immune to the consequences of betrayal.

Lost in my thoughts, I almost miss the end of the ceremony. After the exit of the newly mated couple, we are invited to dine together and rejoice. Well, here goes a couple of hours of eating and pretending to be happy for my brother for something I may never get to experience but desperately want to. All I need to do is get through this celebration, then I can return to searching the grasses for Ryn.

Chapter Thirteen
Bruises and Cuts

RYN

The smooth wood slowly heats in my palm. I stand with my arm lax, watching my opponent look at me with distaste and annoyance. The air within this large chamber is thick with tension. Derision from my training partner causes me to grip the hilt of my practice sword hard enough to turn my knuckles white. We haven't even started yet.

"Are you sure Trev is the best teacher?" I ask Dyne with a grimace.

The man who helped create the fabled red dragon sits against the rough stone wall. He nods. "Your cousin is the one chosen to train all new recruits in combat. He's got the skill and patience for it."

Skeptical, I look at Trev and the hostility radiating from his light blue eyes, making me doubt that patience is a trait of his. I lick my lips and glance around the room. A few others spar, but it's mostly empty. While observing my surroundings, I keep an eye on my cousin because I don't trust him at all. I trust Lady Belra more, and that's saying something.

Trev widens his stance, and I swallow while sifting through the memory of Threy showing me how to hold a sword. My mind tries to stray toward what happened next, but I push it away. Now is not the time to mourn the loss of Threy's love and body. I need to remember the little he taught me because it looks like my instructor doesn't plan on doing any actual instructing. This is going to hurt.

As if to prove me right, Trev steps forward and swings in a movement so fluid that I can't follow him. Desperate, I throw up my wooden blade in hopes of a lucky block, drawing on what I saw Threy do during his practices. I'm not so lucky.

Wood smacking into my knee causes me to bellow in pain before I have the chance to hold it in. He is not holding back, as the throbbing bone in my leg tells me. When he comes for me again, I take a painful step back. My sore knee gives out and throws me to the floor. All air exits my lungs as I pant on the cool stone. The tip of Trev's practice sword touches my throat harder than needed.

"You're not trying very hard," my loving cousin tells me.

I try to speak, but he's pressing down hard enough to make talking difficult, so I simply glare at him. He matches my look. Silence weighs heavily between us, neither wanting to break the stalemate. This is our first session, an idea made of need since I can't shift to defend myself yet.

At long last, I'm able to pull air into my throat. "It's not like I grew up in an environment where I was encouraged to fight. All I know is what I learned watching dragons fight. That isn't much."

"You'll have to learn faster then."

"I need to be taught then, cousin."

His striking eyes narrow. Dyne cuts in before the attitude can spout from his mouth. "She's right, Trev. Don't let your feelings about her get in the way of you doing what you need to do."

"We have different views of needs, Uncle."

"We do not," Dyne says, crossing his arms over his chest. "What's at the top of both of our priorities is successfully removing the king from the throne. We can't do that without the red dragon, so she needs to know how to defend herself. If you can't remain impartial enough to do your job, I'll talk to the other leaders and remove you from training duty."

"I'm not washing dishes or shoveling horse manure."

My mouth curves into a frown at his disdain. I slaved in the stables for years. Without people working with the horses, we wouldn't have them. Every job is important to keep things moving smoothly. The people that shovel horse poop are just as important as he is.

"It's what you'll be doing if you don't instruct her in the correct way. Treat her as if you would any other new recruit. The red dragon is too important to risk her over your pride and jealousy."

"We don't even know for sure that she is the red dragon of prophecy."

I laugh. "I don't see any others around."

Trev turns back to me. "I don't see any at all. Why don't you shift and prove it? Oh, right. You can't. How convenient."

I push myself back to my feet and scowl at the annoying man. "I may not be able to tell what my dragon looks like, but I know for a fact that I'm red."

"Both of you calm down," Dyne says before the argument can continue. "Trev, she was born of a fairy dragon and a drake. That means she can only be one thing; a red dragon. Two, smell her. Her scent is not even close to human, which is the one thing I couldn't mask. She doesn't smell like heat or fire; she smells of ash. Fairy dragons smell like nature. Drakes smell like heat."

"So she smells like destruction. Sounds about right."

My teeth clench so hard that my jaw hurts. Dyne holds up his hand to forestall the angry words bubbling in my throat. My fury turns on him, and I have to try hard not to yell at him and say he has no authority over me because he isn't my father. I bite the words back a second before they almost escape. Father or not, blood or not, he is someone who stands high in this group. If I want to reach my true strength, I need to not destroy that connection. Any other relationship with him doesn't matter.

"Go cool off," Dyne tells his nephew. "Come back when you're willing to take your duty seriously. If you don't find that state of mind, I'll be talking to the other leaders tonight. Please don't make me do that because you're one of the best trainers we have. I won't let your unjustified anger damage our chances."

Trev stomps away. Dyne directs me to sit and take a drink. I quench my thirst, but I don't sit. Telling him I need a few minutes to calm down as well, I walk out of the training room, relieved to see Trev has already disappeared down the hall. I go to the one place I know will relax me.

Beland snorts when I approach him. I'm assured that he gets outside exercise and fresh grass every night, but a cave system is no place for a horse. The fact that I had no choice doesn't matter; I still feel guilty taking him from the stable. To calm, I move toward the old equipment piled in the corner to find a brush.

The bristles are falling out and spread wide. I must work with the available tools. Each swishing stroke melts tension from my shoulders. With a deep breath, I catch enough horse scent to fill my nose. This is home. This is how I spent years after my family was destroyed by a jealous dragon. As I near his flank, I sigh at the further reminder of dragon cruelty.

I run my fingers over the deep scars on his backside. Hunting accident. That's what they said it was. Dragon claws should have been nowhere near this animal. It had to be intentional.

"I was hoping that when I came here, I'd find less cruelty. It doesn't seem that way anymore. I'm a dragon now, or I always was. How can you still feel comfortable around me after this injury?"

Beland turns his head toward me and butts my cheek. I feel love coming from him, which startles me a little. Taking care of animals has always been a talent of mine. They're so expressive that I always wondered how others couldn't read them better. Maybe this is a dragon talent, which only makes me angrier that they did this to him.

Sighing, I lean my head against him. "I'm sorry. I can't stay. Duty calls."

My horse stomps a hoof and pushes into me again. I laugh, put the brush back, and make my way to where I'm supposed to be. Trev meets me at the doorway. He grimaces but motions me to enter first. Inside, Dyne talks to both of us to ensure we're both calm enough to focus before telling us to continue. After expressing surprise when he examines my grip on the sword, my cousin gives me slight adjustments. I don't mention Threy showed me because I feel that won't go over well.

We begin.

Dyne's threat must have worked. Trev actually instructed me and held back—a little. As soon as I'm back in my room after skipping supper, I sigh and lean my forehead against the cool stone wall. I take a few deep breaths before straightening with a wince.

Every single muscle and bone hurts. Yellow mottles my skin, the only evidence of the beating I took from Trev. Faster healing will always be welcome, particularly with an instructor like him. Dyne didn't even insist on practicing my blocked magic today. I must look as done with this day as I feel.

I grab a towel and some fresh clothes, then walk toward the bathing area while hoping it's empty. Dragons don't care much about nudity, but I've only been a dragon for a short time, so being naked in front of strange people still makes me nervous. My life before was to be as meek as a proper slave and not draw attention. Dragons like to collect humans and dispose of them when they're done. It was best to stay fully clothed at every possible moment.

In the cave with the flowing stream, I let out a sigh of relief. It's empty. I place my towel and clothes next to the flowing water in the back of the cavern before stripping. As soon as the water touches my toes, I let out a violent shiver. It's cold. Not that I didn't bathe occasionally in a watering trough, but I got used to Threy's warm baths.

I attempt to summon my magic without any success. With a sigh, I remind myself that this is flowing water anyway. There's no real way to keep it heated. Frustration still runs through me. After all this practice,

I'm still not close enough to summon at will. I can light a candle successfully more often, the strong red dragon that I am.

That brings a chuckle, and I take the rest of the steps leading into the cold water. Washing as quickly as possible, I rush to return to shore and wrap my towel around me. Ever since I first turned into a dragon, chilly temperatures seem to affect me more than they used to. I guess a being of fire doesn't like icy.

As I dry my hair, the scrape of boot on rock jerks my head back up. I'm almost done. Why can't people wait?

No one is there. Frowning, I finish drying off as I watch the doorway. Not a single movement can be seen. With a dark chuckle, I tell myself I'm paranoid. Who wouldn't be with a king that wants them dead? Paranoia is probably what I need to survive. I'll welcome it.

I slip my clothes on and bend down to pick up my towel and dirty garments. Hearing the noise again, I freeze. Terrified, I stand as quickly as I can and try to spin. I'm not fast enough. A strong arm circles my stomach while a sharp blade at my throat paralyzes me.

"Regards from King Darac," a voice whispers into my ear.

Answering will make my throat move. My throat moving will mean I get cut. Looking deep inside, I call on my dragon. She stirs but doesn't come forward. Fear overwhelms me, and I feel this is how the mighty red dragon is going to end. Weak, afraid, and alone.

In one last desperate move, I beg for my magic to come forward. I feel a spark, then pain assaults my throat.

Chapter Fourteen
A Magical Connection

RYN

The pain recedes to be replaced by warmth. I'm not cut; the weapon is growing hot against my shin. If I am cut, it has to be only a little. The fact that it hurt at all means it increased in temperature very quickly. This is proven by my attacker's sudden yelp.

A gooey sound meets my ears instead of the clang of metal on stone as the knife falls. Looking down, I see that the metal is starting to melt. Without further delay, I slam my elbow back into the man's stomach behind me. He grunts and stumbles away.

I take off toward the doorway, but my assassin grabs my wet hair. Pain spreads over my scalp with his sharp tug. Stumbling, I find myself pinned against his chest with a strong arm cutting off all airflow. Someone has to come by. This is the only way to get clean after a long day of training and working. For once, the empty bathing cave feels more like mockery than relief. Just my luck.

At this point, I can't even gasp for air. I struggle, but the arm tightens. Fighting is becoming difficult, and I find myself wishing we would have started with hand to hand instead of the sword. Even though I wouldn't be far enough along in the training to do much, the thought makes me swear in my head. Trev picked the wrong type of combat to start with. He probably did it on purpose.

Desperate, I try to throw my head back. He's holding me so tightly that it does no good. I can't get the leverage and strength to hit him with any impact. My vision darkens, and I feel Rynmoriath come roaring forward. I don't shift, but I feel my strength grow. My heel stomps on the man's foot. All he does is let out another grunt, so I fold my leg, pull it forward, then slam it backwards.

The sound of his leg snapping as his knee bends backward sickens me. I'm not sure if that's a sign of weakness or strength. He's attacking me, so I should be happy about his pain. Instead, I feel guilty for causing it.

A strangled scream bursts from my attacker's chest, and I stumble away as soon as his grip on me loosens. I fall to my hands and knees. Looking back, I see the man I recognize from the halls crumpled on the ground. I yell for help.

Panic takes over his eyes, giving him a second round of adrenaline. I'm not sure how he does it—dragons must be able to take a lot of pain—but he climbs to his feet and limps toward me, pulling another knife from his belt. No one's coming. I must save myself because no one else is here.

I call for my magic, but it remains stubborn and doesn't come. This is how I end. I say my goodbyes to Rynmoriath. She stirs more. As the man gets close, I feel my dragon surge again. Magic bursts out of me, throwing the man across the room. He slams into the wall and falls into a heap. I doubt he's dead. At least he's unconscious. I yell again.

This time, footsteps answer my call for help. Trev is the one that dashes through the opening, followed by a few more of the battle-hardened fighters. Trev murmurs at them to run for others while he walks over to the man lying on the hard stone floor. My cousin barely casts a glance my way.

Dyne and Nova rush in. Dyne ignores the man to find me, which shows a lot more care than the cousin who ignores my very existence. "What happened?"

"I was getting dressed after cleaning off, and that man attacked me. He said he's from King Darac."

"Traitor," Nova grumbles before stomping over to the unconscious man.

"What happened after he attacked you?"

Disbelief fills me as I think of the answer to that question. "My dragon stirred within me, and my magic came. First, I used heat to melt his weapon."

Dyne follows my pointing hand to stare at the cooling puddle of metal on the floor with his mouth hanging wide. "Did you shift?"

I shake my head. "After he dropped the knife, it's like she figured I was safe and retreated. I tried to run, but he grabbed my hair to pull me back to him and try to strangle me. I kicked his knee hard enough to bend it backward. He somehow still managed to stand and come for me. When I was starting to feel like it was hopeless, she came back and my magic pushed him against the wall."

"Both times your magic came, you felt your dragon?"

"Yes."

"That's something I'll need to think about. They may be connected, which would make it hard to summon both at the same time. I hope we can figure out a way around that. Are you hurt?"

"My throat's a little sore, but I'm fine."

The man who is my father by blood reaches for my throat to softly examine it. I don't jerk away, but I do flinch. His soft fingers remind me of the paws he showed me when he changed into his dragon. Everything about him is warm and fuzzy, which only makes his words about fairy dragons ring true in my heart.

Looking over at Trev dampens that feeling.

"If it burned you, you must not have been expecting it, and it had to happen fast. Red dragons are immune to fire, even in human form. It wouldn't surprise me if it's remnants of your human mask still leaving residue. It should occur less as your magic and dragon come out more," Dyne says.

"I'm nothing but one giant enigma."

"I think, at this point, that was a good thing. Your attacker under-estimated you."

My laughter sounds hollow. "Everyone always does. It doesn't help that I was good at hiding behind servitude."

"You did what you had to do."

I bite my lip as I feel my gaze harden. "That's what happens when you grow up not knowing who you are."

"Ryn—"

Dyne is interrupted by Nova shouting a command. "Just do it, Trev. We don't suffer traitors."

When I look over, I see Trev unsheathe his sword. Curious, I watch with fascination. When the blade removes the head from the body of the rebellious rebel, I yelp. Seeing his blood pool beneath him makes me gag and retch. My loving cousin looks back and rolls his eyes. I swear I hear him mutter something consisting of the word dramatic. I ignore him.

Nova walks over to where Dyne crouches over me. "We need to move camp. There's no telling if he told the king where we are."

"What if there are more?" I ask.

She sighs. "He's not the first mole we've found. We have to act as if he was the main threat and move. I'd like to set a guard on you."

"People already question my strength."

"You're too valuable to lose. As soon as this is all over, we'll stop guarding you. This came too close."

Groaning, I nod. I'm too valuable. My entire existence is important because of the stupid prophecy. Does anyone here see me as anything but a means to an end? Dyne may. Atan does. I don't know if they count in this assessment. "Not Trev."

Nova chuckles. "It'll be a rotation, so you'll need to deal with him sometime. We have enough fighters to go a couple of weeks at a time. I'll put him at the end of the list."

Defeated, I climb to my feet. I'm met by a hulking mass of muscle standing out in the hall. When I move to make my way to my room to pack, he follows. This must be the first poor sap to be stuck babysitting. Nova is quick. This is crazy. How did I go from a lowly stable slave, to a personal servant, to a red dragon, and now so important that people have to follow me around to keep me safe? Never in my life did I ever think I'd be worthy of guarding.

I take a deep breath, sobering myself. As stated not long ago, I'm only important until the prophecy is fulfilled. I still find myself wondering if I will live through this war. Nothing in the prophecy says the red dragon comes out of this alive. I'll kill a king, but will someone kill me in return?

It doesn't matter. Life is what it is. What will be will be. If I've learned anything from being at the beck and call of dragons and destiny, it's that I have no say in what happens to me. No matter how much I wish to fight, I end up right where I'm supposed to be, whether I want to or not.

I pack up my meager donated belongings into my bag under the watchful eyes of the brute by my door. I'm pretty sure no one can hide in such a sparsely furnished cave, but I don't have the energy to argue.

"How long will it take for the group to be ready?" I ask.

He blinks as if surprised I'm talking to him. "A couple of hours. We can pack up quickly."

"Do they need me?"

"No. If you want to rest, I can step outside and wake you when it's time to move."

"If you don't mind."

Before leaving, he looks under my thin cot. Like anyone is going to be able to hide under there. It's clear, even to my untrained eyes, that no assassins are hiding in this room. I don't say anything because I know it's probably part of his duties as my guard. As soon as he's out of the room, I grab my journal and write a short passage about my training and near death.

I sometimes wonder why I cling so hard to this life. Will I ever see Threy again? Life doesn't seem worth living without him. As much as we were at odds before, he's one of the rare good dragons. Maybe my death will release him from the bond. Will it hurt? I don't want him to hurt. In the end, I know I have no choice in the matter. This unrelenting prophecy will do what it wants with me.

Sighing, I shove the pencil in the book and put it back in my pack. As tired as I am, I lie in bed, tracing the darker grays that sometimes twist through the rock above my head. Threy's face enters my mind.

His smile when I do something surprising. His chuckles when I say something dirty. I can't help but wonder what he's doing right now.

What's happening in the world above? As a human slave, I wasn't told much. I also was often ignored, so I could at least learn a little of what was happening outside by being silent about my tasks. Now, I have nothing. No news. No clue.

Does Threy still pine for me? Have his parents tried pushing Tiera at him again. That would be interesting since he's already mated. Has he figured that out? I'm sure if he knew before, he would have told me. I'm the only one that knows the extent of our bond, except Dyne.

I'd do anything to fall asleep in his arms again. I don't care how closely we have to hide it. The secrecy used to bother me because I wanted to claim him as mine for all to know. It was too dangerous, so I sulked about hiding and pretending to be his personal servant. Right now, I'd take that back in a heartbeat. If it gives me Threy, I'll gladly accept the deception and secrecy. Anything to have my copper dragon back with me.

A sharp pain stabs into my chest. I bite my lip to keep from making any sound that might bring the man outside the door in. I'm not sure what that was, but it's gone now. I rub the spot between my breasts to ensure nothing is wrong. I run my hand over a peaked nipple and pretend it's his. No one's hands can feel as good as his.

As my thoughts swirl, I feel heat pool between my legs. I reach inside my pants to find wetness slicking my fingers. It's been so long without the man that makes my entire world shine. I need him. My fingers slip further. No one can feel as good as him, but I need the relief.

Chapter Fifteen
Shadows Bite

RYN

A knock wakes me from my sleep too early. Blinking, I sit up and look around in confusion. Dreaming of being back with Threy has both disoriented me and undone what my time before rest had fixed. I rub my eyes and call for the knocker to enter at the next pounding.

It's my babysitter. "Everyone is getting ready to move."

"Okay. I'm ready. Groggy, but ready."

I'm not sure if that's truth or lie. That was not nearly enough rest to refresh myself for hours of walking underground. My blanket gets crammed into my pack. When my bodyguard picks it up, I try to argue.

It's my pack and my responsibility. He has none of it and motions me out the door.

Watching the line of dragons and humans go by, I wait until I see Atan to slip into it. My friend makes room for me without being asked. The person behind mutters annoyance when the hulking man pushes in into the crowd to stay close to me. Atan glances back and lifts a brown eyebrow in question.

I sigh. "They put a babysitter on me."

"Sounds like one is needed."

With a grimace, I look back at my guard and consider asking for a name. I shake my head and look forward again without asking. If they're rotating, I won't have time to get to know him. It feels weird being the one waited on. It feels backwards.

All my adult life has revolved around serving others. Take care of their horses. Fetch the mounts. Follow Threy around and get him whatever he wishes for. This feels wrong.

"And what are people going to think if they see I can't defend myself?" I ask.

"That you're new to fighting."

I hear the man at my back grunt in agreement. My scowl hurts, but I fight the temptation to turn it on him. It's not his fault that he's stuck with me. That doesn't mean he has to agree with my weakness, no matter how true. The scowl turns into a grimace.

"Listen to me, Ryn," Atan continues when I don't respond. "You're important to this movement. If anything, you're the most important part of it. They've been teaching you to fight, but they're not going to let someone take you out before you can defend yourself. Right now, you need men like Synt."

Well, looks like I get a name anyway. Why should I need a name? The likelihood of one or both of us dying is high. Besides Dyne, Nova, and Trev, most of the people in this group either treat me as some sort of divine being that they need to avoid soiling or treat me like someone tested and found wanting. Friends don't come any more readily now than as a slave. I recognize people by faces, not names.

Maybe it's me. I'm so used to being invisible that I don't really know how to interact with people. That's something to think about later. I'm too tired to focus on making friends right now. It's been a rough day, night, whatever it is. Time ceases to exist down here. All I know is what others tell me.

"Until I'm no longer needed, then I can depend on myself," I say with a touch of bitterness.

"You'll always have me to depend on. And Dyne too."

I laugh. "Dyne? He sees me the same as the others."

Atan shakes his head. "You seem blind to the pain and regret in his eyes, Ryn. I fully believe him when he said that giving you up and not interfering was done out of necessity. I think he would have loved and raised you with happiness if circumstances were different. You don't seem to have the same bitterness with your mom."

"My mom had all intentions of going back for me. She died to keep me alive."

"While Dyne fought somewhere else. I'm sure if it wasn't the safest to leave you, he wouldn't have."

"You've always hated dragons. Why are you so quick to defend one now?"

My friend is silent for a few moments before speaking again. "Some have grown on me. Imagine my surprise when I realized that dragons are almost likable when they're not enslaving you. Most, anyway. Some are still cranky and snobby."

Synt snorts behind us, as if more amused than upset over Atan's comment. Maybe he's one of the dragons my friend means. He hasn't done anything to prove any different, so it's possible. My bodyguard has been nothing but kind and respectful. Maybe I can request him again instead of Trev. One less in rotation shouldn't cause too much of a problem for the others.

We walk for a while before I find myself catching hints of fresh air. Curious, I sniff to make sure I'm not simply imagining what I want to feel. I'm not. The crisp scents of night and grass reach me. A little further along, I see Atan take a deep breath and close his eyes. We're heading topside?

The difference when we walk out of the cave system is almost overwhelming. I stop and lift my face to the starry sky to feel the cool breeze blow over me. Crickets chirp in the long grass as it swishes in the wind. This is perfect, and I feel energy return. Lack of sleep doesn't matter when I have the freedom of being outside again.

"Best to keep moving," Dyne says, coming up behind me.

I groan but do as he suggests. "Is it safe to be here?"

"These caves run all through the underground in Sertran, but some of the tunnels have caved in at certain points. We're moving to another section that can't be reached through where we were. It's best to move to somewhere that can't easily be reached by our last known location."

"That makes sense, but is it safe?"

"Not always. It's necessary. Dragons aren't the only predators out here, so keep your eyes open. The grasses can be dangerous at night."

Nodding, I let the conversation die. Nothing in life lacks danger. That's one thing I've learned. It's always best to be aware of your surroundings to keep from drawing the attention of the wrong creatures. As much as I want to enjoy this clean sensation, I hurry along behind the others, Synt not more than a step or two behind.

I know it's dangerous out in the open, but I'm going to enjoy it while I can. Who knows how long I'll spend in the stale darkness, surrounded by stone, when we reach our destination? Might as well take in as much fresh air as possible. This respite is needed, no matter the danger of enjoying it.

Outside, the people around us are quiet, so we follow their lead and keep the silence strong. Anything to avoid any possible watching predators. The only noise made are the horses in the back and the occasional screechy wheel of a cart. Even the dogs are quiet. Then I hear it, a rustle in the distance. Others do as well because the line slows a little. It doesn't stop, but we're more cautious.

"How much further?" I whisper to Synt.

"Another hour I'd say."

I bite my tongue. The darkness may hold an enemy we can't see yet. An hour feels like a long time in the grip of the unknown. What's out there? It could be a couple of rabbits or a sleeping herd of buffalo. My logical reasoning does nothing to quell my uncertainty. It's easy to imagine a monster in the dark, whether human, dragon, or animal.

The maker of the sound doesn't force me to wait for too long. Black shapes spring from the grass, attacking the people trying to hide in the same darkness. Screams and roars echo in the night. All around us, dragons replace where our people once stood. Humans scramble for the safety of a dragon, wagon, or fighter. Synt tosses me a dagger.

It's slippery in my sweaty palm. Attempts to call my magic and dragon are useless, as always. Nothing comes at my bidding. What good is a powerful dragon that lacks actual power? Frustration makes me growl at the same time a black blur leaps for me.

I raise my dagger to fight, but I don't need to bother. Its head rolls as Synt's sword slices into it, landing at my feet. It's a giant black cat, with fangs as long as my middle finger, if not longer. It's hard to tell in the dark. My bodyguard rolls beneath the weight of another feline. A third hits me from the side.

Trying once again to call my dragon forth, I growl at her ignorance of the danger I'm in and the need I have for her. Teeth dig into the shoulder that leads to the hand holding my dagger. Numbness makes my fingers tingle, and I almost drop the only weapon I have. I'm able to grab it with my free hand. I swing around to embed the blade into the ribs of my attacker. It howls and stumbles back.

I know it won't be gone for long, so I swing again before it can pull away. The cat falls limp on top of me, leaking sticky blood all over my shirt. Another comes out of the grass. Struggling, I try to push the fuzzy corpse off me. It's heavy and moves too slow. Death comes at me in a stalking, hungry shadow.

The cat lifts its lips up into a ferocious snarl. I can't defend myself like this. As it gets closer, the scent of its rancid breath reaches for me. My struggling hurts, but I need to get free. It bunches hind legs and readies to end the prophecy before it can be fulfilled. The fuzzy head rolls across the ground, Synt standing over my would-be death with a bloody sword.

Looking at my muscular babysitter, I can see the deep gash bleeding on his cheek. He helps me to my feet, and I notice others milling around. Everyone is still tense, but I sense the immediate danger is over. A wyvern walks around to survey the battlegrounds.

She's all black, with a thin head and sharp, needle-like teeth in her beak. Feathers cover her clawed wings as she uses them to help walk around. Black scales glisten in the moonlight. She stops next to us and sniffs.

"Injured, but fine, Nova," Synt says beside me.

The wyvern nods and continues to walk down the line. "That was Nova?"

"Yep. Any injuries besides the bite on your shoulder?"

"No. Why is a wyvern fighting against a wyvern king?"

"That should heal fine then. Not all wyverns like the way King Darac rules. If you want to know more, it's something you need to ask her. She's pretty open about it, but it's not my story."

Prying into someone else's past isn't important under these circumstances, so I decide to let it go. As he gathers our bags, I watch a couple of dragons dig holes to place the dead. Once that's taken care of, they shift back. We are on the way again before Dyne finds me.

"Are you hurt?" he asks.

"Why? Don't want the rebellion to fail."

Atan, who gratefully found a place to hide in a cart, shoots me a look. I send one right back at him. I don't care what he says. My reaction is based on what I see, not what someone tells me.

"More than that," Dyne says with a sigh. "I know you won't believe me, but I've always loved you as my daughter. I don't want you to get hurt. The rebellion is important. So are you as a person. You don't have to think of me as a father; I understand why. All I ask is that you give me a chance to prove that I see you as more than a weapon."

I lift my gaze to the stars for a few moments. "My shoulder was bitten, but Synt kept me alive."

Dyne thanks Synt for his actions. Everyone remains quiet, exhausted from both the walk and the fight. Grass whips around us. My mind drifts to Threy. It's late, so he's probably in his nice, warm bed. What I wouldn't do to be there instead of here.

A pain shoots through my chest hard enough to take my breath away. I rub it while trying to avoid notice. Luck isn't on my side.

"Is your chest hurt?" Dyne asks.

"I get a sharp pain from time to time. Nothing seems to be wrong though."

"How long has it been happening?"

"Since the attack by the stream. It's not an injury. The only thing that guy hurt was my throat."

Dyne grabs my arm to slow our pace a bit. "That's not my worry. Are you usually thinking about Threy when it happens?"

"Yeah."

"How bad is it?"

"Not bad. Just a quick sharp pain. What do you think it is?"

Synt grunts. "Mating bond."

I stumble, tripping over my own two feet. Word will now spread; I'm sure of it. "But it's not full yet."

Dyne steadies me, careful of my shoulder. "The more your magic strengthens, the stronger the bond will get. This will get worse as you get better with magic."

"Great."

My father by blood is saved from answering as we reach the entrance to the new cave. I'm assured we have at least another hour of walking to get to the safer part of this system. With a groan and tired legs, I follow along. This night is never going to end.

Chapter Sixteen
Breaking Heart

RYN

"Can you feel your dragon?" Dyne asks.

"She feels like a horse excited to be home after a long ride."

He chuckles. "That's good. It means she feels at home within you."

"Why doesn't she want to be free?"

"It's not that she doesn't want freedom. After being suppressed so long, free rein inside of you feels like she's released. It wouldn't surprise me if she's a little apprehensive about coming out. That's the only thing I can think of."

Pressing my lips together, I look around at the empty room. Nova stands by the doorway again, keeping people out because when my magic does work, it is as likely to burn someone by accident as do what I ask. My magic comes easier, but it's wild when it lets me summon it. Frustrated is a huge understatement for me.

"I thought I had to picture her right to summon her," I say.

Dyne sighs. "You do, but I fear that's only one of the issues. She wants you to know her. That doesn't mean she trusts the outside. This is a side effect I didn't think of when hiding you."

"How do we get around it?"

"I'm not sure. I'm going to continue to think about the issue. It may take time. It may take a different way of training, but we will figure it out. I caused this mess, and I'll clean it up."

For once, I'm not angry at him over his actions stunting me. "You did what you had to do."

His blue eyes jerk up to look into mine, as if gauging the truth of what I tell him. I keep my eyes on his to show him I'm not being sarcastic. My tantrum has finally run its course. At the worst, I feel guilty over my treatment. That doesn't mean I'm ready to call him my father. It simply means I've come to terms with the lies of my previous life and the fact there were solid reasons for it.

If anything, my near death at the hands of the tyrant king is enough to push me fully into the rebellion. I've done nothing to the fearful royal wyvern, and he still tried to have me killed. I mean, I know he's had a price on my head since before I was born. It's a little more urgent when I have a knife at my throat.

"Do you think they've done anything to Threy?" I say.

The subject change makes Dyne blink and Nova grin. I'm a little surprised at the direction I went too. A burning fills my chest at the mere mention of him, but I keep my face calm. I know Dyne worries about me. There's nothing that can be done, so I'll have to withstand it.

"I'm sorry. The question just popped into my head. If the king tried to assassinate me, I can only imagine what he's willing to do with the dragon that helped hide me," I say.

"Threy has a little more shielding than you do. Darac does as he likes, but turning the head of the Ildracan clan against him is something he'll take care with. He will get what he wants, but he will do it in a way that doesn't blow back on him. All the fairy dragons were already killed, except the few still with the rebellion. Taking out another type of dragon won't reflect well and may send more to our side."

"If this Jeweled Dracon is so powerful, why can't he wipe out the caves?"

"Multiple reasons. First, red dragons from before warded some of the tunnels before they were hunted down, as we talked about before. The problem with these wards is that they're starting to fail because they need to be refreshed after so many years. There are no red dragons to refresh them." The familiar dark look from our previous conversation passes over his eyes, but he continues before I can ask about it. "Second, there are cave-ins that even the silver fire can't penetrate. It makes it too hard for the fires to flood the entire underground. It's a matter of finding safety quickly."

He's already explained this but still remains patient while answering my question. Something else catches my attention. "Silver fire?"

"Yes. Most dragons haven't seen the flames from the Jeweled Dracon before. It's knowledge that has been passed down through the fairy dragons after the destruction of our people. I've also seen it."

"How many times?"

He bites his lip and looks away. I see the grief in his slack muscles and in his eyes before he turns to look at Nova. "I've seen it briefly twice, but once was a little too close. You aunt Iori was killed by the fire, and I barely got Trev out alive."

"And you lost your wings."

When Dyne winces, I mentally kick myself for the callous comment. I didn't think before speaking, so I hurt unintentionally, but I still caused pain. I no longer live in resentment of this man. I should take more care when speaking to him.

"Yes. Sertran almost lost three fairy dragons at once that day."

"How many are there?"

He looks at me again. "Two hundred, maybe three... I think. There were once thousands."

That's so sad. My gaze falls onto my lap. So many lives lost because of fear and greed. I've always known the world is cruel and unyielding, but I realize more and more how bad it is day-by-day. There's no limit to the amount of evil in this world. It's a plague that must be eradicated, and it's up to me to do it.

"Why would the dragon god gift one dragon enough power to destroy everything?" I ask.

"There is so much more to the gift of Drakyth than destruction. It has immense power that can be used for good and evil. Darac merely uses the power to feed his paranoia. Did it hurt when you thought of Threy a minute ago?" Dyne asks.

Pulling my mind out of the darkness of our conversation, I nod and accept the change in topic. "It's more of a lingering burn than a quick sharpness now."

"I was worried that the more we accessed your magic, the more pain you'd have."

"This needs to be done. I can handle it."

"For now," Dyne mutters. Louder, he says, "Well, let's practice a bit more. You know what to do."

Closing my eyes, I call to Rynmoriath. She focuses her attention on me and sends me a feeling of contentment. As she comes closer to the outside, I feel the magic just out of my reach. I stretch for it, groaning at the fact that it runs through my mental fingers like water. To keep her close, I avoid picturing my dragon. She doesn't like when I picture her wrong, but I don't know how to do better without her coming out the whole way.

The scaly touch of Rynmoriath on my consciousness is warm and inviting. Trying to force her out will only scare her, so I focus more on being welcoming. She rubs against my mind in a way that reminds me of Hunter after my long days in the stable. I'm finally able to grasp my magic.

As told by Dyne, I focus on defensive spells. He tells me the easiest thing I can do is create a small shield. Once stronger, I'll be able to make a bigger one. He can make a full dome around himself, which he says is a rarity among fairy dragons. At this point, I'd take any tiny shield, even if it's as weak as paper to start.

My mind visualizes what I want to do, and I push the power in me toward the vision. I feel a flicker that dies down fast. Rynmoriath flinches at my frustration and retreats deep within me. Letting out a quick breath, I open my eyes. Why is Dyne smiling?

"What?" I ask.

"You did it!"

"What do you mean? All I felt was a short flicker."

"That was it."

Glancing at Nova, I notice that even she holds a warm smile. Confused, I glance back and forth between them. "It barely felt like anything. I got frustrated, so she left me."

"It was tiny," Nova says, "but it was there."

"Really?"

Dyne chuckles. "I saw a short shimmer about the size of my palm. It didn't last long, but it was still there."

"Huh. I thought it was another complete failure."

We try again and again. To my disappointment, it doesn't happen anymore. Despite my dejection, both Nova and Dyne seem excited. I'm reminded that patience is needed, which is getting exhausting. After another hour, Dyne declares that's it for the day. I'm ready to leave all the failures behind. My small success energized me. Rynmoriath's stubbornness to return drained all that energy.

"Let's get a quick meal, then we can meet Trev," Dyne says, making me grit my teeth.

The wooden sword comes for my head, and I manage to block it at the last second to avoid being knocked out. So far, Trev has behaved, but he definitely isn't taking it easy on me because I'm family. If anything, I think our familial bond angers him enough to be harder on me than usual.

Another hit jars my weapon so much that my fingers tingle and turn a little numb. While focused on the sensation, Trev uses his practice blade to sweep my feet out from under me. Sparks flash when my head hits the hard floor. I gasp for breath and make no move to get up. When my vision clears, I find my cousin looking down on me with his sword arm hanging limp and a frustrated look on his face.

"You got distracted," he says.

"That last swing made my fingers go numb."

"You need to learn to ignore those kinds of sensations. Distraction in battle is deadly."

I glare at him. "I need a quick drink."

Trev shrugs and does a few quick moves with his fake sword. Dyne watches me walk over to him. "You're learning."

"I'm still earning more bruises than anything."

"That's only because Trev has to press harder."

I snort and sit to get a drink while catching my breath. Dyne hops to his feet and walks over to talk to his nephew. Their voices are too low for me to pick up, and I don't bother to try to listen in. Trev smirks, which makes me feel suspicious. Dyne walks away from him before I can change my position on eavesdropping.

"What was that about?" I ask, watching Trev from the corner of my eye.

"Nothing important. Just a little strategy discussion."

I narrow my eyes but don't push further. The look on his face tells me he won't elaborate. Deciding to get this over with, I stand and grab my weapon, more cautious than earlier. Before I get back to my original place, Trev charges me. Yelping, I swing my sword up to block his attack and jump to the side. He doesn't give me any reprieve, following my retreat and continuing to swing.

Fear takes over. It's all I can do to keep him from hitting me. I back between others practicing and watching, trying my best not to be hurt by the accidental swing of someone who is not my sparring partner. This only causes more bruises.

Trev knocks my sword out of my fingers with a move I have no idea how to counter. I trip and fall onto my butt. Mania flashes in his light blue eyes as he raises his sword for a blow that will be devastating.

Rynmoriath!

The terror and panic in my thoughts bring her surging forth. Just like during the assassination, a burst explodes from me. Trev flies into the nearest wall, earning a visit from a worried Dyne. When I look around, I see the two closest fighting couples were also thrown. Blood runs from someone's head. Another holds a clearly broken wrist. Someone is unconscious while the last looks around confused.

Looking over at Trev, I see him sitting up, holding his head with his eyes unfocused. Dyne asks him a few questions. When satisfied with the answers, he rushes over to me.

"Are you alright?" Dyne asks, grasping my shoulders.

Stunned, I glance around while shaking my head. "He tried to kill me."

"He wasn't."

"You didn't see the look in his eyes."

"That just means he is a good actor."

My gaze swings back to his quickly. "What does that mean?"

"When I went to talk to him, I told him to attack with everything he has and make it look like he meant it."

"What?! Why would you give him free rein like that? He hates me. He could have killed me."

Dyne mutters calming words that I want no part of. "I wanted to see if your dragon would respond when needed and if you could use magic when in dire need. You did. It gives me more information to think about when trying to figure out a new way to make our sessions a success. Ryn, you grew fangs and claws before you defended yourself."

I'm about to yell at him again, but the last part hits me. "I did? I partially shifted?"

"You did. This gives me a lot to think about."

"Can you do it without me almost dying?"

"He wasn't going to actually hurt you."

"I—" Agony blocks out my next words. I suck in a deep breath, as it feels like someone stabs me repeatedly in the heart. There's no noise possible at all; the pain is too much. Grasping at my chest, I can't even moan.

Dyne's voice tries to break through the agony, but I can't make out anything he says. Tears stream from my eyes as I lean forward. The pain slowly dies down after what feels like eternity. When my vision clears, I see a circle of people around me. Even the woman bleeding from me throwing her into the wall looks concerned. Trev looks slightly worried, which is surprising.

"Ryn?" Dyne says, breaking through my pain.

"That hurt," I rasp.

"It seems that the strained bond is worse after a strong burst of magic."

"Really? I couldn't tell."

My sarcasm is ignored as Dyne murmurs about needing to speak to our leaders and rushing from the room. His frantic eyes cast one last worried glance back my way. Strong hands help me to my feet. The new bodyguard half-carries me to my room. I'm done for today. No supper. No journal. All I want is my bed.

Chapter Seventeen
A Flash of Red

Threy

Mindaine whinnies beneath my gentle touch. Something about being in the stable makes me feel comforted. I'm not sure if it's the quiet, the warmth, or the fact this is where I first saw Ryn. Her beautiful gray eyes drank me in, and I played with her reaction. Delto noticed and cruelly ripped her from her home to be my personal servant. It was either accept the gift or let him have her, which would have meant torture and eventual death.

Sighing, I lean my face against my horse. He butts my head with his nose. I take in the scent of horse and hay, ignoring the undercurrent of manure. For some reason, my horse seems to care that I'm upset. A sharp pain penetrates my chest until I need to suck in a deep breath. I'm not sure what this is, but I haven't told anyone about it. No one would care. It's getting worse.

"Well, Lord Threy. Fancy seeing you here."

Tensing, I turn toward my uncle. All my life, he's been anything but cruel. Always trying to teach us the best way to fight and defend ourselves, he was a good uncle. Right now, the smirk on his face takes all those pleasant memories away. Something painful is coming my way.

"Uncle."

"Training your replacement. I think he'll do well when the time comes."

The snide tone makes me cringe. I guess beating a general in battle will turn him bitter against you, particularly when you use a trick to do so. I've seen him with others, and he's nowhere near this hateful. He was keeping me from saving the woman who stole my heart. Did he expect me to just turn my back on what I consider mine? Wasn't happening.

"I'm sure he'll serve Delto well," I say, turning back to scratch Mindaine's neck.

"You'll need to find something to do that will bring honor to your family. Rumors are already spreading about why you were taken away from your duty. You can come with me. Helping us might afford you a little more respect."

Curious, I turn back to him. "Go with you where?"

While curious, I'm also cautious. Offering to help me doesn't fit the look on my uncle's face or the way he's been treating me lately. I am ready for whatever he's about to say. I don't have to wait long.

"Your father gave me permission to widen the search for your sweetheart. In fact, he expects me to put every dragon on the search.

I'm to take care of her however I need to, even if it means killing her. As long as I have proof of her demise, of course."

My fist clenches in Mindaine's mane. I release my grasp when the horse whinnies discomfort and snaps his teeth at me. It's not until my uncle's hand strays to his sword that I realize I'm gripping my hilt with a tight fist. Calming myself isn't easy. Threysoryth is ready to burn the general of our army.

"You've been flying every night, Lord Threy. Any sightings?" My uncle grasps his sword, preparing for the reaction he expects out of me with his words.

I fight the beast that rages inside me, knowing this is nothing but a trap. If I attack, he'll have a reason to beat me into submission—if not outright kill me—and I can't give him that. I can't beat him in a fair fight. It was a trick that brought me victory last time. A third son can't beat the power Drakyth gifts our generals.

Threysoryth fights for release, my claws gouging into my leather pants. Blood fills my mouth as fangs pierce my tongue.

If he kills us, we can't keep Ryn safe.

The thought reaches my dragon. His rage is still present, but he withdraws with a warning growl that I'm sure my uncle can hear. Removing my hand from the hilt is hard. My joints ache while I force them to release my white-knuckled grip. All my muscles remain stiff and ready for an attack.

Looking disappointed, the general relaxes his stance. "Well? Any sightings?"

My heart floods my veins with fury, but I hold back to avoid doing anything stupid. "None. I go out to hunt."

He sneers but accepts my answer. "I'll let you know when the deed is done."

Pushing the next growl down is hard. Somehow, I manage before it can rumble deep inside me. "I'm sure you will, Uncle."

Annoyed by my lack of response, he stalks out of the stable. I wait until I hear them ride away before exiting and making my way for the keep. Threysoryth begs me to go after them and make sure they don't find Ryn and hurt her. I want that with all of my heart, but it isn't possible. I can't take on that many. Besides, if I can't find her, he won't either. Faith in her ability to hide is the only thing that keeps hope alive.

Instead of returning to the keep, I circle behind it. No one is present, so I find a tree to sit beneath. Ryn is *too* good at hiding. It's obvious she doesn't want me to find her. Does she not love me like she said? Does she not trust me?

Both of those questions fan the flames within me. I gave that woman everything I have, and she doesn't want it or trust it. My family has practically disowned me in private, and my word means nothing to them. All because I chose her over them.

Then she does this. She runs away without even a goodbye. She hides from me while I spend all my spare nights searching for her. Maybe being the red dragon has gone to her head. Maybe she feels like she's too important. Maybe I'm not good enough for her anymore.

"Brother!"

My heart falls. This is the last thing I need right now. "Go away."

"I wanted to find you because I figured you'd be upset by the news of the increased intensity of the hunt. I want to make sure you're alright. Little rabbit had an effect on you."

"Sure you do. You only want to make me feel worse, so go away."

"You're my youngest brother. I don't want your pain."

I scoff. "Oh, please. You orchestrated this whole thing."

"The whole thing? Not likely. It's not like I knew who the insignificant stable girl was."

Clenching my fists, I hold back my desire to tear the heir of Ildracan apart. It can't happen. He's too strong. Even if I accomplished it, I'd be executed. I'm sure he wants to fight though. Delto has always enjoyed putting me in my place.

"Obviously not insignificant," I say.

Delto chuckles. "Obviously. That rabbit has fangs. Although, they're dull. She's easy to scare, isn't she?"

The joy in his voice makes holding back even harder. This man should not have an entire dragon clan under his control due to his ego. The future looks bleak when he takes father's seat. Maybe I'll be lucky and he'll anger the king enough to get himself killed. That would be something to see.

"Go away."

"Do you have nightmares of watching her caught by the king or our uncle?"

"Actually, my dreams are quite nice. They're of me tearing your throat out. I'd tear out your heart instead, but I'm pretty sure you don't have one."

Delto's green eyes darken until they're almost black. I'm not sure if his smirk is from his amusement or the desire to put me down. Either would be a great guess with a high likelihood of being right, so I can't pick one.

"Is that a threat, brother?" Delto asks with a snarl in his voice.

"You asked about my dreams, and that's all they are. The last time I checked, dreams aren't threats, or I bet you'd be threatening Father a lot since you're in a hurry to be in control."

Rakurn chooses this time to run over. "Delto, peace. It won't look good for your lordship if you kill your brother. Threy, why do you have to keep proving to me how stupid you are?"

My eyes find our middle brother, who has a hand on Delto's shoulder. "What makes you think I care what any of you think about me anymore? You've all used me for your own gain. Why should I care what I look like to you?"

"You already angered the volatile one of us. Don't anger the one that has a little leverage with him."

I meet Rakurn's glare for a few moments, stand and head for the courtyard. Delto yells behind me. "Going to search for the woman that ran away from you? You're pathetic, brother. If she wanted you, you'd know where she is!"

That pushes me over the edge. Threysoryth bursts from me so fast that I don't even realize it's happening. I spin and launch myself at Delto. He shifts before I can reach him. My dragon readies his fire while I swipe with claws. Rakurn swears, makes sure he's far enough away not to get trampled, and starts stripping.

My fire blows on Delto's dark green dragon, all my fury behind it. He bursts through, unsinged, and tackles me. When I see his teeth come for my throat, I twist to dig my back claws into his back leg. My brother misses my throat but takes a chunk of dirt out of the ground instead. This isn't some playful fight meant to make me submit. This is real. He'll kill me if I let him.

I'm able to push him off me. Before he can launch another attack, Rakurn jumps between us and screams into our heads. *Enough! Stop this now!*

Delto listens to him, which surprises me. The arrogant heir listens to no one. Regardless, he shifts, as does Rakurn. I refuse, glaring down on them from height. My tail thumps the ground in displeasure, and my belly heats while looking at the vulnerable Delto.

"You're so touchy, brother," Delto says in the tone he's perfected that leaves you wondering if you're being mocked.

I roar loud enough that the hair blows back from both of their faces. Rakurn holds up a hand for peace. "Peace, Threy. It's best to leave this lie untouched. Let it go."

My growl rumbles so loud that my entire body trembles. Delto stands at ease to show me how little he fears me, even in human form. I hiss my anger and defiance, launching into the air with one giant leap. My eldest brother's laughter follows me into the sky, but I ignore it. I need blood, but it can't be his without making things worse. Things are bad enough, and I don't need to add to them.

Therefore, the expendable third son of the leader of the Ildracan clan flies south, away from the keep and away from family. Anything to keep myself from making a deadly mistake. The air pushes against my wings as I beat them to gain height. The town fades below me, replaced by yellow grass that sways in the breeze.

With the distance, my fury cools. That doesn't stop me from diving on a herd of buffalo. I find the biggest one and dive haphazardly into the middle of the herd, no care for any damage I might take. Horns stab at me, but I pull up with my prize and turn east. Instead of landing, I hover to eat, raining blood down on the ground below me before dropping the leftovers.

That's when I see it, a flash of red in the distance. My heart skips a beat. Without thought, despite my earlier anger and frustration, I follow the brightness in a sea of dull grass. As I draw near, I see that it's not her; it's not Ryn. My heart falls. I land with the sensation of squashed hope and heavy disappointment. The red-haired man walks over with caution.

I inhale to see if I recognize him, but nothing familiar reaches my straining nostrils. In fact, the scent is strange, like an enhanced sense of nature. Pure and free. Unsure what is going on, I let my scales ruffle to increase how large I look. Not that this man is of any threat in this form.

He stops and raises both hands. "Easy, Lord Threy. I've heard about your evening flights and hoped you'd find me. We need to talk."

My tail thrashes so hard that I smell freshly cut hay.

"Can you shift? Use all your senses to prove to yourself that I'm alone if needed. I can wait. We need to speak about Ryn."

Her name on his lips makes me roar. The man doesn't flinch. His blue eyes watch me, so calm and gentle I can't find it in my heart to threaten him further. Disgruntled, I listen and sniff to confirm no one else is near. Once satisfied, I allow myself to shift.

"That's better," the man says.

"Where's Ryn?"

"Safe."

"Who are you?"

He opens his mouth, but I notice when he changes his mind about what he was going to say. "My name is Dyne. I'm with the rebels."

"Tell me why I shouldn't kill you where you stand with that confession?"

"You didn't kill Ryn, who is a much bigger threat than I am."

"You're not her."

"No. I'm not the woman you love."

My lip pulls up in the corner, and I turn my back to the man to show him I'm not afraid of him. It also gives me the chance to get my emotions under control. I'm sure he can smell my rage. Dragons need to remain peaceful to keep from overwhelming others with our scent and giving them an advantage. I'm finding calm hard to find lately. My calm is lost somewhere in this grassy sea.

"Is she safe?" I ask after a few moments.

"She is, but she misses you."

I laugh. "That's why she ran away from me."

"Ryn didn't run away from you, which you know. It was too dangerous for her to stay. Has your chest been hurting?"

"How is that any of your business?"

"I want to lead you to her another night."

I spin back to face him again. "Why?"

"As I said, she needs you."

"What if I don't want to see her? She left me behind, after all."

"I doubt you'll give up this chance, but I'm not going to tell her where we are heading tomorrow night in case I am wrong. She didn't want to leave you. It was forced on her. Ryn longs to see you again and won't take the disappointment of you not appearing well if she knew."

"What makes you think that I care?"

He tilts his head. "Because there's something you don't know and understand. I'll let her tell you. I'll give you two days to think over what I've said. If you want to see her, return here in two nights at this time."

"If I bring guards?"

"Then you'll lose your chance of ever seeing her again."

Dyne walks away, calm and collected with an angry man that can burn him to a crisp at his back. My anger is not letting me think clearly. Do I want to see her? Or do I want to make her feel the same rejection I did? Which one is the right decision? Sighing, I shift and head back to the keep. A hot bath and rest may help me think.

Chapter Eighteen
Family Matters

THREY

The long soak in hot water didn't help. The fitful sleep that followed didn't work. Walking around the keep all day and going to market today did nothing.

Here I am, an hour before I'm supposed to meet Dyne, and I have no idea what to do. Logic tells me all my anger is misplaced; Ryn loves me and didn't want to run. The stubborn part of me reminds me over and over that she made the choice to leave. At one point, this news would have made me happy. To be truthful, it still does. But I'm also conflicted.

What do I do?

On the one hand, even if she left, I truly feel Ryn is the woman for me. No one else will do as my mate. I want her and only her. She risked her life to be with me.

On the other hand, Ryn walked away while I was preoccupied. She hasn't sent any messages from wherever she is. It's obvious that the rebels can do so because they had to get hold of Elda. So, why haven't I gotten one? Does she care at all?

Destiny brought a beautiful woman with red hair into my life, then ripped her away as the red dragon of prophecy. Where do I stand in this fate? Was I merely someone to bring out the powerful destroyer of kings? Am I to wallow in self-pity until the end of time; mourn a love not really meant to be?

Hunter jumps onto the top of the couch I sprawl on. I glance up at him. "Why are you so loyal? She left you too?"

The orange cat meows at me and stares with golden-green eyes. His tail moves up and down without a care. When he starts to purr, I give up trying to reason with a cat. He doesn't understand. No one does.

A knock at my door tries to disturb my hateful contemplation. I glare at the entrance into my room but make no move to answer. This isn't me. Sure, I hated politics. I still lived with loyalty to my family. Self-pity was never something to indulge in because it's nothing but a weakness.

That's all I do anymore. I'm a different person. My family doesn't enjoy the respect it once did because of how they treated me. Ryn opened my eyes to what love really is. I never wallowed in my room. The loss hurts too much to do anything else. My life was never full of anger until recently.

It consumes me day and night. How do I go back to who I was? Is it even possible? Doesn't seem like it. All I can see is the endless emptiness that has engulfed my life, destroyed my ability to love.

Another knock makes me sigh. I look at my door again. Yet another new undesirable trait I enjoy; I want people to just go away. Leave me alone to my grief.

Is that what this is? Grief? It's not the first time the word has come to mind. Grief causes anger and bitterness. Ryn's still alive, and I have the chance to see her again. The bitter flavor of abandonment is hard to swallow.

"Threy, I know you're in there. I can smell you. Let me in."

Iara is not the person I wish to see right now, so I say my favorite two words again. "Go away."

"I'm not going anywhere. Let me in."

"Not happening. And I learned my lesson from the last time. That door is locked."

"I can stay out here all night."

"Hope you brought a cot."

Wait, night? My frantic eyes turn to the window. The sun is going down, but it's not night. What does it matter? If I was going, I surely would be on my way by now. Maybe that means I subconsciously decided not to meet Dyne.

Iara starts babbling about childhood memories. The time Rakurn accidentally locked himself in the library. When Delto was so busy laughing that he ran into the door he thought was still open. Me using her dress to wipe mud from my fingers.

She's making me miss my family, which only causes anger to bubble deep down. Instead of reminiscing, I stomp to the door and yank it open. "Stop! I'm not in the mood."

"You never are anymore. Thanks for letting me in."

Iara pushes past me. When I notice that her servant isn't with her, I sigh. "I don't remember inviting you in. I'm not in the mood for a lecture."

"I'm not here to give one. Not really."

"Where's Jarlry?"

"I didn't want him here in case you wanted to talk about the red dragon."

I groan and sit back on the couch. "Why would I want to do that? Everyone else wants me to forget about her."

"But you don't want to."

"How would you know?"

My sister sits down next to me, leaving a cloud of perfumed scent. "We haven't really spoken much, but even my glimpses of you tell me how upset you are."

"So you're stalking me."

"I miss you. You can't let others take your joy away."

I look at her with narrowed eyes. "Last time I checked, you were one of the reasons I'm in this state."

Iara lets out a deep breath and looks away. "And I'm truly sorry for that. My meddling made things worse, even though I was only trying to help. It backfired. Have you heard from her at all?"

Wishing I could confide in her like before, I press my lips together. "No."

"You hesitated. Why did you hesitate?"

Annoyed by her constant meddling, I scowl in her direction. What in Sertran makes her think I'd divulge this information to her, of all people? The woman who told my parents that I wasn't choosing a mate because I was in love with my personal servant. She almost got Ryn killed. The fact she wasn't meant to die that night means nothing right now.

"Come on, Threy, I'm not going to tell anyone," she pleads.

"Why?"

My sister sighs and looks down at her hands. "I met someone at court."

My breathing slows. "Met someone?"

"I fell in love, Threy."

It's not until this moment that I realize I've been tapping my foot. The only reason I notice is because it stops. Every movement halts as I contemplate what my sister is saying. She fell in love?

"There was a man at court, someone I first didn't trust, then began to see as a friend. Not long after that, I felt more. It would never work though."

"Why not?"

"He wouldn't be considered proper material for a mate for a lady. Our parents would never approve."

"Too bad you weren't born first and could rule Ildracan instead of Delto. You'd be better at it and have the freedom to mate with who you choose."

"Well, I'd probably still have to mate for the good of the clan."

Sighing, I lean back and look at the ceiling. "Sometimes you have to do things for yourself. I'm tired of being a puppet."

Silence stretches between us, and neither of us wishes to break it. My mind goes over everything I just learned. Maybe I'm not as alone in this as I thought I was. Maybe someone does understand. It's a strange feeling to consider.

"I never found her or heard from her, but someone found me the other night," I say, taking a chance Iara is Iara again, the sister I used to lean on.

"Who?"

"A rebel. He wants me to meet him tonight, and he'll take me to Ryn."

"You have to go."

"Why? She ran away from me."

Iara grabs my hand. I drop my gaze from the ceiling to her. She watches me for a few moments before speaking. "She had to."

"Why?"

"Because she's the red dragon, Threy. Mother was trying to turn her in. Listen, if anything, my dreadful time at court taught me that we can't let that man keep this kind of power over others."

"What are you saying?"

"You trust me with the information you just gave me, so I will trust you with this." She stops to look around like someone might have snuck in while we were talking. "Someday I'll talk of my time there, but he's a vile, evil man, Threy. I feel the rebels have the right of it."

Silence engulfs the room again. She talks of treason, and we both aren't sure how to handle it. The words spoken can end with us both executed by the very man she speaks. We've never been happy with his rule, but this is something more.

"You have to go to her, Threy," Iara says, leaving the rest hang in the air.

"We'll only be torn apart again. Why are you so for this now?"

"Because I realize it isn't infatuation or obsession. What I see is true love, and you can't give up on that. It was meant to be, which is why it's so hard."

I laugh. "Meant-to-be shouldn't be hard."

"Nothing worth having is easy. You deserve your happy ending."

"This isn't one of your naughty romance novels, Iara."

"It could be." Before I can reply, she continues. "Time grows short. The real question here is whether you can live with yourself after letting this opportunity go. You need her. Go to her."

My sister stands to exit without waiting for my answer. Her question rolls around inside my mind. Do I need her? All the memories flood me at once. The laughter, the joy I feel. Iara's right; I need her. I stand and make my way to the garden. There's little time, and I hope Dyne waits for me.

I'm in the air within moments, doing my best not to look as hurried as I feel. I can't bring attention to my flight. Last night was the first night I didn't fly, so it needs to look like I'm simply restarting the tradition. Nothing but a night hunt as the sun dips below the horizon. My wings beat the air, rushing but seemingly calm. This is almost the most difficult flight of my life, with only the one leading to confronting my parents at the cliff to be worse.

My flight zigzags, as if I'm searching for prey. When I near the spot that I met Dyne last, I hold my breath in hopes of seeing his bright red hair. I'm thankful to find him still waiting. I land and shift.

"I was worried you weren't going to show," Dyne says.

"I wasn't sure I would, but I was reminded that I need Ryn in my life." When Dyne smiles, a familiarity hits me. I gaze over his features again, finding enough to feel like I should recognize him. "Do I know you?"

"We've never had the pleasure, Lord Threy."

"You seem familiar."

He only smiles that jarring smile again. "Do you know the spot by the cliff where a tree stands from a few boulders to look like a...uhh h..."

"Third dragon's horn?"

Dyne looks a little confused. "Is that some kind of euphemism?"

"You can say that."

"Then the answer is yes."

"I know it."

"That's where she is. Tell her that I'll be waiting for her at the entrance to home. I made sure you won't be able to find it. No, don't argue. I know that you won't give her up willingly, but your name is known. She doesn't know you're coming, so enjoy the surprise that brings happiness to her face."

My mouth snaps shut. As much as I want to tell him I wouldn't give her up, I can't beat the magic. "Why are you doing this for us?"

"She needs you, Threy. Now more than ever. She will explain it more when you're together because it's her issue to speak of. Take care."

He starts to walk away. I can't leave my curiosity to stew. "Dyne, wait." He turns. "Who are you, and why do I feel like I know you?"

"I probably remind you of someone important." My quizzical look makes him chuckle. "I'm the dragon that made the red one. Ryn is my daughter by blood only, but she's still mine. You better fly to her before she gets frustrated at my lack of return and heads for home."

If I could speak, I wouldn't be able to resist asking him more. How was she made if fairy dragons are extinct? Then his scent hits me again, familiar yet different. He is one? How is this possible? They were all killed for threatening the king's dominance.

This can't be real. Sure, a red dragon needs a fairy parent, but even that logic doesn't make this wondering any less heart stopping. He's a dragon that shouldn't exist, making others that shouldn't either. I could ask, but I can't bring myself to.

Still full of disbelief, I let him walk away and follow his instructions. Right now, the only thing of importance is Ryn. I hope she waits for me, even if she doesn't know why she's waiting.

Chapter Nineteen
Relationship Issues

Ryn

"You cheated," I say, looking up at Trev from the ground.

"No fight is ever clean."

"I get that, but was it necessary now? Can't you teach me how to fight without hitting me after making it seem like we are done?"

"You must always be on the guard, even then things seem to be safe."

My cousin leans down to give me a hand, but I smack it away. He's probably sincere in his wish to help because Trev has been softer and has even smiled at me a few times in recent days. The more I improve, the less he seems to hate. That doesn't mean I'm going to let down my guard, especially after the trick he just pulled.

Climbing to my feet, I keep an eye on my trainer. He grins. "That's right. Never trust your enemy not to strike when you're most vulnerable."

"While I know you don't like me much, I didn't think you went as far as seeing me as the enemy."

"I don't. If anything, you've done enough to prove that you're stronger than you look."

"Thanks," I mutter.

"You need to get your magic under control, so we can do this in a larger room."

With a sigh, I take a quick glance around without losing sight of Trev. We're in an older storeroom that smells of potatoes. There's just enough room to practice, but not much more than that. The regular training cave is off limits to us after I almost killed more with my wayward magic. Ever since that first time, Trev randomly decides to attack with all he has to try to break the block I have. All I've managed to do is scare people too much to want to train around me and knocked Trev unconscious about nine times. After he ended up needing healing following the last burst, he hasn't tried it again.

Sure, I can create light and heat now, but my magic isn't much better than that. My shield is about the size of half my body now, and Dyne wants to make it so that I can cover myself in a bubble. This is taking too long.

"Are you dwelling again?" Trev says, putting our practice weapons in his bag.

"It's not like I don't have a lot to think about. How can I defeat a king if I can't control my magic?"

"As Dyne says, patience."

"Patience is hard when the entire world is depending on me saving them."

"You're getting better quick enough to impress even me."

"That's a feat."

He grins. "You got that right. Keep this up, and I might actually start to believe you're the chosen one."

Trev's best friend pops his head in. "Are things almost done in here? For the life of me, I can't seem to get the human to understand that he has to attack, not just defend. Could use some help."

"We're done for now. I can come help," Trev responds.

As he walks out, his friend—Rando or Ralro or something like that—sends me a sneer. Most people give me more respect than I deserve. Some seem scared that I might confuse them for King Darac. There are a few that speak in whispers about me, ones that think I fall short of expectations. This is one of those people.

When I enter the bathing cave, a couple is kissing at one end. I grimace and move upstream all the way to both keep me hidden as much as possible and avoid whatever they plan on doing. The noise I make pulls them apart, but they still have eyes only for each other. That's fine with me.

Stripping, I step into the cool water. The wash is quick, so I can be out of here before more eyes can show up. After, I head to the dining area. Atan is already there. Grabbing my sandwich and the surprise of fruit, I make my way over to my friend.

"Another rough day at training?" he asks after my first bite of sandwich.

"What?"

"You have an almost healed bruise on the side of your head."

I grimace. I've never been a stranger to bruises and cuts, but Trev is showing me what sore really is. Every time I feel like I might leave with less residual pain, my cousin picks it up a notch, showing me just how much more I need to learn. At this point, I'm so used to bruises that

I don't even notice them anymore. My dragon heals them before I fall asleep anyway.

As a slave, it was important to be adaptable. That trait comes in handy now. Bland food, sore muscles, cuts and bruises, and lack of light are constants for me now. My situational flexibility helps keep me from becoming depressed. It's better to live life the best you can, no matter what it throws at you, even if you're not even sure to survive it.

"Trev is a good trainer," I say after another bite. "He hurts though."

"He should take it easier on you."

"I'm advancing because of how hard he is on me."

Atan lets the conversation die. He can be upset about my cousin's treatment of me, but I need to see the necessity of it. It's because of him beating on me that I'm as far as I am now, and no one knows how long I have to improve. This is necessary pain.

I save my fruit for last. As soon as my sandwich is gone, I pick out a slice of apple and groan in pleasure at the sweet juices. Meat, cheese, and bread; that's all we usually get, which makes me curious. "Where did this treat come from?"

"One of the scouting parties came across a wagon of supplies. They outnumbered the guards, so they attacked. There's butter too."

My ears perk at the thought. Dry bread is sustenance, but there's so much more to life than eating food to survive. That thought makes me wince. What we have now is an improvement over what we received as slaves. Threy spoiled me.

I can't help myself. "Butter?"

"Yeah. They haven't unpacked it yet."

Well, that explains why that's missing. Butter is as much a luxury as fruit, so I shouldn't feel this disappointed. I spent too long being fed well. No matter how well I adapt to new situations, I still find myself missing the perks I had. One of those being Threy.

A sharpness comes to my chest with the thought. There's always a dull burn that's gradually getting worse, but I've learned to live around it. Trev doesn't give me any understanding over it. Any time Threy comes into my mind, the pain increases. I keep it from Atan and take a deep breath to ease it.

"I want to check on Beland," I say as I stand.

"You check on him every night. Don't you trust them to take care of him?"

"It's more than that, Atan. I feel at home there. For a short time, I can forget that I'm destined to fight a dangerous battle with a power-hungry king. There, I can just be Ryn again."

"That makes sense. I'll walk with you."

Beland is happy to see me. I'm starting to wonder if there's more to these feelings I get around animals. They seem to respond to me as much as I do to them. I keep meaning to ask Dyne about it, but I get distracted. Not like life is full of things to hold my attention or anything.

When I turn away from the horse I've come to think of as mine, I find Atan standing really close. I jump and take a step back to gain a little space for myself. The look in his brown eyes confuses me. "What's going on?"

"Nothing. Seeing the smile you had while giving Beland attention reminds me so much of the stables. You almost seemed happy there."

"Because I was. I hated being torn away from the horses, but it was my own fault for bringing notice."

"Not many men wouldn't notice you."

Uncomfortable, I take another step back. Who is this man? The Atan I know is a joker and whiner, but he's not this. We were friends and fellow stable hands. There were no romantic feelings between us. I barely let myself feel close enough to call him a friend.

"Are you alright, Atan? Did you hit your head?" I ask, hoping it's something as simple as that.

"You're beautiful, Ryn. I've always thought so."

I can't take this weirdness anymore, so I try to slip around him. He grabs my hand as I pass and brings his lips to mine. Shocked, I push him away. "What the hell, Atan?"

"We were so close, Ryn. Don't you want to see where something deeper might lead?"

"You are my friend. I don't look at you in any other way."

Atan's dreamy look fades. "Ryn, I've loved you forever."

"You haven't known me forever."

"It feels like it."

When he takes another step toward me, I hold up my hands and jump back. "I love Threy, and no one else can ever have my heart."

Anger crosses his eyes. "He's not here, and who knows if you'll ever see him again."

Agony pierces my heart as soon as his words hit my ears. I gasp and lean down to press the heel of my hand to my chest. It feels as if someone stabbed a sword through my heart, and I find it hard to breathe. A hand rests on my shoulder. A voice calls my name. None of it matters as I fall to my knees.

One of the horses turns to nudge me. It's all too much. The loss of the man I love. The uncertainty over whether I'll ever see him again. Not being able to say goodbye.

I do all I can to push those thoughts out of my head. I need to not think of such things if I want this agony to ease. The pain slowly recedes, and I can speak again as I hear what Atan and my silent shadow are asking. They speak of whether they should get someone or not.

"No. I'm fine. It's something to do with my magic. You don't need to go get help. You can go back to guarding the door."

"Ryn..."

"No, Atan. I'm not talking about this with you anymore. My heart belongs to Threy."

"He's a dragon, Ryn. He's an enemy that wants to suppress us."

Glaring, I let my anger take over. "I'm a dragon too. Does that make me an enemy?"

The man I barely recognize steps back at my rage. "Never. I'll never see you as one of them."

"Well, I am one. In fact, I'm one of the most powerful dragons alive, if not *the* most powerful. *Them* is me."

"Ryn..."

"Leave me alone, Atan. I'm no longer comfortable around you."

"Ryn..."

"Go!"

Startled at my yell, the man who was once my only friend turns and walks away. I sob, my tears flowing freely. I've lost so much; my true family, Threy, who I once was, and now my friend. Who am I? Who am I supposed to be? Why does everything good in my life get taken from me?

Dyne finds me sobbing on the hard floor and rushes over to me. Gentle hands cradle me as I cry, and I offer no protest. Instead, I clutch at his shirt and dampen the cloth with my tears. I cry for all I've lost, all I might continue to lose. This isn't fair. None of it is.

When I finally calm, I explain what happened to Dyne. He sighs. "Ryn, you are a beauty. You remind me so much of your mother that

I can't help but remember my time with her when I see you. Dragons love forever. This is something humans will never understand."

"Was our friendship only because he thinks I'm pretty?"

"That's not something I can answer. Only he can, and you're in no condition to talk to him. Let's practice magic. Maybe that'll take your mind off of it."

"I'm not in the mood."

"Even if I tell you our lessons will be outside?"

That grabs my attention. Fresh air will do wonders. I don't even ask any questions, picking myself off the floor and following him through the tunnels until we find an exit only one person can squeeze through at a time.

The breeze hits me as soon as I'm free, and I turn my face into it. Dyne tells my guard to stay by the cave before he takes my hand and leads me away. Being the strong silent type, my protector grunts and settles in to wait. I can hear the waves crashing against the cliff, making me believe we're still in Ildracan. It's hard to tell in such darkness. We've traveled so far.

"I need to retrieve something," he says. "Stay here and don't leave without me."

"I can come with you."

"It's safer if you stay here."

Sighing, I concede the point, tired of always being protected at every turn. If this is what being important means, I don't like it. I settle between a rock and a tree, listening to the sound that reminds me of the night prophecy came for me. There was so much fear and anger, waiting for death to come for me. Threy proved how important I am to him when he took on his entire family.

Time passes, and I worry that something might have happened to Dyne. It's been a really long time. He didn't tell me how long it would be, but I worry it shouldn't have been this long. I hope he didn't abandon me or that this isn't some new trick to bring my magic out.

I stand and decide I want to go looking for him. The sounds of wings beating the air startle me, and I dash back to my hiding place, sure Dyne is in trouble. I scent the air, smelling drake. When I look up, I feel myself climbing to my feet without thought, mindlessly pulled by the copper scales lit by the moon. It can't be.

"Threy?"

Chapter Twenty
No More Wasting Time

RYN

The copper dragon lands in front of me, a little distance away. Those familiar green eyes feel like they look right through me. My heart stops as I watch him watch me. He doesn't move; neither do I. It's like we're stuck in time, close but yet so far away. Where's Dyne? I need to tell him about this and hope he isn't mad.

After a couple of minutes, Threy shifts. His blond hair stirs with a strong gust of wind. I drink in the sight of his naked body while he still doesn't make a move to step toward me. I bite my lip, which makes him frown. He never likes when I do that.

One strong arm lifts before my love drops it again. He's unsure, making my heart ache for the distance forced between us. I can tell he wants to run forward, but something unknown seems to stop him, so I make the decision for him.

"Threy!" I say while rushing to him. As soon as I'm close enough to him, I jump into his arms, happy when he catches me.

Sobbing, I bury my face in his chest to inhale the hot scent I've been missing for so long. The feel of his hard body pressed against mine is too much to handle, but I push harder into it. Threy embraces me without saying a word, taking deep breaths as if trying to remain calm. I look up to see tears on his cheek.

"Why did you leave me?" Threy whispers, a sound so broken that I nearly fall to pieces.

"I didn't leave you; I left the danger coming for me. Your mother..."

"I know what she did. Elda told me after I convinced Threysoryth not to eat her." I jump back in alarm, and he chuckles darkly. "She's still alive, but my dragon went on a rampage. Your co-conspirator was the last one to touch you, so she was blamed. I didn't hurt her though."

A breath of relief whooshes out of me. Elda took me from him, but she did it to protect me—and further the rebel cause. Which is top priority when it comes to Elda? I have absolutely no clue. Either way, the end is the same. I'm both alive and working toward coming into my full potential. Both are needed to stop a tyrannical king set on my demise.

"The last thing I wanted to do was hurt you, Threy," I say.

"But you did it anyway. Yes, I know about the impending death, and I'm being selfish. I can't help it because I'm nothing but a shell without you. If our time apart has taught me anything, it's that I'm not fit company to be around if you're not with me."

I wipe his tears away while ignoring my own. This gives me the chance to think of what I can possibly say to him. I've broken his heart, the one I admired long before I wanted more. He's always been different, even if I didn't want to see it at first. Sure, he was still a blind dragon, but there was something to work with inside him, and he was willing to learn.

"I wanted to come to you, leave a goodbye note at least, but Elda convinced me it was urgent to get me out before the sabotage at the stables was taken care of. Threy, I didn't want to leave you, and I've wished for nothing but to be in your arms again," I explain. He must understand. I didn't mean to leave him broken.

His eyes hold a desperate plea, one that searches for the truth in my words. Threy wants what I say to be true; he needs it to be. I place my palm against his strong jaw. When he leans into my touch, I can't take the distance anymore. My fingers move to the back of his head and pull his lips to meet mine.

Threy doesn't fight me, but he does hesitate for a moment before moving his lips. Strong arms wrap around me as the kiss deepens to one of need and desperation. My arms encircle Threy's neck to keep him as close as possible. The kiss almost hurts. Neither of us is willing to let a little soreness pull us apart.

Lifting me, Threy kneels to lay my body in the high grass. It tickles. If my mouth wasn't busy, I'd probably giggle at the sensation. Fingers move beneath my shirt, so I help them by wiggling my way out of it. When Threy pulls his lips away from mine, I whimper at the loss.

Wet heat engulfs a nipple, making me forget my quick wave of disappointment. My back arches into the sensation as my body hungers for more. The other breast enjoys the feel of his strong hands before he moves lower. I'm shocked at how quickly Threy manages to undo the ties of my pants.

The leather that's a little too big on me slips down over my hips like a lover's caress. Once they're off, Threy growls, "Finally."

His hands coming back up feel even better. They slide up the lower half of my leg, moving inward once they reach my thighs. One hand moves back to the outside, but the other keeps its straight course. Gasping at the feeling of his thumb circling my clit, my hands fist the soft grass. All tickling is gone, replaced by the sensation of him massaging in just the right place.

The smell of broken grass fills the air when I pull my hands closer, bringing two handfuls of green stalks with me. I moan at the pleasure of his tongue while the heat builds deep within. Two fingers enter me at the same time, making me moan louder than expected. Tension takes over as the warmth flows through me.

Rynmoriath comes closer to the surface and growls her approval of what Threysoryth's human does to the one she resides in. Trembling takes over as Threy pushes me closer and closer to the top. Tingling washes over me. When his tongue finds my clit while his fingers move in and out, I cry out, reaching down to fist his blond hair and leave a little grass in it. My body shakes and tenses so hard that lights flash in my vision.

I feel my body relaxing, but Threy mutters about not being done with me. Soft lips move over the inside of my hips, sending my body into hyper awareness again. Groaning, I let my body writhe on the ground. A warm, wet tongue moves up to my belly button, leaving a cool trail that my skin reheats in seconds, then up further until he finds my nipple again. He suckles and nibbles, bringing the warmth back to me. It rushes over me in waves, and I growl in my chest again. Threy returns the sound, his chest vibrating on my belly and producing a whimper out of me.

Threy moves up to my throat, stroking it with protruding fangs that tell me Threysoryth is right under the skin. "Threy," I say in the middle of the next pant, "please."

Without a verbal response, he thrusts into me hard enough to throw my head back. My nails dig into his back while my legs circle his waist to change the angle. The next thrust finds me clawing at him like a desperate animal. I forgot just how good this man feels inside me. It feels as if my hands are trying to climb his back. Something warm and wet slides between them, but I can't focus on anything but the tension building inside of me.

Heat from his body reaches for mine, and our warmth mingles in a way that makes us both moan. It becomes too much. My head rolls back again to let his name burst from his mouth. My body clenches around him as he grunts and whispers my name. I dig my nails into him more while he nibbles at my neck. This wave after wave of pleasure feels never-ending.

After what feels like forever, the tightness in my core releases, and I collapse to the ground in a limp heap. My lungs grasp greedily for air as Threy continues to pepper my skin with light kisses before taking my mouth in his. This time, it's not desperation I feel but love. I have my mate back, which reminds me that I still need to tell him about that. In a minute. I want to savor him and the lack of pain in my chest.

Pulling my hands back down, I jump at the sight of blood. "What did I do?"

Threy pulls out of me, sits, and looks at his back. "Looks like your dragon got a little excited."

He twists so I can see. My bloody hands cover my mouth in shock. "I did that?"

As he moves, huge gashes open and spill blood. It's easy to see where each one of my fingers raked over him more than once. Guilt overwhelms me. First, I hurt him emotionally. Now he's bleeding rivers because of me.

"It's fine," Threy says with a laugh. "They only hurt a little. I actually like that I can make you lose control like that."

"But people will see when you get back."

"One," Threy says, laying down next to me in the grass on his side, "by the time I'm home, most of the keep will be asleep."

"Not everyone," I mumble through him kissing the side of my mouth.

"Most," he says, taking my earlobe between his teeth. "Two, stop interrupting me. Three, I'll be mostly healed by then. Four, I want you to do it again."

Gasping, I find myself straddling him. His quick moves shock me. His hardness after such a heated exchange shocks me more. How can he still want more? As I think that thought, his fingers move to my nipples, and the heat returns in seconds.

I groan. "This would mean clawing your chest too."

Threy sits up, holding me close and nuzzling my neck. "I want your marks all over me, my love. It's been pure torture without you."

His words bring back my senses. I push him away from my neck. "Wait. We need to discuss something before I get distracted again."

"I like distracting you."

"Yes, and I like being distracted by you, but this is important."

"So is this," he says, taking another dive for my throat.

"Really," I say through my next moan. "Please, Threy. I have to tell you this."

My copper dragon pulls away, leaving my body to scream at me for being stupid while I move off him. His green eyes look curious and slightly nervous. "How important?"

"Have you been having pains in your chest?"

Threy blinks multiple times in quick succession. "How did you know about that?"

"Because I feel them too."

"Why is this important?"

"Threy, we are mated completely."

Laughter bursts out of him. "That's not possible, Ryn. As much as I want to be mated to you, we haven't gone through the ceremony."

I take a deep breath and ready myself for whatever his reaction will be to my next words. "I'm a red dragon, Threy. According to knowledge of the past, I have so much magic in me that all we had to do was desire to be mates and have sex, which we did—multiple times."

His beautiful green eyes widen. "Really? So we're mated? Who told you this?"

"Dyne. I'm assuming you met him if you're here, which explains his absence that I was worried about. He's been concerned about my pain."

"How would he know?"

"He's apparently pretty knowledgeable. He's been the one training me in magic because he's the only one strong enough."

Threy sighs before burying his head in my shoulder. "How would he know enough to teach you?"

"He's a fairy dragon."

He grunts. "I had that thought, but it doesn't make sense. That's not possible."

"Why not? Because they're extinct? The king loves his lies, Threy. How else do you think I was born the color I am?"

Threy reaches over and pulls my lip from beneath my teeth before I can break skin. He pulls me close. "I didn't mean to doubt you. It's hard to rewire a lifetime of programming. This is huge news. Of course, there must still be some if you were born. I'm sorry. Your father? He dropped that surprise on me before we parted."

"By blood, yes. He's apparently a very strong and very knowledge-able fairy dragon. Being apart grows painful for us. We can do it for a short time, but then the pains start. It's only starting now because my magic is growing."

"Don't tell me details because I don't want the knowledge when I have to go back, but have you met your dragon?"

"Kind of. I know her name. I can't shift yet. Dyne did something to me as a child, so she couldn't come out and reveal me. Both my dragon and magic are still blocked. We're trying to free both." A thought occurs to me. I almost forgot with the distraction that is my copper dragon love. "What did she look like?"

"Your dragon? Absolutely beautiful. She is the perfect shade of red, like the cherries you love so much. Drake, definitely mostly drake, but she's a little smaller. Um, think wyvern size. The only other difference is your dragon doesn't have horns and spikes like other dragons. You're softer, if that makes sense."

I picture what I know of drakes and what Dyne looks like. "It really does."

"Enough of this. If we are only allowed tonight until the pain comes back, get over here."

Threy pulls me back on top of him. I giggle and devour his mouth with mine. We won't waste any more precious time on talk. The night grows short, so it's time to get our fill of each other.

Chapter Twenty-One
Insincere Apologies

THREY

It's early morning by the time I land in the garden. Darkness still reigns, but it gives way to a lighter darkness that hides the stars. I shift and walk over to a bench with a familiar figure lying on it. We spoke of a lot of things between our many moments of bliss, and she was one of the topics.

Reaching down, I squeeze her shoulder. Letting her sleep isn't an option because she holds my clothes. "Iara, what are you doing?"

My sister jerks up, blinking her bright blue eyes. She looks around as if confused, then down at my clothes in her hand. Her gaze finds me, and she holds out my coverings. As I dress, she yawns.

Since Iara isn't speaking, I try breaking the silence. "That's not a very comfortable place for you to sleep."

"Does she hate me?"

Startled by the question, I'm speechless for a few seconds before finding my voice. "No."

"Why not?"

"Do you want her to be?"

"No, but I would be in her position."

Sighing, I settle down onto the bench beside her. I'm tired, but she needs this. "She's not happy with what happened, but she understands why you did it. She's not a hateful person, Iara."

"If you see her again, tell her I'm sorry."

Glad my sister isn't mentioning her name, I keep it the same. We speak low enough that no one can hear, but it's best to take care. The subject at hand would put everyone in danger.

"I already told her," I say. "I figured your apology to me would extend to her as well."

"Good. Are you going to stop flying into the night like a madman?"

"No. Changing my routine will draw suspicion. If I want to see her again, I need to make sure it's like nothing happened, nothing's changed."

"Makes sense. I'm glad you went."

I nod, pausing before telling her about us being mated already. Our relationship used to be so close, and it's hard to remember that I can't tell her everything like I used to. Ryn explained that Dyne dampened the bond to keep it from being used against her, but it's best if no one else knows. I can tell Iara senses I'm holding something back. I'm glad when she doesn't push.

"I need to get some sleep," I say.

"I'm sure you do. You need a bath first though. You smell like her."

Her smirk makes me grin like a young dragon again. "I will. Good night."

I stand to walk away. Her voice makes me pause. "I can't believe it's her."

"Me either."

No other words are spoken, so I exit and walk down the halls to my room. The only people up are the human servants, and I make it back without being accosted by anyone. As I enter, Hunter runs over to me and meows loud and long. He weaves around my legs. Confused, I pick him up. The cat sniffs every inch of me, rubbing his face against my skin and purring.

"You smell Ryn, don't you?" I ask him.

He makes a sound that reminds me of a little chirp before licking me. Laughing, I say, "Alright, Hunter. I know you miss her, and I wish you could have gone with me. Although, I don't think I could have taken sharing her attention. As much as I want to let you get your fill of her scent, I'm exhausted. Down you go."

Putting him down, I swear it looks like he's glaring at me. I slip out of my pants as I walk to my bathing room, Hunter trailing behind. The cat watches me bathe and follows me to my bed. The covers welcome me, and I use my magic to warm the space around my tired body. Hunter Jumps up and curls against my chest. It seems the best way to get attention from the cat is to come home smelling like Ryn. Sleep takes me as soon as I close my eyes.

Pounding at my door startles me awake. I notice Hunter is already gone while blinking sleep from my eyes. There's no way I got adequate sleep in whatever time I slept. The knock sounds again.

Grumbling, I walk out and grab a pair of leather pants. I swing the door open to find a messenger waiting. "What?"

"My lord, your father wanted me to tell you that the noble ladies will be here with their parents for an apology in about an hour. He wants you in the courtyard for their arrival."

"Very well."

After he leaves, I close the door and sigh. I am not awake enough to deal with this. It was a late night—completely worth the torture of an exhausted day. Maybe another bath will wake me up. I need to wash her scent off me better anyway because I can still catch Ryn on my skin. In the room, I start running the water. I adjust the temperature with my magic to make it as hot as I can stand it and slide in when it's ready.

I pace once my bath is done. The last thing I want to do after such a wonderful night is confront the two women that tried to force a mating. They wouldn't have succeeded, but the mere attempt is enough to set my blood to boil. Even before that, I couldn't stand them and their blatant cruelty.

And now they are coming here to offer what I'm sure is a fake apology while their father bails them out with payment. I pity Iara needing to put up with being served by one. Whichever she chooses, their ego won't make this easy. Neither will their spoiled attitude. Maybe I should consider this payback for what she did to me. I can't help but think she's getting the raw end of it.

This is torture. The sun hasn't moved very far, so it's nowhere near an hour yet. Pacing isn't going to help me in the least. Instead of driving myself crazy, I need to occupy my time in some other way. A walk might help. It's worth a try.

The halls are bustling at this hour. Everyone looks more awake than I am, which happens when getting adequate sleep. There is no regret, but the tiredness makes me feel heavy and cranky.

Outside, dark clouds move toward us from the distance. They've yet to reach the sun, but it will happen soon. Fitting for the mood that comes from being away from my love after a night like last. Ryn is my sun. The circumstances we find ourselves in are the clouds. The threat of the king and my family is the storm that darkness brings.

Sighing, I push all melancholy thoughts out and walk toward the grassy area behind the stable to lean on the fence. Mindaine chases another horse around, his black tail flying behind him. Watching the carefree horses rest, run, and eat shows me why Ryn always loved the stables. It's peaceful here, freeing. Even the reddish-colored one lifting its tail to deposit some fertilizer isn't enough to make me walk away.

Behind me, the bustle of people talking and laughing threatens to invade my senses, along with the thuds of various activities and the clang of metal on metal. None of it matters. I close my eyes and focus on the scents and sounds of the horses. Right now, I need this peace more than thinking of the confrontation to come or my family's annoying meddling. The horses aren't just a reminder of Ryn. They're more than that, and I can see why she loves them so much.

I can't stand here as long as I would like because I hear a runner rush by with news of the nobles' arrival. With a sigh, I back away from the fence and walk to join my family on the steps leading into the keep, a position of power. Mother stares at me with cold eyes while Father motions for me to stand between them. The lady of the keep hasn't forgiven me for any of my harsh words, but I have to stand beside her as the aggrieved party.

The carriage pulls in and comes to a rest in the courtyard. Servants jump from supply wagons and rush around to check on everything.

One walks over to the carriage door, and I take a deep breath to fortify myself for what's to come. The noble parents step out. My lungs are about to burst when the girls follow.

Judging by the haughtiness in their dark brown eyes, I'd say they haven't learned to humble themselves after everything. Sule smirks when she sees me standing above her on the steps. I cross my arms over my chest. Lorsa looks at me and glares, as if this circumstance is my fault.

The entire family walks up and bows to mine, the lords in charge of keeping them in line. Lorsa grimaces when her father shoots her a look, then says, "I offer my most sincere apologies for the grievances Lord Threy was forced to endure from me. I should have been more mindful of him and not tried to push mating."

Sule scowls. "I also apologize for my transgressions and beg for forgiveness. Please don't be too harsh on our parents for things we did out of their control. We won't try anything like that again. We've learned our lesson."

My father nods. "Very well, ladies. You are to spend time with my daughter to determine who shall stay. Threy and Delto, come with us. Rakurn as well."

We follow him into the keep. Iara rolls her eyes as I pass, telling me this is the last thing she desires. I grin and walk by. As we enter the throne room, Father slows, probably to embed in these two the power he holds over them. Once in the meeting room, everyone takes a seat.

"We are here to speak of retribution for what your daughters attempted," Lord of Ildracan says. "Forced mating is a serious offense."

"But our daughters didn't succeed," their father says. "That should count for something."

"The only reason your daughters still live is because of that fact. It's clear they wouldn't be able to accomplish what they had hoped against a full-grown male warrior, so it was stupid on their part. That didn't stop the insult from happening. I am the law for our clan, so it is up to me to uphold it. This is a serious problem that needs to be addressed and requires greater recompense than you offered. You know my terms."

The nobleman sighs and gestures for one of his men to bring in a small chest. "Coin that you requested, plus a little more in hopes that we can move past this incident. As also agreed, one of our daughters will serve yours until you see fit to release her. They've accepted this is to be part of their punishment."

"Very well. Threy, do you accept the apologies and terms?"

I want to tell him the apologies aren't sincere and I'm truly gaining nothing out of any of this, but I don't feel like dealing with a lecture in politics later. "It all sounds good to me."

Anything to get this over with.

Of course, I can't say that part out loud. Doesn't mean I can't think it. When we exit, the girls are waiting. That was fast.

Iara looks like she just consumed something sour. "Sule will be staying."

By the emotions flashing through her blue eyes, I think my sister believes she's going to regret this. I happen to agree with that, but it's what Father wants in retribution, and his ruling must always be followed. He probably thinks he's doing something good for Iara. I know the truth behind that blind belief.

The other three deny an invitation for dinner, and we follow them to the courtyard. Servants are carrying trunk after trunk of belongings for Sule. She's going to need an entire chamber just to hold her stuff. It's like she thinks this is a vacation.

Once the family is in the carriage, they begin their trip. Iara mutters for Sule to follow her while everyone else goes about their day. I decide to start my flight a little earlier today. This small change will be seen as me needing to get over what just happened as well as keep my usual hopeless ritual. The truth of it is that I'm tired after a night spent with the woman they don't know I found again.

Chapter Twenty-Two
Shielding

RYN

My wooden blade vibrates under the hit, but it's better the wood than my bones. Trev swings again, met with another block. I swipe my blade at him and almost catch his side. He barely keeps me from giving him a big bruise to match the one fading on my ribs.

We do this for a while. When I see his smirk, I know what's coming. Trev increases his attack speed and strength. I manage to keep up for a few moves before having my legs swept out from under me. I grunt and lie there without speaking, trying to regain the air I lost with the landing.

At least he doesn't pretend to try to kill me anymore. When Dyne realized that it wasn't helping, he asked Trev to stop, so we're now back in the practice cave. My magic slowly improves, but it's still a bit erratic. The fairy dragon believes that's more from the practice than almost being knocked out or gored by a wooden sword. I'd like to think so too, so we can avoid going back to that.

Trev doesn't hate me like he used to, but it still scares me when he goes crazy on me. If I can *not* deal with that during training ever again, I'd be a happy red dragon. So far, my cousin has listened and not forced my dragon to defend me.

My instructor looks down at me. "You're doing well. Being free of the mate pain must be helping."

Ever since the other night, I haven't had any chest pain. Dyne says it will come back, but I probably have more than a couple of weeks. It's not helping enough to keep me off my back. "Not well enough if I'm still looking up at you like this."

"You're learning quicker than most. Must be the red dragon blood."

I watch him for any hint of mockery but find none. Trev seems more accepting of me as time goes by. The brutal trainer even jokes with me at times. It's a refreshing change. I also learned that he's eight years older than me. Old enough to remember my mother, which sparks curiosity. I'm too scared to ask what she was like to him.

He offers me his hand, and I take it. "Again."

Sighing, I grab my weapon from the ground and ready myself. This time, he comes at me somewhere between the skill he showed before and the talent he used to knock me down. It's all I can do to keep him from hitting me; no time for attack. As I do my best to avoid more bruising, I study him, slowly getting used to his speed. After a little while, I'm able to try to hit him. It ends with a welt on my wrist.

I hiss in pain and drop the wooden weapon. "That's going to make it hard to hold a sword right now."

The throbbing quickly grows from my wrist and up my arm. Fingers go numb. My cousin takes my hand in a gentle grip. When he twists it, I have to bite my tongue to keep from crying out.

"Looks like we're done for the day," Trev says. "Your dragon needs time to heal that. The attack surprised me, and I reacted without thought."

"I thought it was safe to try."

"It almost worked. We're done, Uncle!"

Dyne stands from his seat against the wall, ever the loyal taskmaster, not missing any practice. "We'll get some food into her before I start the magic training again."

"I could use something to eat as well," Trev says.

He takes the practice weapons over to the racks, then walks over to us while we wait to leave. We walk through the line and pick up some dried meat, cheese, and bread. At the table, the two men sit on either side of me.

"When we get a chance," Trev says with a mouthful of food, "I'm going to try you out with the swords we have to see if one fits."

"She's there already?" Nova says, startling me by sitting in front of me without warning.

"She is. We need to make sure it's right, so I hope we have one that works. If not, we'll need to find someone to attempt a trade with."

"So, I'm getting a sword?" I ask.

"If we have one, yes. If not, when we do have one."

Nodding, I take a bite of cheese with a smile. I must be doing better than I think if I'm getting a sword. "Will I need to keep my babysitters?"

Nova laughs. "Yes. It's still easy to be snuck up on. Having a sword doesn't make that any different. Where is your guard anyway?"

Dyne answers for me. "We figured they weren't needed when she's in training. One will be back for suppertime."

"Makes sense. There's no shortage of muscle during training."

Everyone laughs. When I look up from my plate, my eyes freeze on a pair of brown ones. Atan looks at me with both annoyance and sadness. He looks away quickly and grabs his food, sitting on the opposite side of the dining area, as far away from me as possible. I bite my lip and look down again, saddened by this turn of events.

Awkwardness is heavy whenever we're both in the same room. There's no undoing what happened between us. His statement of interest. My complete rejection. His unwillingness to accept it. There is no friendship after this. The food now sits heavy in my stomach.

Trev growls beside me, and I see him looking at Atan. Reaching over, I place a gentle hand on his arm. "Let it go."

My cousin blinks and looks over at me. Dyne told him of what happened, which also means Nova already knows as well. I don't want all this attention on the subject, so I hope this group is all the further it's been circulating. No one else needs to know.

"No one should force mating on anyone," Trev says in a low rumble.

"It's not the same for humans," I reason. "They don't see anything wrong with being with others of their kind without mating."

I grimace. When did I start thinking of humans as them? I mean, I'm not wrong. All my life I was human—until I found out I wasn't. Their pain is mine; I've lived it. I've been beaten and oppressed, forced to serve those that killed the humans that raised me as their own. Dragon may be my current label, but I was human in all ways that counted once.

But you're still not one of them.

"It doesn't matter. You told him you don't feel the same, and he kept pushing. He kissed you without asking first and without any encouragement from you. That's despicable."

I force another bite down to buy myself time to think before I respond. Even humans shouldn't force, but I don't think that's what he was doing. "I don't think he understood how uncomfortable I was when he brought it up. I was too busy being nervous and shocked."

"But he kept pushing it."

There is no argument for that because he did become pushy when he realized I wasn't interested. Then there was the dragon comment. That one still hurts when I think about it.

Trev reads my mind. "Then to say what he said about dragons. We took him in, and he still considers us the enemy?"

"I don't think it's the rebels he considers enemies," I say, trying to calm my cousin.

"Dragons are dragons. Yes, there are good and bad, but if you don't specify, you mean all."

"Now you're reaching for something to be insulted by," Nova says around the makeshift sandwich she made.

"You're not insulted?"

"Not at all. That human suffered under the hands of dragons all of his life. It's a hard mindset to unravel."

I let their debate continue, shutting out their words. Dyne pats my shoulder with a comforting touch. The longer I know the man, the more comfortable I feel around him. The words father and friend don't feel so distant now. His love is no longer in question. After all, he gave his daughter a night of pleasure with her mate to keep her heart from breaking.

"I still don't like him," Trev says.

To my amusement, Dyne cuts in. "You didn't like Ryn before either."

"That's different."

"How?"

"I admit I was a little jealous."

I laugh, letting the conversation take a different turn. "Really? I would have never guessed if you didn't just admit it."

"Well, I was. I also doubted who you were because you were so clueless."

"Don't doubt me anymore?"

"I'm coming around to the idea that there might be something special about you."

We all laugh, and I feel the darkness lift from my spirit a little. This is what I need in my life. Love and laughter. It makes the danger around the corner feel more distant. This is what I've been missing, something Threy gave me a bit of. Humans are discouraged from having relationships and friends because you never know when the end is coming for someone. It feels nice to finally have what I was advised against before.

For once, I feel like I have a true home. Not just somewhere to rest my head. Not a single person. A real home. The only thing missing is Threy, and I hope I get to share this with him someday. He's the only thing keeping this from being perfect—minus the impending battle to the death.

Who will survive what's to come? Who will I lose? That thought is too much to endure. Even Trev is someone I don't want to lose. Every one of these people means something to me, even the human man sulking across the room. Danger comes to us all. Pain is right around the corner. I must not let myself grow complacent with what is to come.

Before, it was all their expectations that kept me going. Now, it's something more. The stronger I get, the better the chance these people will survive. Growing strong is important if I want to avoid as much heartache as possible. The entire kingdom depends on me, but it's these people I'm going to fight for.

"Alright," Dyne says, "let's get to magic practice."

Everyone stands to go their separate ways, and it feels like this is how we will eventually end. Atan has already left the room. Someone is already lost to me because of unrealistic expectations. How realistic are the hopes of the other people I'm growing to love?

I'm the mystical, prophesied red dragon. They're my mentors and family. Someday, I may lose them. Not today. I'll do my best to keep them safe. They won't leave me if I have any say in it. With that thought, I follow Dyne to the room we usually practice in.

First order of business, a shield. I'm getting better; it's now bigger than I am. As much as I hate the word patience, it's paying off. If only it pays off fast enough to keep these people safe and reunite with Threy for good. The king will die. The Jeweled Dracon fire will be beaten. Loved ones will live.

This is the promise I make to all humans and dragons. We've all lived in fear and under control for way too long. It's time to end it. I just have to make it happen.

Dyne tells me to make a shield. I call Rynmoriath, who comes to the surface faster now. Maybe someday she'll let me become her again. I want to wear her scales and fly in the sky, but she's stubborn.

Today, I'm able to conjure a shield right away, much to Dyne's pride. It grows until it's taller than me. I've yet to figure out how to round it into a dome of protection.

"Great!" Dyne says. "Soon, you'll be able to create big enough shields to cover the passages. Then we can start on wards while also working on covering yourself. Perfect."

I smile, but my heart's not in it. I'm learning to protect myself. What happens if I can't protect those I love? No shield is big enough to cover my newfound family.

Chapter Twenty-Three
Urgent Message

THREY

The breeze feels good against my skin. Today, I'm hiding from everyone in the garden. It's been tough having no duties to perform. I've been expecting Father to give me something to do, but he hasn't. Maybe boredom is part of my punishment.

"I don't care who you think you are."

Uh oh. Iara sounds angry, which has been her constant state since Sule became her servant. Not that I'm surprised by this reaction. Both sisters are a handful and infuriating, to say the least. I wonder what happened this time.

"I don't care," Iara responds to something I didn't hear. "Jarlry is my personal servant, and you will not treat him that way. If I hear of it again, I'll make sure you face consequences for it. Now go retrieve my laundry."

After a moment, I see my sister slip into the garden and look around the corner as if hiding. I say, "Having problems?"

Iara jumps at the sound of my voice before spinning. "Don't do that."

I grin. It's not often that I see my sister flustered. If anyone could do it, Sule is fully equipped to handle the job. The evidence is staring at me with blue eyes that shine with annoyance. My sister is not happy.

"I couldn't help myself," I say.

Iara sighs and takes a seat next to me, smoothing her purple dress to look more composed. It isn't long until she has her emotions under control. There's no hint of her frustration in her scent.

"It's not nice to take enjoyment in others' suffering," she mutters. I may not be able to smell her annoyance, but I can still hear it.

"Why don't you tell Father that it's not working out?"

Iara lifts her hands and looks at her nails. "Sure, that'll work. Let me tell the lord of the Ildracan clan that his brilliant idea isn't as smart as he thinks it is. I'm sure he'll be understanding when he finds out his punishment is not good enough. I don't even know why she wanted to be here."

"Wait. She wanted to be here? I figured waiting on you would be beneath her."

My sister shakes her head. "It's obvious that she thinks so, which only baffles me more. While her sister did everything she could to make herself seem incompetent—I'm not at all sure it was an act—Sule was dripping with sweetness and almost seemed like she was willing to do this. I'm not sure what her angle is, but it was either her or the woman who couldn't even pick up my dress without cringing."

This is curious. Nothing I saw in their town told me either one would be willing to wait on someone. They expected to have everything done for them, not the other way around. This is curious, and not in a good way.

"I'm going to try to get back to my room before she's on her way back. I really don't want to put up with her more than I have to, so maybe I can make myself look busy. I do have some inventory things Mother wants me to look at."

With a pained scrunch to her eyes, my sister stands and quickly exits, in the biggest hurry I've ever seen her. I shake my head. I'm not sure what Sule is after, but I am sure it's nothing good. Both of those women are nothing but trouble. I hope Iara can handle her.

One thing I do know, Iara is right. Father won't give up his brilliant punishment over Iara being frustrated. It's best for her to figure out another way to handle her new servant until it's proper to let her go. I'm just glad it's not me in her position.

Standing, I stretch and decide I need a change in scenery. I really need something to do that doesn't involve wandering around. Mother used to give me things every once in a while to help her manage her workload, but she stopped when I was training to be the future general. Right now, she isn't the place for me to go for tasks. Neither of my parents are happy with me at the moment.

"If it isn't Lord Threy," a too sweet voice says from behind me.

I freeze, hoping I'm imagining it. When I turn to find a pair of brown eyes watching me with hunger, I realize my wish is not coming true. I narrow my eyes. "I thought Lady Iara told you to get her laundry."

Sule spreads empty hands. "I'll get it, but I was really hoping to get a chance to talk to you."

"I'm not interested."

She waves a hand at me. "Nonsense. I know the reason you rejected us is because you didn't want two."

"And you thought by taking your sister out of the picture I'd change my mind?" I cross my hands over my chest. "It doesn't. I'm not interested in any woman who feels cruel is the way to be. You ingratiated yourself to make my sister pick you for no reason."

"A general's mate is what I was destined to be, my lord."

I laugh. "If you haven't heard, I'm no longer in my brother's good graces. You're flying for the wrong prey, and now you're stuck."

"Someone as smart as me can get you back into position. All you have to do is ask."

"Again, not interested. You better get back to your duties."

Sule grins. "We'll see. I can be pretty persuasive."

As she walks away, my new stalker swings her hips back and forth, trying to be seductive. I shake my head with a sigh. It's times like these that I really wish I could announce I'm already mated. Alright, I always wish that. To publicly call Ryn mine would be a dream. Not yet. Soon.

I hope.

Delto rounds the corner. When he sees me, he smiles brightly. Rakurn follows behind, looking between us with a clear warning of needed peace.

"Brother," Delto calls before I can duck down another hall.

I resign myself to this encounter. "Delto."

"I've been reconsidering your position. It seems that this whole fiasco will be behind us soon."

Rakurn shoots him a look. "What is spoken in confidence needs to remain in confidence."

I didn't care when Delto spoke, but the aggravated look on Rakurn's face tells me there's something here I shouldn't know. Nervous, I pay better attention and look between my two brothers. Rakurn grabs Delto's arm, but the eldest brushes him off.

"Enough," the heir says, clearly annoyed. "You are my advisor, not my minder. It's imperative to see if our youngest brother has learned the error of his ways and has become loyal again."

"Or you're trying to lure him into a situation to get him into more trouble."

"Whichever, this is happening."

"What is happening?" I ask.

Delto's smirk sets me on edge. "The king has found the red dragon and will be marching on the rebels soon. It won't be much longer. Then you can mate Noble Tiera like you should have to begin with. I'll even let you be my future general again as a reward for your loyalty."

"Delto!" Rakurn says while my heart drops into my chest.

"He needs a chance to prove himself, Rakurn. Do you think one third son is enough to stop the king and his might? Anyway, good day, brother. I'll be watching."

Rakurn continues to argue with him as they walk down the hall. Despite the secret already brought to light, the advisor is trying to rein in the wayward heir. Another sibling I don't envy right now. I wait for them to disappear from sight before hurrying back to my room.

On the way, I stop a messenger. "Tell the kitchen I want food brought to me, and I want Elda to be the one to deliver it. I don't like how others do it as much as her."

I'm proud of the haughtiness I manage to put in my voice, despite my current panic. I've never been one to hold my position over someone, but it is useful now. Angering a dragon is never in the best interest of any human. My orders will be followed.

In my room, I pace back and forth until I hear a knock. Elda stands on the other side. "Place it on my table."

Elda bows her head and enters. Once the food is down and the door is closed, she turns to me. "Is there something else you need, Lord Threy?"

"They know where Ryn is."

Her hand goes to her throat. "Who?"

"The king. Delto just told me to lord it over me. They're going for Ryn. Do you have any way to get word to them? They need to move."

"This is bad. I can send a message, but it goes through multiple people. If I mark it as urgent, I hope it'll get to them in time. Did Delto give a time frame?"

"No. He said he's testing my loyalty."

"Despicable dragon," she mutters, her eyes going wide. "I'm sorry, my lord."

"It's fine. I happen to agree with you. Hurry."

"Yes."

Elda rushes to the door, pausing to make sure she looks like the proper put-together servant before opening it and exiting. To keep up appearances, I lift the lid on the tray. Even her famous bison dip isn't enough to coax my appetite out, but I try to force myself anyway. If I ask for food and don't eat it, they'll know something is up.

As soon as the snack is finished, I sit the tray outside on the floor to be picked up. Pacing is going to wear a path into my floor. I wait for as long as I can, sure it's late enough to halt any suspicions. Learning the joys of lifting off from the garden, I work my way there. My clothes are off in seconds, and I'm in the air as the sun dips below the horizon.

Shadows stretch beneath me while I weave back and forth through the sky. The flight is lazy. I'm trying to decide where I want to go. I know I won't see Ryn again so soon and don't want to risk her, but our spot draws me. It probably still smells like our lovemaking. The desire is strong, almost forcing me to change course. The scent would calm my racing heart.

Something grabs my attention and makes me abstain from heading toward our spot. It's a small sound, but I can still make it out above the chirping bugs in the tall grass. Wings; that's what I'm hearing. Avoiding looking back, I do everything I can to make it seem like I'm only out for a leisurely fly. If they know I'm on to them, I won't learn anything.

Loyalty test.

The words echo in my head. Is the raid really happening, or was this an attempt to use me to help them find it? No. Rakurn, while a rule follower, wouldn't be able to lie like that. He's the one that makes Delto's gloating feel real. This is something else.

My straining hearing catches something new, so I turn that way, catching a glimpse of a dark shadow further back but acting like nothing is amiss. Whatever I do, I'm not leading them to our spot. Shadow would mean a black dragon. I clench my teeth until my jaw hurts.

Uncle.

His search is bringing up nothing. Yet another way I'm besting him, so he hopes for me to make a mistake. Maybe he wants to find her before the king can attack to prove he's better. This is the only thing that makes sense. Or he wants to catch me unaware and do away with me. No. He wants to teach me a lesson, not kill me.

I'd bet my left wing that it's the first option. Instead of giving myself or him away, I follow the sound I heard before to a herd of buffalo. Grinning, I dip silently, taking one at the edge of the group without fuss. I take my time to eat, wondering if the general will reveal himself.

He doesn't, so I lift back up when I'm done, licking the blood off my lips.

For the rest of the flight, I make lazy circles. At one point, I swear I catch the smell of frustration. I'm careful to keep my smugness to myself. My uncle wants to play this game, then I'm ready for him. I hope he enjoys exercise because he's getting no clues from me tonight. My only worry is how careful I'm going to need to be from now on. I'm not any safer than she is.

Chapter Twenty-Four
Familiar Magic

RYN

At breakfast, I find myself with the same group again. Laughing along, I continue to let my heart grow fond of those around me. Good never lasts forever, but I'm treasuring it for as long as I can. I can only hope that this happiness lasts a long time.

Someone runs up. "Nova. Dyne. You're wanted for a meeting. We just received an urgent message."

The two asked for stand and rush out. Trev looks over at me. "Guess we should wait to start training until we know what's going on."

I nod and eat some of my toasted bread, dry without butter. My mind goes over everything, worried about what might be ready to destroy my peace. An urgent message doesn't automatically mean something bad though. It can be anything, right? It's never anything good.

Trev elbows me. "It'll be alright. If it was something terrible, we'd be evacuating already."

"Yeah. You're right. It's just that we've had it good for too long. I don't trust that to last."

"You call this good?"

I laugh. "Well, no attacks. I haven't been almost assassinated in a while. We've been in the same spot for a long time. You don't hate me any longer. It's better than it's been."

"Who says I don't hate you?"

I bump his knee with mine. "You have."

"I have said no such thing. When have those words ever left my mouth?"

"Your actions said them."

"Misinterpretation then."

Feeling all my anxiety melt away with his teasing, I grin at him. "Whatever makes you feel better."

"I don't need anything to make it better. I always feel great."

We fall silent for a while, and I can't help myself. "What was my mother like?"

Sure he's going to get mad at the question, I hold my breath. My mother has been a touchy subject between us, so I may have just made him hate me again. I'm not even sure why I feel the need to ask. It's been on my mind for so long, but why now? Why ruin a great moment?

To my surprise, he doesn't seem angry. "She was a great person. Independent. Strong. Caring. She saved me and my uncle. That's how they met. I was too young to remember, so I've only heard stories about it."

"She loved Dyne?"

"So much so that she gave up the hope of having children by mating with him."

"What?"

Trev laughs at my confusion. "You don't think crossbreeding is common, do you? Can you imagine how many red dragons we'd have if it was? Hybrids are rare, so they didn't expect to have kids. She took me in as hers because my mother died in the attack that led Dyne to her."

I remember being told that, but it slipped my mind amongst everything else going on. Dyne must have been very special to her if she made a choice like that. I can see it. Despite our rocky start, he's calm and collected; kind and gentle. His entire heart is in this rebellion, but I can tell that he wishes for peace. We've grown close through training, and I can see why she would fall for him.

"That means I was a surprise," I whisper. "I thought female dragons choose when to have children."

"They do, but she wasn't exactly guarding against it. The unexpected is often not expected."

I snort. "You don't say."

"I do because I'm wise like that. Unexpected does not mean unloved. Both of them were so excited when you came along. You could see the glow on both of them. That's probably when my jealousy first started."

That makes sense. It's clear Trev loved my mother and looked at her as his own. They were a family. When I came along, I was nothing but an interloper to him, someone to take attention away from him. Someone stealing his love.

"I shouldn't have been though," my cousin continues. "Your mother never gave me less attention. It was just the potential of someone who was actually a piece of her coming into the world. It made me feel insecure."

"I'm sure she loved you."

"She did. Raya loved you so much though. It was hard to watch as a young boy who didn't have a mother of his own. The day she disappeared after the attack, I was terrified."

"Then you learned she died to hide me."

Trev falls silent. No wonder he hated me so much. First, I took the security of her love from him. Then I took her life. I can understand his hostility now. As a young boy, it would have been even harder to process her loss, particularly after losing his direct family already. I was the only thing left to hate besides the king, but he already hated royalty.

"I'll admit I harbored resentment," Trev says. "It's hard to keep hating you, unfortunately. You remind me too much of her."

I laugh. "Nothing you said about her sounds like me."

"It all does."

My laughter dies, and I let silence take over. He can't mean that. In all the time I've known him, I've never heard him sugarcoat anything, but he can't mean it. She sounds so perfect, and I wish I could have known her, but I'm not like her. I'm not admirable. All I'm trying to do is survive; that's always been my goal.

People run in, calling for an evacuation. I look at Trev, who says he's sticking with me and calls for a friend to gather his things. We rush for my room, and Trev helps me fill my bag. As we exit, Trev takes his supplies from waiting hands. Dyne catches up with us.

"What's going on?" I ask as we move along.

"Threy."

I trip, saved from a face plant by Trev's quick hand. Threy? My heart plummets at the thought that he is responsible for anything. That can't be right. He had no idea of our location, so he couldn't have told anyone. Besides, he'd never put me in danger. Something else is going on. Something else *has* to be going on.

Dyne continues. "Threy overheard the king knows of our location, so we're on the move again. He gave the information to the cook in the keep. Elda, right? Good. It had to change hands multiple times. There's no telling how long we have. We need to move. They wanted to ask me if I thought it was a legit warning. I see no reason for him to lie."

Nodding, I let out a relieved breath. Threy is helping, not going against us. I'm not sure why I even suspected it in the first place. My copper dragon would never do anything to hurt me. He's only ever wanted to protect me. My mind is a cruel place, full of doubt. I should know better.

"Are we going topside again?" I ask, pushing my thoughts down.

"No. We are only moving to a different part of this system. There are no blockages, and we don't want to risk being seen in the daylight. There is an old ward that may still be holding. We are heading there to get ahead of the king's army. They're weakening, but some still hold back the flames."

I wince. If I had the ability to do what I want with my magic, I could easily strengthen the old wards. My failure is keeping everyone in danger. Anger fills me, and I send it deep down. I have what is needed to keep people safe, but I can't use my abilities. Nothing I try works. Rynmoriath holds the key.

Please, help us.

My dragon stirs but doesn't make any other move to listen. Instead, I feel her nestle deep down again, comfortable to hide away and remain quiet. She's comfortable inside of me and doesn't want to break free. Even reminding her of the feel of the air on her scales isn't enough to bring interest. Rynmoriath is happy as she is and in no mood to change it.

Frustrated, I scream into my head. Nothing I say or do moves the heartless beast within me. To her, she's safe within me and not willing to budge. After so long locked inside of me, she's made it her home and isn't willing to change that now. I need a reason to convince her otherwise. So far, that has proven impossible.

Word comes that an attack is happening, followed by the barking of dogs. A few brave men and women hold the entrance. It seems that Threy's word came just in time. We hurry along as Dyne shows me different marks that will lead us to safe zones. Moving past one, he tells me that ward has already fallen. Everyone moves quickly, unwilling to be caught behind if the king uses his main weapon.

We reach another warded passageway. Dyne moves through, and I notice a faint shimmer. As I pass through, I feel something grab hold of me. I pause to contemplate the strange sensations while others rush past. Reaching out, I let my hand stroke the permanent shield in front of me. Something calls to me; something feels right.

It's hard to describe what it is that I feel, but it's a sense of oneness. Rynmoriath stirs, reaching with me for the strange power that feels familiar. My magic rises up to mingle with what I feel. Both parts of me silently examine the strange sensation.

It feels like family. It feels like home. My dragon comes close to the surface without threat or coercion. She wants to feel this as well, and she wants to savor what she feels. Dyne has used magic around me many times. So has Threy. Magical power has never felt like this. It never called to me. This is different. Magic made by a red dragon feels the same as what I attempt to use. This is me, but not me.

This is the feel of those red dragons that came before me, my ancestors from another line. Despite different bloodlines, we are one family. What would it be like to know another in the flesh? Mentored by one of my own. Would Rynmoriath be more willing to break free of the prison my father made for her? Would she want to know the feeling of air beneath her wings if one of our own showed her?

Trev grabs my arm and pulls on me. I stumble after him, not wanting to leave behind the feeling of kinship. Rynmoriath grieves in my head as we're dragged further from the familiar feeling of those that came before. The further we get, the more we want to go back. Distance is dulling the connection between us and whoever made that ward.

Dyne steps in front of me. "We have to go. There's no telling if that one will hold the fire back."

"It will," I whisper.

"How do you know?"

"It's still strong. I could feel it when I touched it. Time has passed, and it has weakened, but it's still strong enough for a few more blasts."

Dyne looks at me as if hoping I'll say more. What can I say when I'm still processing it myself? Even now, it reaches for me. Or am I still reaching for the power? No. Rynmoriath is sulking in the back of my mind. The ward is pulling to me.

Shaking my head, I push away the unspoken questions that I can't answer. I need to examine this feeling more, but now is not the time. People push by us, and I think I even see Atan glance back from the crowd. None of it matters. All that matters is finding safety. The people I'm beginning to love need to be protected.

Until I can learn to copy what I felt, they'll always be in danger. My curiosity needs to wait. Alone in whatever temporary room comes next is where I need to be to contemplate what I felt. Maybe my dragon will be more willing to help me investigate. She welcomed the touch of the strange magic, longed for more. I'll talk to Dyne about this later. Right now, we have to get to our new camp.

I guess there will be no training today. There's no telling how long we have to travel yet, but these moves usually last a day or more. The further we can get from where we last were found, the better for all of us. We've lost the ones that stayed behind—there's no doubt about that—but we won't lose more than necessary. I need to figure this out. Rynmoriath needs to help. If only I can convince her.

Chapter Twenty-Five
Strange Magic

Ryn

I take the time to put away my meager possessions while exhausted. We traveled for three full days, only stopping to eat and sleep. There was no time to talk or think about the strangeness at the ward. We passed through two more on the way, and every single one gave me the same feeling.

Rynmoriath is restless, but I can't take the time to examine it anymore. I need sleep. By the scent, this room has been vacant for a while. This mustn't be a well-used camp location. That makes sense if it's where we are choosing to hide. Maybe there's no close exit. I'll need to ask about it when I'm able to speak to Dyne.

Tired of the effort it takes to repack everything, I only remove my blankets from my bag. My journal comes out long enough to write the events of the last few days and my thoughts on them. As usual, I include a passage about Threy to keep him fresh in my mind. Not that a night like our last visit is easy to forget. I miss him already.

Stretching out on the cot, with my guard standing outside, I ready myself for the first uninterrupted sleep in the last three days. It's much deserved. Only... I can't sleep. Rynmoriath strains for the nearest ward, but it's not close enough for her to feel it. That doesn't stop her.

Groaning, I roll over and bury my face in my thin pillow. I need sleep. Training restarts tomorrow, and Trev doesn't give me any leeway when I'm exhausted. He reminds me that not all fights happen when I'm feeling my best. I force my mind away from the wards and think of Threy instead. The way he looks. The way he sounds and smells. The way he feels. That distracts her enough to let me fall into slumber.

The knock at my door to signal the morning shift switch comes much too early. I moan and yell that I hear but don't make any move to get up. I wonder if Trev and Dyne would give me the day off. That's wishful thinking that has no chance of coming true. No rest for the red dragon of prophecy. Everyone needs me at my strongest before it all comes crashing down.

Not a great pep talk, but it works. I push up, allowing myself to breathe fresh air instead of old pillow. Giving myself a long and exquisite stretch, I yawn. Time to get up and get dressed for the day.

At the dining cave, Trev and Dyne already sit at a table with some bread and cheese. I grab my meal and join them. "No Nova?"

"She's supervising some of the planning and setup. She took hers to go," Dyne answers. "Listen, I want to talk to you about your reaction when we crossed the first ward."

"It wasn't just the first one," I say. "I felt it on the other two as well, but I was too exhausted by that point to spend time focused on it."

"What did you feel? I know you say you could tell that the ward was strong enough to keep us safe. Anything else?"

"Kinship. Don't look at me like that. I don't know how to explain it better. It felt like I knew the magic wielders that made the wards, like they were a part of me. My magic called to them, and their power responded. Kind of like I could sense the dragon behind the ward."

Silence falls, so I take the quiet time to eat a little bit of breakfast. Trev watches Dyne as if waiting for some breakthrough knowledge. The older fairy dragon stares at me in confusion before turning back to his food. I look for something else to say between bites but come up speechless.

"Maybe all red dragons are connected somehow," Dyne says after a while. "It's hard to tell because of how rare they are and how long ago the last one lived, before even I was born. Not much is known, let alone passed down through the generations. That's the only thing I can think of because I can guarantee no one from our lineage put those wards up."

"So, we're like a family?"

"In a sense. Red dragons have so much magic potential that it's possible their magic connects them. Were you able to figure out how to make them?"

Sighing, I put my cheese down. "No, unfortunately. The magic felt familiar, but I couldn't learn it. I just felt like it wanted me to touch it. My dragon wanted me to too."

"How did she react?"

"Excited," I say, trying to put the emotions into words. "That doesn't feel strong enough. It's like she found an old friend, one she thought was gone forever. She came forward without any begging from me and pushed my magic toward the ward. Her reluctance to leave it is what made me want to stay close. She wanted to revel in whatever she felt."

"This gives me an idea. We'll try it after lunch."

"What is it?"

"I'll tell you when it's time. I need to go ask some questions."

Dyne jumps up, forgetting to take his plate with him. Trev reaches over and dumps the leftover food onto his. When I raise an eyebrow, he shrugs and mumbles something about being hungry. I let it go because food can't be wasted anyway.

My mind goes over what ideas Dyne could possibly have, but I come up with none. Exhaustion makes me feel foggy, and I don't look forward to sword practice today. I want to ask Trev if we can skip it but know better. The torture will go on as scheduled.

"I finally found a few swords that might work. I'd like you to try them out," Trev says.

My heart leaps with hope. "So no practice?"

My cousin laughs. "Don't sound so excited. After we find one, I want to try some moves to make sure the balance fits you correctly. The right sword can make all the difference in a battle."

"But you're not going to beat me up?"

"Not today. We will start that again tomorrow."

One more day of no bruises. I can deal with that. Anything that keeps me from possible knocks in the head is something I can agree with. Thankful for an easier morning, I finish my breakfast and follow Trev out of the dining cave. We stop in the room that's serving as the armory. The human manning the place nods our way as Trev leads me toward a few swords he has lying out.

"Try these," Trev says.

Looking down, I count four. If this is all he thinks will work, I hope one does. It's not like supplies are plentiful. The first one I lift makes me grunt with the weight, but I still force it up.

Trev shakes his head. "If it's that heavy for you, it's not the right one. You can't have a weapon that fights against you. Try another."

Happy to follow the suggestion, I let the weapon fall back down. The metal thumps hard on the table, and I cringe at the sound. Since that one was too heavy, I try the smallest one. Much lighter.

"How does it feel?" my cousin asks.

"Very light. I feel like I can throw this one."

He sighs. "You need somewhere between. Your weapon needs to be heavy enough to cause damage but not fatigue."

That one goes back to the table easier. The last two look similar in size, so I decide to just pick one at random. As my fingers slide around the hilt, I'm shocked at how it feels as if made for my hand. I lift it, finding the heft just right.

"I like this one," I say.

"Get into your attack stance and take a few swings."

I do as he says. The first swing slices through the air with little effort. A backhand swing is next. It feels right. To make sure, I try a few of the more complicated maneuvers Trev has taught me.

"Any strain? Balance feel off at all?" Trev asks.

"Not at all. It feels perfect."

"Great. Let's get you a belt."

Following him over to a shelf, I wait while he examines each one for any damage and tests length. With a grunt, he turns to try one around my waist, but it's too long. A few more rejections lead to a proper fit.

He cinches it tight enough to keep it from sliding down my hips but loose enough to allow movement, then shows me how to sheathe my chosen weapon. Next, he makes me take it out and put it back in too many times before he's satisfied. I'm a little bored by this point.

In the training area, Trev has me unsheathe it and runs me through a few smaller moves. After that, he does some sort of slow fighting, increasing speed every once in a while. As much as I was happy for what I considered an easy practice, this is just as hard. Weeks of fighting fast don't prepare you for slow motion moves. By the time we call it quits, my arms feel like jelly.

Dyne shows up right on time. "Ready?"

I sheathe my sword. "Yeah. What are we doing?"

"Walk with me?"

Curious, I follow him through the halls. We walk until traffic begins to thin out, then it stops altogether. "Where are we going?"

"There's a ward this way. It's not close, but it's walkable. We usually like to stay close to warded passages, but we're hoping where we are is safe. This camp hasn't been used in a while, and we would need to cross other camps to get out of the caves."

That's kind of what I was thinking earlier, but I don't mention that. He simply confirmed my theory. "Are we still in Ildracan?"

"We are, but more toward the eastern border, close to Wyvthin."

Something in his voice catches my attention. "Why does that seem to upset you?"

Dyne shrugs. "Nothing important. Just old memories best left buried. Anyway, I'm hoping that being close to a ward will make it easier for you to work with both your dragon and your magic. If she is more agreeable around wards, it's worth a try."

"That's a good idea."

Rynmoriath stirs with his words. Excitement returns. She wants to feel the magic of red dragons long gone. This is the last thing I have left to try because picturing her as Threy described brought her closer, but I still failed. My dragon does not want to leave inside me. She wants to stay hidden, which I guess I can understand. I used to want that too.

It's easier to stay safe while hidden.

Too bad it can't stay that way. We have a prophecy to fulfill, no matter what that fulfillment brings my way. I've given up thinking I have any say in what destiny has in store for me. I must do my part.

At the ward, we stop. Dyne asks, "Can you feel this one?"

Rynmoriath leaps for the opportunity. "Yeah. It's weak. This one won't withstand an attack."

"Let's see what you can do."

Nodding, I sit so that one part of my body touches the glimmering shield at all times. I close my eyes. The picture of my dragon comes faster now, drawing her out to the surface. I can feel her admiring herself, so I know I have it right.

Come out, Rynmoriath.

She balks and retreats a little, but not so far that she can't feel the magic. Even the lure of what she wants to touch isn't enough. Sighing, I open my eyes. "She's not interested."

"What about your magic?"

I close my eyes again and reach for my magic. Rynmoriath comes closer again and feels for the ward. At the same time, the foreign magic reaches for me. Gasping, I find my mind pulled somewhere. I'm no longer in the cave. Instead, an elegant room sits before me. A man in rich clothes paces back and forth while yelling at a group of people. I can't see clearly enough to make out words or faces.

Fear is a prominent emotion, soon replaced with awareness. This isn't me. I'm in someone else's head. I feel the other person reach for me. Panicked, I try to withdraw, but I'm stuck in whoever's mind I've invaded.

Shock takes over the curiosity that isn't mine. A hand flies to the mouth on the stranger's face. That's when I catch the sight of a strange ring with a large ruby in it. Two dragons frame the gem, their tails forming the band. It's a pretty ring, one I've never seen before.

"The red dragon..."

The whisper catches the man's attention, and he turns to look at the me that's not me. She gasps and pushes me away. I may have not been able to break free, but the force she thrusts at me sends me spiraling back to my mind. Yelping, I fall over.

Dyne appears above me. "You did it, Ryn. You formed a dome shield."

"That's not all I did."

As I explain it to him, his eyes keep getting wider. "That's not possible. There's no way the dragon that made this ward is alive. All red dragons are gone, except you."

"The connection felt weak, so I don't understand it either. She felt familiar, but she didn't feel anything like a red dragon."

"I need to think about this. The magic worked, so I'm going to send messages to search for any kind of talisman that was made by a red dragon. Maybe if you're wearing something, it would help. They're not numerous because, like the wards, they break over time. There should still be something."

"Sounds like a good idea. From what I got from this, I don't want to try again here. I didn't feel it elsewhere, so it's only this ward."

"We'll figure something out."

I trust him. What I don't trust is the strange thing that just happened. Who is that woman? How can she feel me? I'll have to add this to my list of mysteries I'll probably never solve.

Chapter Twenty-Six
Playing in the
Rain

THREY

"If you keep this up, people might mistake you for Rakurn," Iara says from behind me.

Yawning, I stretch and look up from my book. The bench is making my butt go numb, so this interruption gives me the chance to stand. Birds tweet among the ornamental bushes and trees. Wilted flowers give way to fresh splashes of color. It's peaceful here. So peaceful that I can almost forget everything sad and disappointing going on.

"It's not like I have much else to do," I say with another yawn. "I'm the disgrace that needs to be hidden away."

"Things will calm soon."

"That's a lie, and you know it."

My sister looks away. "Maybe it's best to be beneath their notice."

The tone of her voice sounds of deep sadness. Even her eyes look misty. I glance around to make sure no one is close. "What's going on?"

"Mother is pressuring me to pick a mate. I'm where you were not long ago. I have received multiple letters of interest, and our loving mother expects me to pick the male perfect for Father's rule. She wants to arrange visits soon."

"And there's no way the man that you wish to mate is in this group."

"Not a chance."

It seems like none of the Ildracan children get to mate for love. Well, I did, but very few know it. They won't until it's safe for both of us to declare it. I won't endanger Ryn in any way.

"I wish you could have the mate of your choosing," I say.

"I know you understand what I'm going through. Care to take a walk to the market?"

"Where's your noble servant?"

"I set her to reorganizing a closet that doesn't really need it."

"Then let's go. I need to stretch my legs anyway. Just let me return this book to the library."

Rakurn is there when we enter, as usual. He glances up at us. "Surprised to see my younger siblings in the library. Do you need anything?"

Shooting him a cool look, I make my way to the proper shelf while Iara speaks with the middle son of Ildracan. I have nothing to say to either of my brothers that won't end in a fight, so it's best to keep my mouth shut. Our sister still gets along with all, even if she spends as little time around Delto as possible.

"Ready?" I ask, walking over to Iara without a glance at Rakurn.

"Yep! Let's go."

She waves goodbye to our brother, and we walk out of the library. Dark clouds are moving in from the west as we step into the courtyard. It seems like my time reading in the garden wouldn't have lasted much longer whether I stayed or not. The threat from the sky doesn't bode well for our walk.

"Looks like we'll need to be quick," Iara says.

"Are you looking for something in particular?"

"I'd like to get Jarlry a small gift to reward his service, and I'd like to browse for anything purple."

"Of course you do."

She laughs and leads me forward. Iara loves the color purple because it reminds her of her dragon. My sister wraps her arm around mine. Humans and dragons bow with respect when they recognize us. We walk through the street, talking of inconsequential things. It's almost like our childhood, but with a cloud darker than those threatening to ruin our market trip hanging over us.

Iara finds some trinket for Jarlry to use to decorate his room and some purple fabric for a new dress. I stop by a table full of carefully crafted stone figures. An orange cat draws my attention.

"Oh!" Ryn says, running toward a certain blanket.

Gritting my teeth, I follow my human. My servant lifts a wooden cat in her hands, painted orange with swirled stripes. The quality brings a grimace to my face. If she'd like a cat sculpture, I could find her one made of ceramic and painted to look lifelike. This one is lopsided and the colors are dull. It's an eyesore.

Gray eyes glitter as she turns to look at my chin. "Can I have this, my lord? It reminds me of my cat from the stables."

I take it from her hands, ignoring the hopeful eyes of the human manning the threadbare blanket. "Are you sure you want this one? I could commission a very beautiful piece if you'd like."

Her lips press together, and her gaze falls back to the dirt. "I'd love this one, my lord. Its quality is more familiar to me, and this man needs the coins more."

The memory comes unbidden. This is the type of object I would have had commissioned for her if she would have let me. Instead, she taught me more about who she is; kind, generous, thoughtful. It was Hunter she saw in the wooden cat, and it's what gave me the idea to have the animal brought to my room as a gift.

"That's pretty. It looks like your cat," Iara says from behind me.

"It does." I look at the woman selling the piece that brings back memories. "How much?"

After handing over the money, I ask the seller to wrap it in burlap for me to carry. She does and also slips it into a bag to make it easier to hold. Thunder echoes in the distance. We need to get back before it rains. Iara has the same thought and grabs my arm again. We make our way back much quicker than the trip here.

Lightning flashes in the sky, and our feet pick up their pace even more. I'm careful to keep the bag tight in my fist to avoid dropping it. The price doesn't bother me to lose, but I don't want to break something that invokes such a strong memory in me. Anything that reminds me of Ryn needs to be kept safe. I wonder what she'd think of me buying it. I hope to eventually get to show it to her.

The sky opens up without so much as a mist for warning. We make a dash for the keep. Water splashes up over our feet and ankles. Iara giggles, and I can't hold back my chuckle. We haven't been caught in the rain like this in years. It's invigorating.

By the time we reach the courtyard, the muddy ground is a giant puddle. We slow and hop in the mess a few times for no other reason than that we can. Entering the keep, we're breathless and laughing. For the first time in a long time, it feels like the world is right again, simplicity at its best. How I long for more moments like this repeating and stretching to fill my days.

Of course, it can't last. Mother steps over to us, sending both a strong glare. "Iara, you are supposed to be looking over match correspondents that I gave you, not out running around in the rain like a pathetic human. You are the daughter of a lord. Act like it."

"Yes, Mother," Iara mutters before hurrying along.

I'm the next target of her ire. "And you! I'm tired of you constantly undermining me. Think what you will, but I am your mother, and you will listen to me. I'd expect this from you, but don't you dare put your thoughts into your sister's head."

"I've always been a disappointment, Mother. I figured you'd be used to it by now."

Scoffing, she walks away after tossing her hair back. I scowl in her direction long after she disappears. This proves to be a huge mistake.

"Lord Threy."

The voice makes me cringe. She's trying her best to be seductive, and others might find it so. Not me. I feel greasy and soiled by the sound of my name on her lips. My teeth clench, all signs of my perfect afternoon gone.

"I'm not in the mood, Sule," I say without looking at her.

"Men are always in the mood."

Her meaning doesn't miss its mark. Without looking, I try to walk away. The annoying woman jumps in front of me. "Why don't we check out one of the empty storerooms?"

"Why can't you take a hint? I'm not interested. I will never want anything out of you but for you to leave me alone."

Voices echo down the hall, and I freeze. Sule takes this chance to step closer and lay her cold hand on my soaked chest. "So strong."

I snatch at her wrist, but instead of pulling away, she leans into me. Giggles grab my attention. I look past her to see two dragon women laughing behind their hands as if they walked in on something unseemly. I'm sure I don't need to push Sule away as roughly as I do. Her smirk makes me realize that I probably just made this worse with my attempts to hide it.

Growling, I stalk past all three women. In my room, I realize that I'm still clutching my bag tight enough for my knuckles to hurt. I remove the cat and set it on my desk, where I can look at it any time I'm working on things. Well, if I ever have anything to work on again. I'm a wayward dragon drifting in the wind right now.

The storm continues outside, so I put away any thoughts of going for a flight tonight. Lightning is dangerous to a flying dragon. I've only ever braved it to reach Ryn that one night. Instead of my nightly ritual, I take a bath to remove the chill from me. I take my time, soaking up as much heat as possible. A steam bath would be great, but I haven't had a chance to visit them recently. I have all the time in the world. Yet, I don't feel like dealing with the gossip when I enter a very popular room in the keep.

An annoying knock disturbs my thoughts of just going to bed early. I open the door to be told my father would like to see me now. The emphasis on the word now is enough to make me wonder what I've done this time. This doesn't sound like a nice evening father-son chat. I take a deep breath and make my way there, sure I'm about to be chastised for something stupid.

I'm proved right when I enter his study. "Can't you make the right choices about anything?"

"What did I do now?"

"You're supposed to be courting Tiera, not Sule."

I burst out laughing. "What?"

My amusement doesn't make the Lord of Ildracan happy. His scowl darkens the entire room. "I'm pretty sure I was clear."

"I don't want to mate with anyone but Ryn. You know this. The last woman I'd ever consider is Sule."

"You were seen in an intimate position in the entrance hall. It's all some people are speaking of."

Rumors spread fast, quick enough to shock me. It couldn't have been too long. Yes, I lost track of time, but I'm pretty sure that much time hasn't passed. How has this gossip found its way to my father already? I wonder if it was intentional. Sule strikes me as the type of woman to force this. Wouldn't be the first time.

"Sule cornered me when I returned from my trip to the market with Iara," I say in my defense.

"Like her and her sister cornered you in their home?"

I press my lips together and let my breath out through my nose in frustration. "Yes. These women are determined to force your hand to name one of them my mate."

"You're a full-grown warrior male, Threy! How could they force anything? Once I could understand, with the shock. Either you're lying now, or you're weaker than I thought. Whatever is going on, it ends now. Tiera is going to be your mate when this prophecy talk is over."

"Nothing is going on!"

Father slams his hands against his desk hard enough for my muscles to jerk in reflex. "Stop making it look like it is then! Whatever is happening, it's up to you to bring it to a stop. I don't care if she's pushing you or if something is going on between you two. Grow up and accept your fate. Protect the reputation of your family for once."

"Nothing is happening because I refuse to mate with anyone I don't choose."

"You will do as you're told, or I will make you. Get out of my sight!"

When I walk out the door, I slam it hard. Servants and a few dragons in the hall jump in shock. The humans move along quickly, but the dragons look on with curiosity. What could the lord have said to his son to upset him so? This is the question I see in their faces. They can keep speculating. I couldn't care less about my soiled reputation; too many more important things hold my attention.

Too angry to return to my room, I make my way into the courtyard. The storm is dying down, still throwing light and noise but more distant. I no longer care how dangerous it is. Without bothering to strip, I shift into my dragon form. With a roar, I launch myself into the sky and head northwest. I need to get away from here for a while.

Chapter Twenty-Seven
Dirty Floor Water

THREY

I duck behind the stables, breathing shallowly to ensure she can't hear me. Since the other day, this woman has not left me alone. Father is angry at me—well, angrier. Mother is annoyed, which is normal for her. Delto finds it hilarious. Rumors are flying all over the place.

Not for the first time, I berate myself for not arguing with Father over this stupid idea for the perfect punishment. This is ridiculous. I can't win with anyone but Ryn anymore, and she's not here. I need to escape, but dragons can follow scent.

"Lord Threeeeey," the slimy voice comes from around the corner. "I know you're here. What a pleasant place you chose for us today."

Panicked, I look at the horses grazing in the pasture, wondering if I should steal one and use it to ride into the grass outside of town. She'd probably follow. I'm at the point where I fully believe she'd do anything to get what she wants. Vile creature.

She's close enough for her shadow to extend into my inadequate hiding place. My breathing stops at the lump in my throat. As her footsteps draw even closer, my heart thuds in my chest. I can practically smell the glee of my stupidity right now. It *is* the perfect place.

"Sule! What are you doing back here? You're supposed to be ordering afternoon tea," a familiar voice says, coming to my rescue.

"I apologize, Lady Iara. I must have gotten turned around."

"I know exactly what you're doing. You are supposed to be my servant. Therefore, you are supposed to be following my orders. I am tired of finding you places that you shouldn't be. Get back to your duties."

"Yes, my lady."

Relief escapes me in one long breath as her shadow disappears. I'm scared of a small female intent on making me hers. How does she think this tactic is going to work? All it's doing is annoying me and making me jumpy. Every time I turn around, she's there. It's nightmare inducing.

"It's safe, Threy," Iara says around the corner.

Straightening my shoulders, I step out. "I know it is."

"Did you think I couldn't smell you there?"

"Even if you couldn't, it would be a good guess that she's here for me. Haven't you heard all the rumors?"

"Don't look at me like that. It's not my fault she is the way she is."

I try to push down the anger I didn't realize I was feeling until she pointed out the look of rage on my face. My emotions are such a mess right now that I don't even know which is more prominent. The desire to fly away for good is strong, but father would only force me back for punishment. I have duties to the family as the third son.

Instead of calming, I throw her a scowl. "That woman is your servant. You should have better control over her."

Iara scoffs. "You try controlling that wild beast. This isn't fun for me either."

"Then tell Father you don't want her anymore."

"I did! Why don't you?"

My anger cools at the question. She knows for a fact that I did try to speak with Father about sending Sule back. Absolutely not happening. He simply told me to grow up and deal with the woman. His rule is the law, and he isn't showing weakness by ending the retribution unfinished.

"Why don't you put an end to it?" Iara asks. "Be firm and stop hiding like a child."

"You sound like Father."

"Maybe I agree with him for once. Put Sule in her place."

"I've tried! I've told her to leave me alone. I've threatened her. I've even gotten rough with her. Nothing works with that woman. She somehow finds a way to turn the situation around. I don't know what else to do!"

"Then how do you expect me to do what you can't? I'm tired of being blamed for that entitled lizard. Her actions are her own. I have nothing to do with it, and if this is the way you're going to treat me when I come to help, you can handle her on your own—like you should be anyway."

Before I can reply, she's gone. Now Sule is making me insult the sister I just got back. This is getting out of hand, but I don't know how to fix it. The woman is unbelievably dense and stubborn. Nothing I do gets through to her. What else is there to do? It's hopeless.

I walk out of the keep gates. I'm not sure if she'll be brave enough to enter town without permission, but it's worth a try and easier to avoid her. All the scents will cover mine. It'll also give me enough peace to think. Anything is better than the stares of those in direct contact with this conflict.

The streets are busy on the nice day that is this afternoon. Children run up and down the spaces between buildings. Dragons, in both forms, bask in the sun and socialize with their own. Humans scurry with their heads down, in various states of dress. A flash of red hair makes my heart skip a beat. My eyes search out the familiar color, finding a young girl dashing into a pottery store. Curious, I follow.

I enter the store to hear, "Girl, how many times do I need to tell you not to run? Everything in here is breakable."

The owner of the voice is a woman with gray in her red hair. She notices me and plasters a smile on her face. By her scent, she's human, so her presence in this part of town means she has skill. The young girl blushes and scurries into the back, leaving me to wonder why I followed her to begin with. It was a spur-of-the-moment decision, fueled by bright red hair.

"Can I help you, sir?" the woman says.

"I was merely curious about your shop and would like to browse."

"Feel free to look around all you like. I put a lot of work into my goods and aim to please."

Nodding, I step over to a shelf and wonder how long would be proper to make my story be more plausible? I feel like an idiot for following the girl in here. I knew she wasn't Ryn. She's too young, and there's no way the red dragon would return here like that. Being hunted is a good reason to stay away.

I guess I simply couldn't help myself. It's been so long since our night in the grass. I find myself longing for Dyne to contact me again.

The desire to be with her grows every single day. Finding anything that reminds me of the woman I love has become a quest.

That's when I find another reminder. A vase catches my eye. It's a shiny white with reddish-brown horses galloping around it. My fingers trace the realistically painted animals. Ryn would love this. The price makes me wince, considering it's human made. I consider having a prettier one commissioned.

The girl comes back through the door to the private area. "Mommy, I can't find any sugared pastries."

"We ran out. I can't afford more right now. Sales haven't been the best. Go find something else to snack on."

The girl disappears and returns with a handful of crackers and water. Ryn's previous words enter my mind.

"I'd love this one, my lord. Its quality is more familiar to me, and this man needs the coins more."

It's not the first time this has come out of the dark recesses of my mind, but I feel it's wisdom to be considered here. Ryn loves human crafted items. That's one of the reasons she'd love this vase. It's clear this family is struggling. She'd want me to buy it.

That settles my indecision. Picking up the vase, I take it to the counter and start rummaging through my coin purse for the right price, then add a couple of extra gold pieces to it. The woman's eyes widen at my generosity.

"Thank you," she whispers.

"Thank you for such beautiful work." On the way out, I drop a copper into the girl's hand. "I believe there's a sugared pastry stand not far from here, if I remember right. Why don't you go and get yourself something sweet?"

The girl squeals and rushes from the store, coin in hand. The woman stares with wide eyes, probably astounded by a dragon showing such kindness to a human. Ryn has made a great impression on me. I have the money, so why not help those that need it most? With a smile, I exit the shop with my purchase.

Mood improved, I make my way home and place my vase on the windowsill. I return to my table, grab the copy of *The Dirty Dragon* my sister left, and read some of it as a further reminder of the woman missing from my life. Her absence darkens the world to my eyes, but I know she's safe. I can feel that much from our mate connection.

A knock interrupts me after a few chapters and the latest mention of 'his third dragon horn.' I place the book face down on the table by my couch to hold my place. As soon as the door opens, a hurried Elda rushes into my room.

"Sure, come in," I say, my voice heavy with sarcasm.

She drops a small tray on my table and turns on me. "How could you do this to Ryn?"

Blinking, I try to figure out what she's talking about. "Excuse me?"

"I've heard the rumors about you and that servant dragon. Ryn loves you so much. How could you do this?"

"I can only guess what you've heard—"

"And it's not pretty. Ryn is five times the woman she is."

"Ryn is a hundred times the woman Sule is."

Elda raises a finger to scold me with, but confusion shows in her eyes before she drops it again. "Then, why?"

"None of the rumors are true. Look, I appreciate your loyalty to Ryn, but nothing is going on between me and Sule. She and her sister tried to force a mating when I visited them. That didn't work, so now she's trying to pressure me another way. It's quite annoying, if I do say so myself."

"So, you're not falling in love with her and meeting her in secluded spaces to enjoy each other?"

"Never. I can't stand the woman. I'm disgusted by her." The older woman examines my face, as if unsure whether to believe me or not. I decide to take a chance. "We're mated, Elda. Ryn and I are made only for each other."

"But you didn't have a ceremony."

"I've been told red dragons don't need one."

Her hand covers her mouth. She looks between me and the tray with a frown. "You probably don't want to eat that then."

She walks over to the tray, removes the cover, and dumps the food into a bag for trash. I feel my brows furrow. "Why not?"

"I may or may not have sprinkled dirty mop water over it when I heard the rumors and came to lecture at you. I'll remove this garbage. Please wait until enough time has passed to avoid suspicion before you set the tray outside your door. I apologize."

I laugh. "No need to apologize. I'm glad Ryn has such a loyal friend. I'm also glad you didn't let me eat that."

"Friend... I never thought of it like that. At first, I just wanted to help her. She's so sweet and generous that I guess she grew into more than someone to look after."

"She's easy to love."

Her eyes find mine. "You should know, I suppose."

Before she can open the door to exit, I ask, "Any word?"

"Messages are few and far between, Lord Threy. It must be that way to keep their locations secret. I'm sure they're fine though. Someone would have said something if the red dragon was found."

I nod, and she leaves. That makes sense, but it doesn't help my aching heart in its quest for any word about the woman it's bonded to. I loved her long before this feeling; it's just more apparent now. I feel a small ache in my chest. Returning to my book, I settle in to imagine the characters are me and a certain redhead.

Chapter Twenty-Eight
Attacks

RYN

Entering the bathing cave, I notice its emptiness. What luck. I strip and slip into the water quickly. While alone, I lift my hand and summon a flame. With it comes a slight pain in my chest, but I haven't told Dyne it's returning. So far, it's not that bad, and he doesn't need to worry.

My magic is coming easier, even if I'm making no progress with shifting. The shifting is worrying me. Without my dragon form, I don't think I can beat the king. All he'd need to do is shift and eat me. I'm as useful as the human I once thought myself to be, despite my growing magic.

I let the flame dance on my palm, moving it to my fingertips and watching it bounce from one to the other. Fire is becoming easier. Warmth is second-nature. A shield is easy. Dyne says there is a lot more at my disposal, but these should be easiest. He wants to start on other things when I master these. I'd like to think I'm close.

He also told me that he can't help me with everything. A fairy dragon doesn't have the magic potential of a red. A camp not far away had a talisman, and it's been helping me a lot. No one knows what it does, but I can feel the power within it. Rynmoriath examines it constantly. I twist the gold ring on my finger. It's nothing more than a yellow chain. Still, the power in it calls to me.

The fire flickers out in my palm, and I climb from the underground stream. Dyne says that all camps have one. It's a needed commodity for a group of people that spend all day fighting, so every camp is built around running water. I'm thankful to have the ability to bathe.

As soon as I'm dressed, I catch a familiar scent. My heightened senses seem to come and go with my dragon. I can always make out if someone is human or dragon, but I can't always catch what's under that. With my new jewelry, my abilities are much more consistent.

Atan freezes in the doorway with fresh clothes in his hands. I sigh, depositing my towel in the bin in the corner. "We can't avoid each other forever. These groups don't seem to be that big."

His laughter sounds forced. "Not a lot of space either."

"Listen, I miss talking to you. I hate the awkwardness between us."

"It's my fault for expecting more from you. I'm an idiot."

"You're not."

Atan grunts. "I know my mind. At this point, I just need more time to process everything. When I'm ready, you'll know. I can't be around you when my hopes were shattered so recently."

Instead of moving for the stream, he turns and leaves, bath forgotten. I throw my head back and look at the ceiling with frustration. This was the first time I've tried talking to him. As much as I want to have my friend back, I can't force it. His advances aren't welcome because my heart belongs to another. If he can't deal with that, this friendship can't be salvaged.

When I exit, Prill jumps to attention. "My lady."

I close my eyes and count to ten. "How many times do I need to ask you to call me Ryn? I'm no lady."

"You're the red dragon."

"I've heard that happens under the right circumstances, but it doesn't make me better than anyone else."

Prill's mouth opens and closes. He's stuck between listening to the mighty dragon of prophecy and arguing with me that I'm special. He's one of the awestruck rebels. Nothing I do can be wrong. He barely stops short of worshiping me. It's a little aggravating. Never in my life have I ever been treated as special. This isn't something I'm comfortable dealing with.

Dyne saves me from adulation. "There's a letter from the supreme council. Leadership wants to invite you to start joining meetings."

"Really?"

"You need to know where we stand with things if we're going to train you properly."

"Maybe I should have been included before then."

"They wanted to make sure you fit in well."

I grin. "That I could be trusted? I get it. Now?"

"Yes, follow me."

Prill follows behind us, his hand on his sword at all times. Mine hangs heavy on my hip, but I'm grateful for the weight. I've yet to use it. Being armed still reassures me. Learning how to use a sword comes easier than magic or my dragon.

"Any hint of what this meeting is about?" I ask.

"We're just discussing where the rebellion stands. What move is best to make next."

"I thought making me powerful was the only move."

"You'll always be more powerful," Prill cuts in. "Red dragons are the strongest."

"Tell that to all my failures."

"There is no failing for you. Only learning."

I grit my teeth until I'm sure I hear them grinding. Dyne chuckles beside me, and I look over to see him grinning like a madman. When he catches me glaring, my mentor tries to hide his smirk, making it look worse. I'd give anything to knock the look off his face. Maybe that would show my babysitter that I'm not as great as he thinks I am.

When we reach another door, I'm grateful to have Prill asked to wait outside. As we enter, I see dragons waiting at a table that I vaguely recognize. Leadership keeps mostly to the shadows, besides Dyne, to protect the chain of command. They're all here now, right in this room. Greetings go around, and I'm directed to sit.

As exciting as it is to be included, this is a bit boring. Inventory reports are read in detail, along with recommendations. After a long day of training, this is torture. I'm second guessing my excitement to be here as we move toward the subject of our progress of training new recruits. Wonder if I can feign sickness at this point.

"Ryn," the man at the end of the table says to grab my attention. I really should have paid attention to introductions. "How do you feel about your training?"

Talk about putting me on the spot. All I know is how I feel, which I know is what he asked. Is this a test to see if I'm paying attention or a test of character? If I mention what my instructors tell me, will I be branded a braggart? If I don't, will I be thought of as a liar?

Well, he asked how I feel about it. "I feel like it's slow going, even though those around tell me I'm doing well. Trev gave me a sword, and I'm close to mastering basic magic skills. I'd be lying if I said I'm doing it patiently."

The man nods, taking in all I said. "And your ability to shift?"

I wince. "My dragon is being stubborn. The increased magic training is making her feel more comfortable, but she still has no interest in flexing her wings."

"So, you've only shifted once?"

"Yes, and I don't remember it much because the pain rendered me unconscious. When I woke up, Threy told me how to shift back. I haven't been able to turn into a dragon since."

I can tell by the looks on all the faces around us that this isn't what they wanted to hear. Dyne steps in. "She's making progress, Chelor. I can assure you of that."

Now I have a name.

"Without her dragon, all hope is lost," Chelor says.

My heart skips a beat. It's not like I wasn't expecting it. To have my exact same thoughts spoken out loud is a blow, one that's hard to take. What use is a mystical dragon that won't come out?

Dyne pats my hand under the table, telling me my emotions are clear on my face. "All we need is time. I'm sure Ryn can figure it out."

"Time isn't something we have in abundance."

"What are you saying?" Dyne says. "We have been stable for a long time."

"Not anymore." Chelor tosses Dyne a couple of letters. "Darac knows we have her and is hitting everywhere he can in search of her. He knows death waits in these caves. The coward is striking blindly.

Multiple attacks at once. Luckily, the Jeweled Dracon was only used in places they think we are."

This is new. By Dyne's expression as he reads the messages, it's new to him as well. We need to do something. We can't just sit and wait for him to come for us. That would mean certain death.

"We need to start thinking about moving forward," he continues. "Trev tells us she's good enough with a sword. We'd like you to cut that training back to three days at a time instead of everyday. Spend the next four days working on both her magic and dragon at every chance. Ryn needs to be able to shift. It's our only hope. We are talking about a good time and place to start gathering."

Dyne grunts. "We're getting ready to move on him?"

"Not yet, but we need to soon. Time is of the essence. Get her ready."

Everyone takes this as an end to the meeting. I have one more thing that I wish to speak of. I never see these men and women outside, so it needs to be now.

"I want to thank you for allowing me to meet Threy," I say, halting their exit.

Chelor looks at me. "We weren't expecting you to be mated already, but we understand the need. We can't have you distracted by the mating pain. How is it now?"

Dyne watches me with interest. I ignore the slight burning that comes with the thought. We don't have time for my weakness right now. If these missives tell us anything, time is short and growing shorter by the day. King Darac is breathing fire down our throats, and it's not one most of us can survive. To beat him, I need to spend all my time getting strong enough to fight him.

"It's fine. Thank you. I'll be sure to tell Dyne if it returns," I say.

Everyone mutters agreement before walking out. I follow them, less than ecstatic to find Prill waiting for me outside. We make our way back to my room, and I'm happy to close my door between me and the adoration that beams smiles at me. I pull out my journal.

The war wants to happen whether we accept it or not. The evil king is killing people without thought in an attempt to reach me and save himself from the threat of the prophecy. Attacks are more frequent and deadlier than before. It's all because of me. Without me, there would be no increase in death. Without me, there would be no chance for an end.

There must be a way to save those I care about. I'm the damn red dragon. I'm supposed to stop this evil. What good am I if I can't even follow a magical prophecy?

Throwing my pen down, I growl at the scribbled words. This can't be it. There has to be more. I need to do something. I need to be stronger, and it needs to be now.

The closest I've come to what we need is by the ward. This ring helps, but what if both will be even better? Dyne won't approve, so I won't tell him. It's not like I'll be going alone. Even if I want to leave Prill behind, he takes his duty of protecting my sacred self seriously.

Something needs to happen, and it's not going to do it without a push. What good am I? That's a question for later. Right now, I have a plan of action that might work. I can't let anyone hold me back, not even the man in charge of my training. To protect those that need it most, I need to take risks. That's what the red dragon is for. Isn't it?

My resolve hardens. This must be done. I summon a magic light to guide the way through the dark caves. It's not as bright as others, but I'm making progress here as well. Even this late, some people will be out. Most, including Dyne and Trev, will be secure in their rooms. It's now or never. They'd tell me to wait until tomorrow—if I'm allowed to at all—but time grows short. It's my failure that leaves us in this position, so it's up to me to fix it.

I step out of the room. "I need to take a walk."

Prill, ever the follower, doesn't ask any questions.

Chapter Twenty-Nine
Forceful Exit

RYN

"I thought we were just going for a walk," Prill says behind me.

"We are."

"I don't think we're supposed to be leaving camp."

Sighing, I keep walking without a response. Prill won't dare touch me to drag me back. That's one good thing that comes from his near worship of me. I can also count on the fact that he won't run back to tell on me either. My babysitter won't neglect his duty and put me in danger. This is happening.

The issue is getting there and back before someone comes to relieve him. I don't want to scare anyone by being missing. I simply want to try my theory without wasting time or worrying about an argument.

At an intersection, I pause and try to remember which way we went. The direction pops into my head, so I turn right.

"Can you at least tell me where we are going?" Prill asks.

"The nearest red dragon ward. I notice I feel different near them, so I want to try being close to one with the talisman on me too."

"Why can't you do that with Dyne?"

"Dyne has his own ideas. At this point, time is flying by too fast. I need to do it now to keep from wasting more of it with failure."

"You're not failing."

Arguing will do no good here. This isn't the first time I've had this conversation about my shortcomings with this man. I'm sure it won't be the last. Right now, I'm not in the mood to repeat old arguments. I just want to get to the ward and get back.

I begin to worry that we've gone the wrong way, but then I see the symbol Dyne showed me on the first trip this way. Relief overwhelms me, and I turn down the path that I know leads to my objective. Let's just hope I can find the way back.

After a few more turns, I see the familiar shimmer. Rynmoriath stops poking at my ring to perk up and strain toward the ward. Her excitement grows. Having two previous red dragon artifacts close is more than she could imagine. I'm starting to wonder if she realizes she's one as well. Connecting with her would give us both more to work with than dragons long past.

I settle in against the ward. "You might as well get comfortable. I don't want to take too long, but I want to make sure I give this a good try."

"I'll watch for any dangers. Alertness is needed. You won't come to harm as long as I'm on duty."

It's extremely hard not to roll my eyes right now. We're in the middle of a dark cave system, far from any unguarded exit. We would sense if anyone was close, particularly with my over heightened senses. I thought my hearing and sense of smell got better when I received the ring; that's nothing compared to now. No one is close.

Rynmoriath seems divided by which magic to focus on. The next challenge is how to focus on both at the same time. I've never tried to split my magic before. I touch the ring first before moving my attention to the ward. It's difficult, but I manage to touch both at the same time with my stubborn power.

My dragon circles inside the confines of my skull. Her presence spreads through my body. We still don't shift, but this is the closest I've ever been to connecting to her. For the first time in my life, I feel whole. I hadn't even known a piece of me was missing until now.

I revel in the feeling of fullness, chasing Rynmoriath around with my mind. She rejoices and nudges against my thoughts like Hunter used to do to my face when I was trying to sleep. Before, I could feel what she felt, but now we are one. Her joy at being close to me is overwhelming and brings tears to my eyes. This is who I am. This is what has always been missing.

I'm not a human slave. I'm not a scared little girl with a dragon hiding inside. I'm not a failure about to let the world I've come to enjoy die terribly. None of these are me, and they never were. I *am* the red dragon of prophecy.

Strength and power run through my veins, and I soak it all in. This isn't weakness. This is the strength needed to take down a tyrant king. I am Rynmoriath. She is me. It's now that I also realize that it's as much me holding her back as herself. My fear is hers. My uncertainty leaks into her confidence. To be her, I need to trust in her. At this moment, that feels easy. Outside of this peace, I feel the weight of hopelessness pulling me down.

I won't let the unknown pull me down. Right now, I will revel in my dragon as she does the same in me. Nothing outside of ourselves matters. All that we focus on is each other. That's all we need.

A sound breaks through the euphoria, and the moment passes. Sighing, I let Rynmoriath go back to examining the two sources of familiar magic. My eyes find Prill staring at me with his jaw dropped. If anything, the wonder in his eyes is stronger than before. Great...

"What?" I ask.

His mouth opens and closes a few times. Speechless seems to be a state I put this man into pretty often.

"You almost shifted," he says. "I saw the line of scales, claws, and fangs."

My brows furrow. "I did? I felt close to my dragon for a bit, but I didn't think I got close to shifting."

"It didn't seem to be enough to send you into dragon form, but it was still so beautiful. You're stunning."

Taking a deep breath, I look back at the ward again. I don't want Prill to see the annoyance in my eyes. It's not his fault I can't do more than almost shift. "I want to try something else."

Closing my eyes, I reach for my ring with my magic again. Establishing a connection with the ward while holding onto the talisman comes easier this time. Rynmoriath gets excited again, but she doesn't meld with me like she did. I feel closer. Not close enough.

Since I know both sources help me, I want to examine the ward a little more—see what makes it work. My magic flows into it and roams over the shimmery surface. At the edges, I find a strange thread of power. Without it, the ward is nothing more than a tied off shield. This thread is the key to blocking the Jeweled Dracon.

Excited, I follow it. The magic in me connects with it. Wonder takes over frustration as I feel the ward strengthening. The power in me that keeps me safe from the deadly flames flows through the channel I found, building it stronger. I have no idea how I'm doing it.

Knowledge of how is less important than the fact that I'm doing it in the first place. This old ward now has more life left to it. Pride washes over me, straightening my weary shoulders. I did it. The how can be examined later. I can't believe I did it.

The familiar feel of the magic itself draws me closer. Who made this? How long ago did they live? Were they one of the ones executed, or did they die another way?

The questions bring me to the center of the shield. I find my consciousness traveling across the kingdom again, dropping off at a mind that I recognize. She's bathing now, and I grimace at the bruises I see on her skin.

Then she notices my presence. "Red dragon?"

"Who are you?"

A noise in the other chamber startles her. "You must go."

"Wait. Tell me who you are first."

The door slams open to reveal a blurry figure. It growls at the woman in the bath. In a panic and full of fear, she pushes against me. The burst of power sends me flying back just as the figure raises a hand to swing at her. I fight the current, wanting to offer whatever comfort I can for what she's dealing with. Her power pushed too hard. I'm falling back without a chance to stop or even slow.

When I slam into my body, I feel a wave of magic burst from me. Screaming, I find myself rolling across the floor as if hit by a physical force. Prill stumbles back against the wall as the ground shakes. The world stills around us, and I pant to catch my breath.

Groaning, I roll over so that my face isn't against the hard stone. I stare at the ceiling, trying to make sense of what happened. My entire body aches, and the walk back is going to take longer than it should. How long do I have left?

"How long was I gone?" I ask.

"Gone, my lady? You didn't go anywhere. You were quiet for a long time though. Maybe a couple of hours."

A couple of hours. We need to get back. As soon as that thought crosses my mind, the aftershock rumbles through our current position. Cracks form over the ceiling, and my eyes widen in fear. Small pieces of stone fall around us, getting larger with each shake. The entire ceiling crumbles. Prill throws himself on top of me at the same moment I think of throwing up a shield.

Not before a chunk hits me on the head and knocks me out.

Moaning, I try to grasp my throbbing head. Something heavy prevents the action. The ringing in my ears doesn't help the pain bouncing around in my skull. Each blink brings my eyes to a more open state. Whatever is on me moves and conjures a magical light.

"Prill?" I say while looking into his eyes. "I can't breathe with you on top of me."

"I can't move."

My focus moves to the shielded dome shimmering around us. How did I hold onto that? Rynmoriath pokes my mind to remind me that she's still there. If she's the one who has been holding it up, I am extremely thankful. Heavy rock presses against the shield. Both of us feel weak and tired.

That's a scary thought that prompts action. "We need to get out of here. I can't hold the shield forever."

"I'm not sure how we can do anything as we are, my lady."

"How long was I out?"

"I can't say for sure because I lost consciousness as well, but you've been out quite a bit longer than me."

"Enough that they may be looking for us?"

"I hope so."

As if answering the question, I hear rocks shifting to my right. Is that the way we came or the other? The roll disoriented me until I can't remember which way is which. A small light shines through the cracks.

"Ryn?!"

"Trev!"

"Oh, thank Drakyth. We felt a burst of power and came to look when we couldn't find you. Dyne said the ward is the only thing this way that might lure you. Are you alright?"

Dyne is going to be so mad at me. So much for not scaring anyone. Not that it's entirely my fault that the world imploded around me. There was another power at play. Somehow, I don't think he'll accept that excuse.

"I managed to throw a shield up before we were crushed, so both Prill and I are alive and well enough considering. I'm not sure how long I can hold it though."

When Trev doesn't answer right away, I worry something happened to him. I'm relieved to hear his voice again. "Dyne can move the rocks, but things are going to shift quickly. Keep the shield up like your life depends on it because it does."

Laughing doesn't work well with a heavy man on top of me. "Will do."

Rocks roll away, some hitting my shield hard enough to put strain on it. Holding the dome is beginning to hurt, so I'm happy when the last of them roll away from me. I let the shield fall.

"If you can do that, why are there so many blocked passages?" I ask as Prill climbs off me with apologies for squishing my smaller body.

"It takes a lot of power and the rocks need to go somewhere. I only moved them to block another path," Dyne says. "What were you thinking, Ryn?"

"That time is growing short. I had an idea."

Dyne sighs and rubs his face. "We could have done whatever you had in mind in the morning."

"And wasted time. Besides, you already said you didn't want to mess with the ward more."

Prill helps me to my feet. The world spins, and I blink some more to clear the fuzz covering my vision. Dyne examines me for any injuries, ignoring my murmurs to tell him I'm fine.

"Did whatever you tried work?" he asks.

"Somewhat. I almost shifted, and I was able to strengthen the ward."

"What? Tell me everything while we walk back."

Walking is going to be fun. I seem to have developed a limp from stiff muscles. On the way, I explain what happened, including the short conversation with the woman at the other side of the magic. Dyne listens to it all with interest.

"Let's not do that again," Dyne says. "We need some of the cave system clear if we want to get out of it."

"I wasn't expecting that to hap—"

Pain pierces my chest. Gasping, I bend over and rub the area over my heart. Dyne utters soothing words while I wait for the agony to recede. It feels like it takes forever.

"That much magic must have opened your connection wider. I'm going to need to find Threy," Dyne says when I can make out words again.

Well, this was an eventful outing. At least it's leading me to more Threy time.

Chapter Thirty
Tricks

THREY

It's been a while since I've been out, so I decide it's a good time to go for a ride. Mindaine is agreeable. This will be a good thing for both of us. I let him trot where he pleases, only guiding him away from danger when it shows up. The sky is bright as birds pass between me and the sun. Nighttime flying isn't the best because of the damp and chill, but it's the only real chance I have to see Ryn.

So far, I've heard nothing from Dyne about Ryn. Yesterday morning, a severe pain stabbed my chest hard enough to wake me. I can only hope to receive word soon.

The day wears on, and my stomach rumbles in an effort to gain my attention. Unhappy with my hunger for breaking up this leisurely ride, I turn Mindaine for the keep. Despite my growing starvation, I don't hurry. My horse isn't in any more of a rush than I am. It makes me feel guilty for keeping him in the stable for as long as I have.

A carriage sits in the courtyard when I return, spiking my curiosity. Maybe Iara talked Father into sending Sule home. Wishful thinking. After all her attempts to corner me and get me in trouble to force mating, I'd be happy to see her gone. I know my sister would be too. She gave Jarlry a black eye the other day.

I take my time to see to Mindaine, giving him enough attention to satisfy him and promising to go riding again soon. Once done, I exit to find the carriage still sitting in the same place. With a shrug, I figure I'll find out soon enough and walk up the steps to the keep.

Iara stands in the entryway, chastising Sule about mud. I try to walk by, but my sister grabs my arm. "You have company."

"What?"

Before she can answer, I hear, "Lord Threy!"

Oh no. Turning, I see Tiera standing with my parents. Rage builds within me that they would ambush me like this, but I manage to hold it back. "Lady Tiera."

"You honor me, my lord."

Sule looks between us, her eyes darkening with anger and jealousy to the point I worry she's about to shift and challenge Tiera. Iara seems to sense it too because she sends her noble servant on an errand. One less discomfort is always welcome. There's plenty remaining.

My mother steps forward with a smile. "Iara, dear, please take our guest to the garden while we speak with your brother. He'll meet you there."

"Yes, Mother."

Iara leads the invading female away as my parents motion me into a room off to the side and chase a couple of servants out. Father turns stern. "Don't argue with us over this, son. Once the red dragon is done, we expect you to court Tiera like you really want to mate her. This pairing is best for the clan."

"I can never love her."

"Love is unnecessary," Mother says with a scoff. "Neither of you needs love. You only need mutual understanding."

I open my mouth to argue, but my father interrupts. "This is what will happen, Threy. Obey us in this or find yourself punished. We've told her that any ceremony needs to be held off until we take care of the threat, and she understands."

The easy way he speaks of ending Ryn brings my claws out to cut into my fisted palm. They exit before I can recover from my anger enough to argue. How dare they think they can control how I act? There is no getting over Ryn, so they're mistaken that any of this would be easy if I let it happen—I won't. This is ridiculous.

I remain in place until my fury subsides enough to avoid scorching anyone I meet in the halls. Iara and Tiera are chatting pleasantly in the garden when I enter. Tiera notices first and smiles with joy in her eyes that makes me swallow. Iara stands to leave, patting my arm and sending me a warning look as she walks away. The message is clear.

Don't make a scene. You can figure things out later.

I bow and sit next to Tiera at her bidding. "I wasn't expecting your company, my lady."

"It was a bit of a surprise to receive a letter from your parents to open up discussion for our ceremony after not hearing from you all this time. I felt the need to visit. I feared you had changed your mind."

I prepare a lie to placate her, but the words stick in my throat. Why should I tiptoe around a family that doesn't care about me and my happiness? This would never work between us. Even if they manage to divert the prophecy, I'm mated to Ryn. The pain would put me into mourning for much too long, and Tiera would never be able to deal with someone else having my heart.

"To be truthful," I say, damning myself, "it's my parents that are pushing for this match. I'm not interested in mating."

"Is it the red dragon?" she whispers.

Guess rumors travel fast. "Yes. I love Ryn and have for a long time."

"I suspected as much, but I didn't want to accuse you in case I was wrong. The fact that she's a dragon puts a whole new meaning to it."

Her calmness takes me off guard. "You seem okay with this."

"I suspected it to begin with, so it's no surprise. As much as I do not wish your heart broken, both your father and the king are searching hard for her. Love isn't needed, Lord Threy. I think we could be a very happy couple together, feelings or no feelings. If this ends in a way that doesn't leave your current choice possible, I'd like you to keep me in mind. There's no love, but I am fond of you. I feel it would be a good mate match, even without the stronger ties between our families. Would you like your mate gift back?"

It takes me a minute to realize she's talking about the gift she picked out in the market when I was trying to buy time to think of a way out of the commitment my parents put me in. "No, keep it for all the trouble and possible disappointment. Maybe as a bribe not to tell my parents either."

"I'm not going to tell them, but I'd be lying if I said I didn't hope you'd come around in the future. Farewell. I couldn't stay long, so please don't worry about your parents getting suspicious. I simply stopped in while traveling between cities. Thank you for being truthful with me."

"I'm sorry it came to this. If it wasn't for Ryn, it would be you."

"That gives me a little hope."

After she exits the garden, Iara runs in. "Tell me you didn't insult her."

"I didn't. I simply told her the truth. She responded with grace and asked me to keep her in mind if needed for the future, then promised not to tell Mother and Father of what I said."

"Wow. She's a better dragon than I am. I would have been jealous."

"That's what I was worried about as well."

Iara takes a deep breath. "I need to invite her to more events. She seems like a noble I can really get along with. I've known she was a good one, which is why I approved when you lied about picking her, but this shows me there's even more to her than I thought."

"I didn't lie. She was who I chose from the list. She just wasn't who I truly wanted. How's Jarlry?"

My sister grimaces. "Healing. Humans heal slowly though. It seems to pain him a bit, but I'm not sure how to make it better faster."

"It'll heal in its own time. Figure out how to get rid of Sule?"

"Don't you wish I did?"

"Definitely."

"I better go deal with her."

We say our farewells, and I make my way back to my room. Before I can get comfortable, there's a knock at my door. This is turning out to be a long day. I haven't even gotten the chance to eat yet. If it's a servant, I'll need to ask for something to stop my stomach from grumbling so much.

It is a servant. "Elda?"

"My lord, you've been out all day and I felt you might need something to eat. I went ahead and prepared your favorite."

I open my mouth to question her, but something in her eyes tells me not to. "Thank you, Elda. I am feeling a bit hungry."

She bows and walks away before I can close my door. At the table, I start by lifting everything to check for any notes but find nothing. Maybe Elda was just being thoughtful like she said. It wouldn't be the first time. I lift the lid on the plate to find a buffalo steak, roasted carrots and potatoes, and some fruit in its own bowl.

Definitely my favorite meal, and I devour it without thought. When I lift the bowl of fruit, I find a small, folded paper underneath. Of course. If it's about Ryn, it's going to deal with fruit. Now I feel like an idiot.

When the sun goes down, meet me at the stack of boulders that looks like a rabbit.

I have to think hard, but I eventually remember where he speaks. The last time I was there, I was around ten. I glance out the window and realize I have time for a short fly first. There's no doubt in my mind who this came from.

Moving back to the garden, I strip and shift before launching into the sky. At first, I merely weave back and forth in all directions. As the sun dips low enough to make visibility difficult, I feel a tingling that penetrates my scales. I'm being watched.

Pretty sure who it is, I make a few lazy turns until I catch his scent. Uncle again. Now is not the time for him to follow me because he'll find something this time. Taking on a general won't go well, even if I can gain some kind of minor advantage. I need another trick.

While I zigzag, my mind works quickly. I know just what to do. My wings bank to take me west. I'm glad when I sense my uncle following. Drawing near to the cliffs, I pick up speed and dive. This location has a chunk of rock that hangs over the edge enough to hide a dragon. Below, the tide is moving out to reveal a rocky beach. I hover and wait.

As expected, my uncle takes the dive to chase me. His neck passes my hiding spot, and I use all my possible speed to take him unawares.

We both roar in fury as we plummet. He bites at my legs, opening up multiple wounds. My focus isn't on the damage he does but what I can do. I keep feigning in and leading him to think he's winning, right up until the point we almost hit the ground. I spin my uncle until he's positioned to smack his head off another overhang.

He's dazed enough for me to avoid a fight when I flip us until he's below me. We slam into the rocks below. My uncle is knocked out, but he won't be for long. I move through my dizziness to climb over the cliff and make my way east, careful to keep my senses strained. He won't be able to track me from the air, so the best thing to do is get as far away as possible.

I find the peculiar formation and land close without shifting. Dyne steps out of the shadows. "Threy, nice to see you again. Head straight east. I'm sure you'll be able to find her without trouble. She's making progress, so the pain is growing. We are working on a better solution, but the mate bonds are known for not being forgiving."

Nodding, I launch into the sky again and move east. My heart waits for me. I'll move as fast as needed to see her again.

Chapter Thirty-One
Fire

RYN

This time, I know what waits for me at the end of our trek. The pain is growing faster. As much as my training needs to take the forefront of our efforts, I'm getting distracted once more. I hate this weakness, even as I'm excited to get to see Threy again. In the end, we can't keep doing this.

I need to figure out how to make my magic and dragon cooperate, and I need to do it faster. Dyne won't let me go back to the ward after what happened, so what I learned that night is all I gained. Not that it's not useful information; I'm just not sure how to utilize it. I managed to strengthen the ward by connecting my immunity to it. How? I have no idea.

"What if we try a different ward that might be made by someone other than that particular red dragon?" I say into the silence.

Dyne sighs and picks his way over a couple of large rocks, leaving me to wonder if this entire cave system will eventually collapse, not just certain parts of it. It definitely will if I let my power get out of hand too much. I nearly killed me and my bodyguard—a different one than the guy following behind us. At least this one doesn't think of me as some kind of all-powerful dragon.

"We can't guarantee the same thing won't happen again," Dyne says. "We don't know who you are connecting to or why. Another accident like that may kill you."

"Not if you're with me. You're better with shields."

"We need more information before we can attempt something like that again."

This conversation feels as hopeless as the others we've had over it. To say that he was upset over what he called my carelessness would be an understatement. Why can't he understand? I won't stop bringing it up until I get some kind of concession that doesn't involve looking for knowledge that no longer exists.

"But," I say to continue annoying my fathering dragon, "that's the closest I've ever been to shifting that didn't involve being bathed in dragonfire. I felt the magic in the ward and somehow strengthened it. I was able to connect to the fire immunity in it and feed it. That's important. If I can do it again, maybe I can figure out how. Don't you think that could be useful?"

"Of course it would be, but it's not worth losing you over."

"Right. Can't risk the kingslaying weapon, even if it's to learn how to actually kingslay," I mutter, unable to hide my annoyance and resentment.

"It's more than that," Dyne says with a sigh.

Neither of us says anything else because this is another argument we both grow tired of. It's hard not to feel like a tool to be used for the rebellion while being trained to be a weapon every single day. The pressure isn't easy to endure, even if some of it comes from myself. I'm growing tired.

What's wrong with wanting nothing but a peaceful life with a certain copper-colored dragon? That thought brings more pain with it, and I stumble to a stop. Dyne turns with concern. "How bad is it?"

"Bad enough to make it hard to breathe. Why did it get so bad so quickly? It's only been a couple of weeks."

"Your magic is getting stronger."

"There are lots of couples with full-blown magic that don't feel like they're dying so fast. Threy told me his mother went away for a couple of weeks to retrieve his sister. His father didn't feel like he was dying."

"I can't answer that with anything but theory. It's possible that since your magic was suppressed, it's all hitting at once because of the time spent blocked. It might have something to do with you being a red dragon. It might also have something to do with the two of you not being able to properly adjust to being mated. Anything could be causing this. Right now, our focus has to be on ending the tyrant's reign. After that, we can try to figure this out."

"Right," I mutter, letting my hopeless frustration through in the single word.

"Ryn, we will figure it out. Trust me. I won't let you live like this. For now, we need to get you to Threy."

Nodding, I start walking again. Further down the passageway, I find myself stopping to examine the wall. I brush my fingers over the rough stone, feeling for heat that isn't there. Darker spots that look like flames mar the surface, as if fire lived on the rock for a long time. Whatever did this carved into the hard wall, eroded it a bit. The depression isn't deep, but it's easily visible.

"The Jeweled Dracon is very powerful," Dyne says behind me.

"That's what did this? It eroded the rock."

"And it only raged for a few minutes. It took many lives."

The sadness in his voice pulls my attention from the marks. Grief darkens his eyes as he looks at what no longer holds my attention. It's an old grief, by the looks of it, one that lives forever in nightmares.

"What happened here?" I ask, almost afraid of the answer.

"I was here when it happened. I lost many friends. Come. We need to get you to the meeting place by nightfall, so I can hurry to meet Threy."

That's his way of changing the subject, and I allow him to. At an intersection, I feel something tingle at the edges of my senses. Rynmoriath grows curious. Crouching, I run my fingers along the floor where the paths split. It's familiar, yet something different.

"There used to be a ward there," Dyne says.

"That explains it. It feels the same but different, weak to the point I can barely make it out. The flames destroyed it?"

"It was too old to hold. Escaping this tunnel after it collapsed is what cost me my ability to fly."

The pain in his voice brings tears to my eyes. I stand and let him lead me away. This time, he's the one to stop and crouch. Tears fall down his face as he places his hand in a deep divet in the floor. He mutters what I make out to be a quick prayer to Drakyth before standing.

"What is it, Dyne?"

"This is the spot Trev lost his mother, your aunt Itori. I wanted to help her to the ward too, but we heard the roar of the flames. If only I could have carried both. She made me promise to save Trev."

I place my hand on his shoulder. "I'm sorry my weakness is making you relive all this."

He covers my fingers with his. "Itori and Trev were the last of my family. Leaving her behind was hard, but she was right when she said we'd never make it. I barely made it out without dragging her along. This is a day that will forever live in my mind."

"I'm sorry that happened to you."

"Me too, but it led to a positive. Without this happening, I never would have met your mother. She saved my life many times over. And without her, I wouldn't have you."

Dyne squeezes my hand in a way that tells me it's more than what I am; it's who I am. I've found it hard to believe, but I do understand now. Yes, I'm a weapon to dethrone a king. I'm also his daughter. This is what he's tried to tell me over and over that I almost grasp before forgetting. He lost almost all of his family, and he had to give me up for my safety and for the sake of the prophecy.

Finding value in yourself is hard when you've been abused your entire life. I was nothing for so long that it's hard to understand that I can be something again. The humans he left me with raised me and loved me, but I lost that due to dragon jealousy. I never thought I'd find family again, so I pushed it away when offered. I was so stupid.

Dyne begins walking again. I follow with my bodyguard behind us. This place holds dark memories for him, but he's willing to revisit them to help relieve my pain. His agony is less important to him than mine. This gives me a whole new perspective to think about.

Before I can think more about it, the scent of fresh air hits me. Through this desolation made by silver fire is the clean of the world outside. We emerge in a stand of trees behind a large rock. Dyne tells the guard to stay here and leads me out. More trees are to the right, and that's the way he moves us. I also see forests to the north.

"Where are we?" I ask.

"Where Ildracan, Fayimos, and Wyvthin meet. The forest of Fayimos has recovered from the ravages of Darac's jealousy and fear better than my people have. Wait in the trees here. I'll send Threy your way."

Nodding, I settle in to wait. For some reason, I feel nervous to see him again. I pick up a stick and break it into many small pieces before plucking a blade of glass from the ground and tearing it apart. It feels like forever before I hear wings beating in the sky.

The copper dragon lands outside the trees to shift. Threy runs into my arms, lifts me, and spins me in circles. When my feet touch the ground again, I find my mouth devoured by his. No greetings. No awkward words. Instead, I find myself losing clothes faster than I can remove them myself.

Threy grips my hips to lift me, and I throw my legs around him without thought. Our tongues don't stop dancing as I find myself pinned against a tree. The bark digs into my back, but I don't have a care besides the tip of his cock poking at my entrance. As he slides in, I moan at the pleasure that fills me.

He moves his hot mouth to my throat, biting and licking as if he needs to taste me. I feel my claws form and dig into his back, which makes him growl. Threy's fingers dig deeper into the flesh of my thighs as he continues to hold me up. Pressure builds with each forceful movement of his cock. I'm gasping at the heat and pressure.

My body tenses and trembles as I clench around him and cry out. He spills his heat inside me, grunting his release. This was an act of desperation and need. One fueled by the beasts inside us. One I'll never forget.

When he lowers me to my feet, I feel my legs buckle. He falls with me, both laughing as we land on the ground full of dead leaves. We kiss again, running our hands over each other's naked bodies until I feel him grow hard again against my thigh. I wrap my hand around his length, listening to him moan into my mouth.

Threy rolls until he's on top of me, taking his time to worship my body this time. His mouth moves to a pebbled nipple, sucking and pulling until I'm writhing beneath him. One hand moves between us to stroke my sensitive clit in circles. He moves his mouth up to my throat while inserting two fingers.

I throw my head back and arch my body to meet his as the pressure builds once more. The sensation is too much to endure, and I get ready to let go. Before I can release, he pulls his fingers out, making me whimper.

"Not yet," he whispers into my throat as he grinds against me without entering.

"Please."

"Not yet."

His shaft strokes my entrance and clit. I groan with frustration, making him chuckle at my throat. My body pulses with the need to have him inside me again. A strong hand moves to my breast, squeezing with enough pressure to make me moan. Fingers pinch my nipple and pull. I gasp.

"Threy..."

"Are you ready for more?"

"So ready."

"What if I'm not?"

This teasing is getting to be too much, so I use my strength to roll us again. Before he can react, I grab his cock, position myself over it, and lower myself over his hard length. He sucks in a deep breath as I slide him deep inside. Moving my hips, I lean down to consume his lips with mine. It doesn't take long to push me over the edge this time.

Once my body stops clenching around his dick, he flips us again, not done with me yet. I wrap my legs around him. When he pins my hands above my head, the pleasurable sensation increases. Breathing and kissing become hard to do as my breath comes in gasps and pants. Each thrust pushes me further and harder than the last. My entire body tingles and heats.

I'm not sure how much more I can take, but I hold on to the ledge. Biting my lip, I feel my fangs dig into tender skin and taste blood. Lifting my legs higher brings a new kind of pleasure that takes my breath away. Threy lets go, and I take the plunge with him.

My entire body trembles with my release. Wave after wave hits me, leaving me gasping and moaning. I squeeze my legs harder, helping him remain buried as far into me as possible. Our bodies slowly come down from the high.

My love rolls to his side and pulls me into his arms, kissing my forehead. "I need a break."

I laugh through my own panting. "Me too."

"I've missed you more than you can imagine."

"I'm sure I can imagine it."

After a moment of silence to catch his breath, he asks, "How is training going?"

I tell him everything, including the incident at the ward. "I feel like everything is within reach but keeps slipping through my fingers."

"You almost have it. Just a little more time."

"We're running out of time. The king is picking up attacks on the rebels. I need to be full strength now."

"It will come. What about going to another ward?"

"Dyne says it's too dangerous without more information that we have no way to obtain."

My frustration brings tears to my eyes. Threy leans down for a kiss to distract me. "Be patient, my love. If you try too hard, it might make it more difficult to break through. You'll sabotage yourself. You will come into your powers. We will be able to put all this behind us. Then you're all mine."

"I want that so bad. I hate this distance between us. Sometimes I wonder if the heartache is all in my head."

"Me too, but soon. I'll be waiting for you on the other side of all of this."

"Promise?"

"Promise. We belong together forever."

Chapter Thirty-Two
Losing Time

RYN

Beland blows my hair back as I brush his neck. If I hate being stuck in this cave, I can only imagine how he feels. Horses are meant to run free, and I wish I could give him that. Those that care for the horses walk them regularly, but we're not close enough to an exit for that to be outside. My horse still seems grateful for my company. The fact I'm the one that trapped him in the caves doesn't bother him at all.

"My lady, Dyne approaches."

I turn to my latest bodyguard, a man with long dark hair and deep-set blue eyes. "You don't need to be so formal."

"It is in my duty to protect you and give you the proper respect."

Sighing, I try to decide if Prill's constant excitement and need to make me feel better is worse than someone acting like they're speaking to a queen. I'm nowhere near the status of queen, and I don't want it either. Dyne interrupts the comparison when he walks through the doorway. I put the brush away before joining him.

"Did you need something?" I ask.

"The supreme council is here. They'd like you to attend a meeting with the rest of us."

My groan makes him smile. I am not a leader and have no desire to be one. These meetings are so boring. Why do I have to attend all of them now? "What's this one about?"

"More bad news and new plans, by the sounds of it."

"Of course. Now?"

"You have time to eat first."

"Good."

He follows me as I make my way to the dining area. Before breakfast is the only time I have to visit Beland because the rest of the day is fully scheduled. Morning is either sword practice with Trev or trying to convince my stubborn dragon of how great it is outside of my head. The afternoon is all about magic and communicating with Rynmoriath. By the time supper and a bath are done, all I want to do is write a quick entry in my journal and pass out.

Trev is already at the table with our plates waiting for us. I raise an eyebrow, but he only points his fork at Dyne, so I turn to him.

"We have time to eat," Dyne explains, "but it needs to be fast. I figured you haven't had breakfast yet. I asked Trev to grab our plates before coming to tell you about the meeting. It saves time."

Well, I can't argue with that. Since it seems that we are in a hurry, I don't waste any time filling my empty stomach. "Looks like no sword practice today, Trev."

My cousin grunts. "You were to work on your dragon anyway."

"Wait. I thought today was a sword day."

"More pressure to focus on your dragon," he mutters.

I turn to Dyne, letting my eyes ask the question in my head. He shrugs. "They're getting desperate."

"So am I not allowed to practice the sword anymore?"

"One morning of sword, then three of magic and dragon."

As if I don't have enough pressure on me, they're mounting more? I'm not sure what else we can try at this point. "Maybe we should—"

"No," Dyne interrupts.

"You don't even know what I was going to say."

"You were going to mention the wards again."

Trev laughs. "You're becoming predictable, Ryn."

"I don't see what else we have to try. We know it worked."

"And almost killed you in the process," Dyne says.

"Did not. I handled it."

"If it wasn't for your dragon..."

"Then assign more babysitters. I can do this."

"The fact that your dragon even was able to help while you were unconscious is unheard of. Let's not try it again." Dyne's tone tells me he's done arguing about this.

I'm not. "I'm a red dragon, remember? You tell me all the time that you aren't entirely sure of what I'm capable of."

Yet, he has more confidence in me than I do. So far, there's only a little I can do on command. Although, it is getting better. I'm not bringing that up though.

Trev chuckles beside me. "You're not going to get him to change his mind on this subject. He's stubborn."

"So am I."

"Agreed. In most cases, I'd even say you're more stubborn than he is. When it comes to your safety, I'm going to have to say he wins this one."

I huff and go back to finishing my food. Sulking isn't normal for me, but this subject brings it out of me every single time. Not that I give up on the subject. We all know I will bring it up again. This is too important to ignore. Unless we come up with another idea, this discussion is far from over. Maybe I can annoy him enough to give in.

Breakfast is barely finished by the time Dyne is motioning me to hurry. Trev takes our plates, giving up more precious seconds not to make the all mighty rebel council angry. I'm not even sure anger over my eating would happen, but Dyne doesn't seem to want to test that out. The entire rebellion depends on my strength, so I think I should be allowed to eat as needed.

At least a full belly is something I have going for myself.

We enter the meeting, Dyne telling my guard to wait for us outside. The table is full, except for the two seats at the end that we take. This many dragons, all focused on me, makes me more than a little nervous. This is the brain of the rebellion, where all the strategy comes from. They're the ones that determine what our next move will be and how much I need to train. My mouth goes dry.

"Now that everyone is here," says the man at the end that I don't recognize. "Let's begin."

Everyone settles in while I examine the man who seems to be the spokesperson. His hair is so light that it's almost white. Eyes so dark of a green that they look to be only a shade lighter than black examine me in return. My thumb pushes on the ring as I take a discreet sniff. I'm able to isolate his scent.

Wyrm. We have one or two here that have given me practice recognizing the watery essence. I've never seen one in their dragon form though. Dyne says it's because land walking is difficult for their little legs. It must be hard for them to be away from the ocean for so long.

Something in my eyes must give away my thoughts because the man at the other end of the table smiles. "Most of the people at this table know me, except our guest of honor. Ryn, I am Abril. Our decisions are always debated and made between all of us, but I'm the voice of the council."

"Pleased to meet you," I say.

"You as well." His attention moves around the table. "We are meeting with your leadership because things are escalating past our control. Darac knows we have our red dragon and is pushing hard. We need to move, and we need to move as soon as possible."

"But we can't be ready," one of our leaders says.

"We have no choice. The tyrant is devastating our numbers. If we wait too long, we won't have the manpower to provide the red dragon support. We've chosen the camp closest to Wyvthin to gather, and we will gather six days from now. It was fifteen, but you're our last stop."

My jaw drops. "I don't know if I'm strong enough yet."

"Yes, we've read the reports. Unfortunately, we don't have the time to waste if we want to stand a chance. You must be ready in six days. Pull out all stops. Halt physical combat training and focus on magic and your dragon. We have no choice."

Fear overwhelms me, and he must notice. "It will be fine, Ryn. The prophecy knows what it's doing."

"The prophecy won't do any good if she is killed before Darac dies," Dyne says, squeezing my hand for reassurance. "She's getting better, but she's not ready."

"Then make her ready. We have no other choice. Also, besides supervising her, we need you to start enchanting objects for the humans to use in battle."

Dyne winces. "That will severely weaken my magic. It takes time to recover from enchanting."

"Which is why we haven't asked it of you before, and every fairy we have is on this duty. We don't want to take time from training Ryn, so you'll need to do both at the same time. You're one of our strongest fairies, Dyne. If anyone can make it happen, it's you. Observing your work may help her. Without adding the humans to our ranks, we don't stand a chance because our numbers are dwindling too much."

Dyne looks like he ate rotten meat. Abril notices and says, "We know this isn't ideal, but we're out of options."

"I understand, and it will be as the council orders."

Conversation moves to preparation, and I find myself losing focus. How can I be ready in six days? I can't fully control my magic. Rynmoriath still snubs the world outside with everything she has. What they're asking is impossible.

By moving this forward, they've doomed us. My failures are much higher than my successes. This simply isn't a scenario where it's possible for us to come out on top. A tyrant with a magical weapon that can kill all. A stunted red dragon who can't even shift. This will not end well.

My hopelessness peaks to an insurmountable blockade against everything. There's no time to do anything. My journey is going to end at the mercy of a crazed wyvern full of jealousy and rage. We are doomed.

"Ryn?" Albin's voice startles me.

"I'm sorry. My mind went elsewhere."

"That's fine. The meeting is over. You have some time to practice before the day ends."

Nodding, I say goodbye as they file out. The room is empty, except for Dyne, before I think to even stir from my seat. My father grabs my hands. "I know it seems hopeless."

"Because it is. I'm not ready now, and there's no way I'll be ready in six days. This is crazy. Are they *trying* to make the prophecy fail?"

"We will get you to where you need to be."

"How? The ward isn't possible because you have to make things."

Dyne's eyes harden. "Not the ward. I'm not discussing that with you anymore. We have a limited time to get you ready. Injuring or killing you isn't an option. Those things—as you put it—may give us a bit of an edge."

"I can't do it."

He grabs my face between his hands. "I believe in you. We all do."

"Even Trev?"

Dyne laughs. "Even Trev. Listen, six days is still something to work with. Give it a chance. As Albin said, we don't have many options now."

"But you're going to be too exhausted to train me if what you say is true."

"I'm only guiding you as it is. You can do this. If anyone can, it's you."

"Because I'm the red dragon..."

"No." His denial brings my gaze to his. "Because you are Raya's daughter, and I see so much of her in you. She fought for what she believed in. She protected those she cared about at all costs. I see that in you. You are so much like your mother that my heart aches."

Tears fall from my eyes. Dyne pulls me into his arms, hugging me tightly. Instead of pushing him away, I cling to him as if my life depends on this closeness. It very well could.

"Focus."

"Easy for you to say," I mumble.

Dyne glances at me before picking up another weapon. He can only do eight a day, which he assures me is more than others. Swords, bows, and leather armor cover the tables and floors around him. There is no system to what he enchants, leaving it all to instinct. This is our second day of doing this. Watching his exhaustion last night wasn't easy. Trev had to carry him to bed.

I purse my lips and go back to sitting on the floor behind him in silence. My magic comes easy now, but I'm not always able to direct it. Giving up, I move on to trying to summon Rynmoriath. It's hard to focus when Dyne is pouring magic into something else. Giving up for the moment, I stand and move to a piece of armor.

"What does this one do?" I ask.

"It adds extra protection to the wearer."

"Like a shield."

"Yes, but not as helpful. It'll help against wayward magic and arrows. Not much more. You're supposed to be practicing."

"I will return to it, but I want to take a look at what you're doing. I was able to examine the ward and see what it was made up of, and I'd like to see if I can identify yours."

"Very well."

My fingers run over the worn leather. Rynmoriath comes at my call to look with curiosity. When she realizes it's not red dragon magic, she grows bored and restless. I keep her close to the surface and push my magic into Dyne's.

"Oh," I say, shocked.

"What?" Dyne asks.

"I can connect to your magic."

"Really?"

Excited, I reach out and touch his enchantment. "It feels just like you, and I'm able to slip my own magic into it. This is neat."

"Maybe it's because you're my daughter."

I shrug. "Maybe."

Remembering the ward, I find a good place to insert my magic. While there, I reach for the same part of me that strengthened the ward. To my surprise, something happens. Part of my essence fills the enchantment that Dyne already added. My eyes widen as I realize what I just did and how easy it was.

"Dyne!"

"I'm trying to get these done, Ryn."

"I warded this piece."

"What?!"

He runs over and touches the armor. "It feels just like the ward. Can you do it again?"

"Can you tell me how you put the shield on the armor?"

We move to another set. With his direction, I figure out that I can place an enchantment as well. I fill the newly made shield with my immunity. "I did it again!"

"How many of these do you think you can make?"

"I don't know, but I'll do my best."

"This may just help us turn the tide of the war."

Giddy, I move to the next one as Dyne calls for Nova to bring more armor and send messages to the council. I ignore everything around me. For once, I can do something useful. I can help after all.

Chapter Thirty-Three
Dracon Proof

RYN

Beland whinnies as the wagon is attached to him. After three days, we're able to outfit a few hundred warriors with the enchanted armor. They add extra protection from swords and arrows, as well as protect the wearer completely from the Jeweled Dracon fire. These pieces are being moved to the gathering point while I make more.

I lean my forehead against the horse's. "You can do it, Beland. You'll help us succeed. I'll see you there."

He pushes against me and blows a breath out of his nose. After giving him a good rub, I back away, waving to my former friend holding the reins. Atan simply nods acknowledgement, which makes me sigh. Dyne wobbles over, still exhausted from last night but prepared to start again.

"You need more sleep," I say, watching the men lead my horse away with life-saving armor.

"We don't have time for me to sleep."

"Now you sound like me."

"Maybe you're rubbing off on me."

"One can only hope."

He laughs, and we both stand in silence until this batch of armor is gone. Once the wagon is out of sight, we head for breakfast. As has become customary, Trev has our plates sitting at the table beside him when we enter. It's mostly meat and cheese. I've been told protein is important for dragon magic replenishment.

"How is the enchantment going?" Nova asks as we sit across from her.

"It's going," I reply.

"Dragon?"

I wince. "Working on it."

We fall silent. We are halfway through our allotted time since the council came with the dangerous decision. I'm still no closer to calling Rynmoriath out than I was then. If I can't grow scales, I can't defeat the wyvern king. The more that time passes by, the less hope that we have. Three days is all that's left before the attack.

Part of me wonders if Trev had it right the first time we met. I mean, I know I'm a red dragon. Maybe I'm not *the* red dragon. The prophecy surely expects a chosen one that knows what she's doing. Or maybe Dyne blocking me destroyed our chances. It's hard to tell which is true. One thing's for sure, I don't have what it takes to fulfill what is expected of me.

Trev pats my shoulder. When I meet his light blue eyes, he says, "You can do this. This is the job meant for you and you alone. I have faith you'll figure it out."

I laugh, but my heart isn't in it. "Aren't you the one that said I wasn't the chosen one when you first met me?"

"Let's just say you made a believer out of me."

"And I've made an unbeliever out of myself. Things seem backwards."

"I'm not someone you want to take after. Ask anyone."

"I can agree with that," Nova says.

"Same," Dyne says.

Despite my growing melancholy, I find myself smiling. It's hard to doubt yourself with such strong allies. I may not be able to do it for me, but I'll do it for them. It's surprising how much having steadfast companions can do for your confidence. They give me something more to fight for, something to protect.

"We can only work during the morning," Dyne says.

"Why?"

"We need to start moving toward the meeting place after lunch. We have one more cart. You're to ride in it and work with your dragon on the way."

"What about all our supplies?"

Dyne shakes his head. "We are moving to the end of the prophecy. Whether we win or not, we won't need them, so only what is needed for the trip is being taken. Right now, your shifting is most important."

"I can work on armor too."

"We received messages yesterday. Most humans are covered. Dragons will mostly be in their dragon forms. Whatever we make this morning is to be used on our people during transport to protect from any rogue attacks. You need to be able to take on the king. I can guarantee you that he won't leave his dragon form. Dragons mean strength, and he will do whatever he can to hide his fear and weakness. We need you to be able to shift."

And it all comes down to this. I've protected as many people as I can. Now, I need to figure out how to protect myself and take down a king with the power of Drakyth behind him. No pressure. None at all.

Most of our people have already left. We've been sending groups with armor shipments. Only a small amount still remains. This will be our last shipment, and we will be traveling with it. It's time for Rynmoriath to stop hiding. We need her.

"I'm your babysitter today," Trev says.

"I'm not sure you qualify as a babysitter. You're a bit rough."

He chuckles. "That's what makes me perfect for the job."

Standing, I return my plate. The people in charge of food are already packing up what we need, and I doubt these plates will make the cut. I still place them on the counter out of habit. We make our way to the area holding what we need. The armor I now wear isn't warded because red dragons don't need magic to be immune to the silver fire. I only need to worry about physical weapons.

Dyne looks over what he needs to do today with tired eyes. I worry that he's going to wear himself down too much to make the journey. Maybe he'll need to be in the wagon with me. I'm sure we can make room for two if we're only taking what is needed to make the trip. He deserves an easy move after how hard he's been working. I can see why enchantments aren't done more often. It drains him.

I move to grab a few pieces of leather armor with Trev's help but stop when I hear a shout. Nova pops her head in. "Evacuate now."

"Attack?"

"Yes. The king has been spotted, so we need to get behind a ward as fast as we can."

I flinch and drop the piece in my hands as Trev drags me out. This is another failure of mine. While I can make a shield, I can't set it to make a ward. The armor is different because it's an object that is smaller and I can soak it with my magic. Creating and sticking a shield over an entire passage isn't working for me yet.

We join the few left as we run toward safety. Every fighter but Trev and Nova rush toward the fighting. They're charged with keeping us safe. One other moves with the other group to protect them, but all others stay to hold back the king's men. We leave the camp behind, running as fast as we can. I match my pace with Dyne's to keep everyone close and avoid losing him.

Someone ahead of us falls, and that's when I realize that the other fighter is Trev's most trusted friend. He falls back. "We need to move faster if we're going to make it. At least get her ahead of the group."

"I'm not leaving Dyne," I growl.

He rolls his eyes. Before he can utter the smartass remark I see in his annoyance, we hear a roar. Dyne's eyes widen. "Run!"

"We won't make it," Nova says. "We're too far away from the nearest point of safety."

"I'll buy you time. Go!"

The fact he said you instead of us tells me he's not planning to make it out of this alive. "I'm not leaving you."

Trev grabs my arms. I look to see tears in his eyes, and I shake my head in denial. Nova grabs my other arm.

"We don't have a choice," Trev says.

When I fight him, he pulls me along. The roar grows louder. I see Dyne turn and throw a shield over the tunnel. It won't work. He's too drained. "He can't hold it alone."

"He can't hold it at all," Nova says with grief in her voice. "We have to get you to safety before it reaches him and before the shield fails. Quit fighting. You might not be killed by it, but we will, and you need us to find the next camp."

"I can help."

"With your ready-to-use magic and dragon?"

I slump in defeat, following as fast as I can. As soon as Trev releases my arm, I elbow him and turn. I use dodging techniques he taught me to get past a shocked Nova. My feet move so fast that I reach Dyne before they can stop me.

"Go!" he screams at me.

"No!"

The flames hit the shield, dropping my jaw wide. Silver fire batters at the transparent barrier Dyne holds. It flickers, and he screams for me to run. I run but not in the direction he wants.

I might not be able to make a shield this strong, but I can still help. Touching it, I let my magic feed into his. Closing my eyes, I look deep into myself and find the immunity within me. As soon as it touches the shield, my magic flows into it until it shimmers stronger and brighter. I feed it until I have nothing left. It's as if my magic has a mind of its own; I'm only here to urge it on.

Trev catches me when I fall back while Nova checks on Dyne, who sits on the ground and pants. The silver flames beat at the ward. It holds. From what I can feel, it won't get through.

"You did it," Trev breathes into my ear in shock.

My cousin sits me gently on the ground. This must be what Dyne feels like after a day of enchanting. I'm exhausted and feel like I can't go on. Trev whoops and jumps while throwing a fist toward the death that won't break through. I want to smile, but I'm too tired to.

I did it, but I'm going to slow us down. Looking at Dyne, I realize I'm not the only one, so it's not too much of a loss. The most important thing is that I made a ward. It took Dyne's help, but I still did it. Even my exhaustion can't stop the triumph and pride pulsing through me. Rynmoriath circles my head with joy. Even she's subdued. I've worn us both out.

"We better not stay here. Once that stops, he'll send in his warriors," Dyne says. "It won't kill Ryn, but it may weaken her in her human form. He'll send them in to find her. We need to move."

"Can you both walk?" Nova asks.

I climb to my feet and stumble when I manage it. Trev throws one of my arms over his shoulder. Without protest, I allow him to coddle my weakness. This isn't a time to be stubborn. As Dyne said, we need to move. I feel a tingle of magic from Trev and look at him with an eyebrow raised.

"What? I can't use magic?" he asks.

"I've never felt or seen you use it before. I'm just surprised."

"I'm a fairy dragon. I have magic. Dyne usually does it because he is stronger. He can't right now, so I'm stepping in."

"What are you doing?"

"Covering our scent. We'll take a few twists and turns that aren't expected to hide us from his men. The good thing about this cave system, there's more than one way to get to where we are going."

"If I wasn't so tired, I'd examine what you're doing to try to learn it."

"Maybe later I'll let you learn. Right now, focus on putting one foot in front of the other."

Nodding, I look back to see Nova carrying Dyne like Trev is with me. My father looks so small against her. He also looks wilted worse than the nights after enchanting.

When I trip, I focus on looking ahead. Trev's friend leads the way, leaving everyone else to stumble behind. This is going to be a long journey, and I hope we can stay ahead of the warriors behind us. We need to make it to the rebel gathering. I somehow need to figure out how to shift. We aren't clear yet.

Chapter Thirty-Four
Split

RYN

Someone nudges me, and I'm not even close to being ready to wake up. Opening my eyes is like dragging sandpaper across them. Blinking doesn't help. I feel stronger, but not well enough to be moving already.

I look up at Trev. "When you said we needed to stop and rest, I assumed it would be more than five minutes."

"As far as I can guess, it's been a few hours. We need to move."

"It doesn't feel like a few hours."

My cousin pats my shoulder and moves to Dyne, who is as unconscious as I wish I still was. Despite my complaining, I know we need to get moving. There's no telling how far into the caves our attackers will search. I made this argument before being forced to rest. That doesn't mean I am going to want to get up after being forced to recuperate a little.

Stretching, I hear my joints pop from my uncomfortable position on the hard stone floor. My stomach rumbles too, but it's not like I can do anything about it at this point. We didn't have a chance to grab food when evacuating in a hurry. The only way to stall starvation is to get moving in the direction of food.

With a yawn, I stumble to my feet. Nova grabs my elbow to help steady me. "Is it too late for that wagon?" I ask.

"It's probably nothing more than ash now."

"I'll take that as a yes."

Dyne grumbles and stands faster than I did. Walking is easier to do myself, but I still stumble from time to time. No wonder Dyne looks as he does after a day of enchanting. This is exhausting.

"You probably didn't need to put that much into the ward," he says.

"Are you a mind reader now? You said before that you aren't, but things can change."

"No. I can tell how tired you are."

"Well I was just thinking about how tired I am too, so lucky coincidence."

We're quiet for a bit before he speaks again. "Once this is over, we're going to have to teach you to moderate your energy more."

"Might be helpful. All I was thinking about was protecting you and the others. The rest just happened."

"And I'm grateful to still be breathing and knowing everyone is safe. Still, we need to teach you how to give just enough magic. You were able to enchant so much because red dragons have immense stores of power, more than any other dragon. The ward was just too much after slowly draining yourself. You got carried away. I know it wasn't on purpose, but we need to figure out how to teach you moderation."

"Sounds good to me. I don't want to ever feel like this again. I can see why you argued with the council about it."

"It's not pleasant."

"Hopefully there is an after this for me."

Nova looks back at me. "What do you mean?"

"Well, the prophecy only says I'll defeat the king, which seems doubtful at this point. What it doesn't mention is if I survive the slaying of royalty."

Everyone pauses and looks at me. I shrug, then push through and keep walking through the exhaustion. It shouldn't be that big of a surprise. War is dangerous, and I'm the key weapon in this one. Weapons break all the time. They miss their mark. They don't withstand the strain put on them. This is the way of war. If it will keep those I've come to love safe, I'm willing to do what is needed. That doesn't mean I need to be optimistic about my chances of survival.

Dyne hurries to catch up while the others fan out behind us. "It also doesn't say you have to sacrifice yourself."

"The closer we get to the day, the more it seems like that's going to be how it ends. What's it going to take to get my dragon to come out? At this point, I think something big has to happen for it to do so. I just hope it's me that pays for my failure and not you or anyone else I care about."

"Fate guides the prophecy, and nothing we do will stop what's to happen. Also, none of us knows what destiny has in store for us. Your mother refused to believe in destiny until you came into this world."

"She did?"

Dyne chuckles. "She was a stubborn one, moreso than you. Raya always tried to convince me, and herself, that destiny had no say in our lives. We do what we want; that's how things happen. It's not pre planned because she refused to follow someone else's idea for what should happen with her life. She almost had me convinced before we conceived you."

"And my birth changed that?"

"A drake and a fairy dragon with no chance of meeting were thrust together in circumstances neither of us could perceive. Raya was hiding away in the forest because the king executed her parents. All she wanted was to be left alone. I was living with the rebels since birth. Our group just happened to be in the area near where she lived. The king attacked us and drove us out of the exit closest to her. She found me while hunting and managed to keep a bear from killing us just in time.

"After that, wyverns found us. Despite her desire not to make trouble, she killed them to keep us safe, driving herself into the arms of the rebellion. All of our time alone with Trev brought us close until we mated. Then you, something so rare it almost never happens, shows up. I feel like everything that happened since then is all the work of destiny bringing us to this point. We're meant to be here."

"And my mother dying?" I ask.

Dyne winces, and I regret my question. "Raya dying was regrettable. I mourn her every quiet second of my life. It happened to put you where you had the greatest chance of surviving, and you were born to a father with the capabilities of hiding what you are. Destiny is real. Your mother tried to fight it and still ended up being claimed by fate in the end. It was all to bring us to this point, to kill the one man who should never have received the power of the gift from Drakyth."

Biting my bottom lip, I don't voice an answer because I don't have one. Everything he says makes sense the way he states it, but I'm not sure I want to believe it either. Maybe I'm as much like my mother as everyone keeps telling me I am. I can't deny it. That doesn't mean I have to accept it.

My entire life has been led and controlled by others. First, my parents' strict rules to keep me safe. Next, the king's stable master ordered me around. With Threy, I had some freedom but not nearly enough. It's time for me to start living my life the way I want to. If that aligns with the prophecy, so be it. That doesn't mean I have to let destiny dictate my life.

We come to a split in the cavern. There are three ways to go, but I have no idea which is the right way. Feels a bit like my life—responsibility without true guidance. Each tunnel is dark, giving no clue to what lies at the other side. Some may lead to a dead end, disastrous for our mission. How do I know which is the right way?

"So, which way do we want to take?" Trev asks.

"Maybe we should split up," Nova says.

"Aren't we safer together?" I ask.

"Not in this case," Dyne replies. "I know you want to argue with me, but you're the most important person here, Ryn. Trev, you and Ranlor should take Ryn one way. Cover your tracks. Me and Nova will go another without hiding. I doubt they'd follow us this far, but it's best to be cautious."

"After everything, you want me to just walk away from you?"

Dyne grabs my shoulders. "It won't be for long. I promise we'll meet at the new camp. Ask around. Anyone should be able to help you find me."

But what if you don't make it?

I keep that question to myself. "I'm tired of everyone trying to sacrifice themselves for me."

"This isn't a sacrifice. It's misdirection on the off chance they are still tracking us. I will see you again."

Unable to take it anymore, I pull him into a hug. "Make sure of it, Dad."

Dyne pushes me back, searching my face with uncertainty. "Did you just call me what I think you did?"

"Yes. You may not be the one who raised me, but you've shown me just as much love in the little time we've been together. I'm sorry for the way I treated you when we first met."

He pulls me back into a hug. "You did nothing wrong. You were stressed, and it was kind of dropped on you. I didn't expect any less. You're my daughter and always have been, but I wasn't there for you. If I could have done it any other way, I would have. I love you, Ryn."

"I love you too."

When we pull away, I see Nova wiping her eyes. Trev smiles. Ranlor has the same scowl he usually directs at me on his face. None of it matters. I finally found out who I am, and the man who helped me is going somewhere dangerous that I can't follow. Too bad I wasted so much time being mad at him.

I watch them walk away until I can no longer see them. Trev allows me this time to silently say goodbye before guiding me down another path. I feel the tingle of his magic.

"I just found him," I say after a few minutes of silence.

"And you'll see him again. Once we get outside, it's about a day's walk straight south. It won't take long."

"We're going outside?" Fresh air will be nice. Maybe it'll distract me from the sense of loss I didn't expect.

"Yeah. We just need to get there. Are you still tired?"

"Very much so."

"When we're halfway there, I'll let you rest again, then we'll move on."

We walk for a little longer. Trev finds a good spot and tells me to lie down. I do as he directs, but I have trouble falling asleep. No matter how hard I try, worry over Dyne keeps me awake. What if he doesn't make it?

He and Nova have become such pillars in my life. Losing either one would be a blow I'm not sure I'm strong enough to come back from. More loss will destroy me. I've had so much already and can't take any more.

Please be safe.

After what seems like forever, I fall asleep and leave the two men to talk softly in the silence.

When I wake again, my exhaustion is down to a mere buzz of tiredness while my stomach grumbles and twists worse. If I don't eat soon, my stomach may consume itself. At one point, a few days without eating was expected. Threy spoiled me, and the rebels fed me three times a day. My stomach isn't used to being this empty anymore.

"We'll hunt once we're outside," Trev says to my grumbling stomach.

"Good. I feel like I could eat a dragon."

"Good luck with that in your human form. Let's get going. The faster we get to camp, the sooner you can practice shifting more."

"Oh, yay." It sounds like I'm joking, but I'm really not. I know I need to bring my dragon out, but I feel like I've tried everything. She's not coming out anytime soon.

Fresh air blasts my face. *See, Rynmoriath? Wouldn't it be nice to fly in the fresh air? Feel it caressing your scales?*

A wave of annoyance greets my words. I think she might be getting tired of my constant prodding. I don't care. If she'd just come out, everything would be so much easier. Doom wouldn't hang over my very existence. The people I love wouldn't be in as much danger.

Ranlor drops back while I walk next to Trev and contemplate my next move. Maybe I can make my own ward and test it with my dragon. No, that won't work. It's the connection with others like us that interests her. Our ward will only show us ourselves, not another dragon.

What do you need me to do to convince you?

She doesn't get a chance to answer. Pain blossoms in the back of my head, and the world goes dark.

Chapter Thirty-Five
Resolve

Ryn

A rough kick to my side brings me out of unconsciousness. Coughing, I try to moan away the pain in the back of my head. This is not even close to a pleasant awakening. What happened? I remember exiting the caves and expecting a nice meal to come soon, then nothing. Only blackness. My stomach twisting reminds me that it's still empty but not ready to eat yet. Pain in my skull makes my stomach feel unsettled.

"You bastard! How could you?!"

That's Trev's voice. It's enough to wake me further. Something is going on, and I need to be awake for it. Moving tells me my hands are tied in front of me. Something cold presses against my throat. Memories of the man almost killing me in the caves send panic coursing through my veins. The mere thought of being in the same position is enough to bring my eyes open to the painful world.

But not enough to see clearly. Blurry figures move around at the edge of my vision. Voices shout through the ringing in my ears, and one blur tries to launch itself off the ground at another. Blinking gives me a little more clarity. No one is near me, so this isn't a knife at my throat. That much is a blessing.

"You're the one trying to go against the natural dragon order, Trev," says a familiar voice.

I blink a few more times, glad to feel my headache recede. Ranlor stands in front of Trev, who is being held down by two others that I don't recognize. My gaze travels across the area, seeing multiple men that smell of wyverns and a richly dressed figure staring at me with a smirk.

"You're a traitor," Trev says to Ranlor, spitting on the ground in front of him.

"You're the traitor, and I'm glad to be done pretending."

Ranlor kicks Trev in the face. I cry out and try to jump to my feet. Two men run over to hold me down, as if a young woman fresh out of forced slumber can give them any kind of challenge. The man watching me smirks and walks over to the pair.

His dark eyes glance my way again, the grin widening. "Who is he to her?"

"Her cousin, my king."

"Ahhh."

King? This is Darac. It would make sense for him to be close. The Jeweled Dracon wouldn't be far from him. Dark hair blows in the wind. His nose and chin are sharp, and everything about him screams thin. Despite his plain black shirt and leather pants, he looks regal.

Something about the way he moves strikes a memory I can't place. Right now, he's fixing me with a triumphant gaze.

"Ryn. Pleased to finally meet you," Darac says.

"Darac. I can't say the pleasure is reciprocated."

"That's King Darac to you, peasant."

The disgust in his voice tenses my muscles. "I've never considered you my king, even when I thought I was human. All I've ever seen from you is cruelty that doesn't show any kind of nobility. You don't deserve the title."

Pain blossoms in my cheek when the back of his hand meets it. The sharp sting makes me hiss, but I try not to let any other reaction show. Whatever happens, I know this is the end. There's no way this coward will let me out of this alive. I'm a threat to his rule, one that must be dealt with. Ranlor betrayed us. Although, I guess he was never truly one of us.

This is the man that keeps me from spending a life of peace with Threy. He destroyed an entire clan for nothing more than the fear in his black heart. Dyne's lack of flight can be laid at his feet. He took my sister from me. My mother died trying to save me from him. Anger rises too high to contain.

"Guess you're not afraid of me when you have me safely bound. How do you know it'll hold?"

Darac laughs. "Because of the magic of your own people. That new necklace you have on? Well, it keeps you from using magic or shifting. Your cousin has one on too. You are no threat, all because of the red dragons of the past. Ironic, isn't it?"

To prove his point, the tyrant walks over to Trev and kicks him in the side of the head. I cry out and try to lunge for them, but those hands holding me down are too strong to break free from. I'm pushed onto the ground, a knee in my back holding me flat against the rocky dirt. Darac lands another brutal kick to Trev's ribs. The crack I hear brings tears to my eyes. My cousin tries to stand, but he's held down like I am.

"You coward!" I scream at him. "The only damage you can do is to those that are made helpless. You're weak!"

"I'm not the one unable to fight back because I'm coming at you from a position of strength. Weakness belongs to those under my boot."

To emphasize this, Darac places his foot on the back of Trev's neck. He presses down, and my cousin squeezes his eyes shut to hold back the yell of pain that tries to escape him. My struggles are hopeless, but it doesn't stop me from trying to get to Trev. To my relief, the pressure on the back of his neck releases. I fall limp on the ground with a sob I can't stop.

Darac walks back over to me, using his boot to push me onto my back. "Something you will learn very quickly, my dear. Listen carefully because I don't like to repeat myself. I'm in charge. I have the power of Drakyth behind me because I deserve it. You will learn what that feels like before I put you down, just like I did with your mother."

My body trembles with fury. "You may have the Jeweled Dracon, but Drakyth obviously doesn't approve of your greed and cruelty. How else would I have made it to maturity, despite all your efforts to hunt me down?"

Anger makes his jaw tick. I'm ready to withstand whatever he throws at me. When his anger turns into anticipation, fear takes over my mind.

"I really hate fairy dragons. You know, I tried to exterminate them a long time ago. They're like rats, hiding in the darkness and breeding. It's really infuriating, which is why I enjoy getting to take another out with my own hands whenever I get the chance."

He pulls a knife out of his waistband. "No," I whisper with horror.

Trev sees it at the same time I do. He looks at me. "Get out of this, Ryn. I'm sorry I doubted you. You are the chosen one. You will prevail. I'm proud to call you my cousin."

"No!" I struggle to get up, only to have the wind knocked out of me when I'm forced back to the ground.

Every ounce of my strength is thrown into trying to stop what's about to happen. To my surprise, I almost break free. The only thing that stops me is another wyvern to hold me down. Three is impossible to escape.

Trev fights those holding him, and it takes four to still his fight. Darac throws back one last satisfied look at me before opening Trev's throat. My cousin jerks as the blood gushes from the wound. I hear myself screaming his name over and over, but I can do nothing to stop the sound.

Frantic feet push into the ground to give me leverage. I must reach him. He can't die alone. Nothing I do brings me closer to the cousin I gained only a little while ago. My heart breaks as I watch those stunning light blue eyes grow dim and unseeing.

I collapse, the men holding me relax enough for me to see that there's now four of them. I'm not sure if it is only a precaution or if my raging grief forced strength even I didn't expect. Right now, I couldn't care less about the reason. The only thing on my mind is the loss I feel deep inside. The emptiness where my family once sat grows larger with the death of another.

Darac crouches by my sobbing frame. "You see, I hold the reins. Whatever I say happens. You were never going to be able to bring me down. When I'm through with you, you're going to wish your end was as quick."

His words can't damage any more than the body of my cousin does. Emptiness takes over, filling the space left by the loss. I've never thought nothingness could fill a void, but it does in this instance. It's a strange feeling, numb and wanting to tear the world down at the same time. How can these two feelings coexist within one person at once? It makes no sense to me.

Another wyvern lands, shifting without pause. "My liege, the rebel army is marching on the capital."

Darac growls and glares at me as if it's my fault. He's probably right. Without me, they wouldn't be marching. This means today is the day of the attack. They didn't wait for me. Do they think I'm dead; that this is their last effort to go down fighting? Do they hope I'll still show up?

"I'll take care of them quickly. Everyone this woman has ever loved will die today, and I'll make sure to give her the details. Bring her in the back way. Lock her up well. The mighty red dragon will fall at my hands in front of everyone when I'm done with her. She will be a great lesson."

Does my death even mean anything anymore? The rebellion is lost without me. Trev lies bleeding not far from my gaze. I can't take my eyes off his pale face. Tears blur his familiar features. Darac whispers something into my ear that I refuse to hear past the roar of anguish coursing through me. He shifts and flies away.

This isn't fair. It isn't right. All my life, I thought I was human. My family was taken from me, leaving me alone. I thought that was it. I was alone for so long. Then Threy came along, giving me someone else to love and care for. The king's hatred of me took that away. I gained a family. A father. A cousin. A friend. The cousin was murdered right before my eyes. Darac will finish what he did to my father when the king unleashes the Jeweled Dracon on him again.

The man takes everything from me. He destroys all he touches. He's a plague on all of Sertran and must be stopped. No one else can die at his hands, and I'm the only one that can stop him. It's up to me, and he believes he's safe with me in the hands of his men.

Fury rages deep within. It takes a few moments to realize it isn't all mine. Rynmoriath fumes, filling me with fire. She rages at the object keeping us down. When her anger turns to curiosity, I follow her to investigate. She pokes at the thing around my neck, noticing the familiar feel of red dragon power. Reaching for the ring, she touches both at the same time.

Power floods me, burning in a way that brings both pleasure and pain. I gasp, pulling the attention of the men ready to move me to the city. I pay them no mind. Rynmoriath channels the magic in me, but she isn't able to use it right now. Instead, she pushes it at the collar around my throat. It grows warm, hot enough to burn anyone that's not us.

Magic trickles out. Before I can examine that, the metal around my neck shatters. Red scales grow over my arms as my body increases in size. The bindings holding me break while the men start yelling and shifting around me. The fire is already in my belly, built by rage, so I unleash it before most of them can change.

Screams fill the air. A weight hits me from the side, rolling me across the ground. Teeth pierce the scales of my shoulders. Magic explodes from me, and I see a wyvern slam into a tree. A sharp beak pecks at my head, so I turn toward it and snap my jaws around the other surviving wyvern's face. It screeches and tries to pull away, but I tighten my grip until the bones crunch. My opponent goes limp.

The other hits me again. Claws tear at my wings, and I roar my fury and pain into the air. We battle, biting and clawing for too long.

I eventually get my teeth around his throat and end him the same way Trev was killed.

Looking around, I see no other wyverns. I got most in the first blast of fire. A whimper draws my attention, so I follow it. Walking on four legs with a giant body feels awkward, but I'm sure I'll get used to it over time. My first shift didn't involve moving. This is a completely new experience for me. I find Ranlor trying to scramble away from me.

This is the man that betrayed us and handed Trev over to Darac. He's the one that made me feel unwelcome at every turn. My cousin trusted him, saw him as a friend. He repaid that by bringing his death to him. Anger makes me roar in his face.

Ranlor scrambles back, his burnt legs useless. He must be too damaged to shift at the moment. "Please. I only did it because he would have killed me if I didn't."

Lies. He reveled in the death of the man that considered him a friend and comrade. It's because of him that I'm one less family member; that the void where those I once loved is made larger. Despite his begging for mercy, I close my jaws over him, feeling his warm blood enter my mouth. He screams, but it's short. The fact that he slides easily down my throat doesn't bother me at all.

After the short meal, silence takes over the area. Even the birds are quiet in the fury of a wronged dragon. My tail thumps on the ground with annoyance.

I need to decide what to do. A red dragon flying through the sky will make a clear target. I can travel by land, but it's best done in my other form. I can only hope that Rynmoriath will listen to me from now on. Her nudging my mind is a sign that makes me believe she's out for good.

First, I turn to Trev. I can't let the predators have him and have no time for a burial, even as a dragon. Instead, I turn him to ash and watch what's left blow away. It's time to fulfill my part of the prophecy. Darac is evil and doesn't deserve the power given to him. It's time his reign comes to an end. It's time to avenge those I've lost.

Chapter Thirty-Six
Trapped

THREY

"Lord Archon wants to see you, my lord."

Sighing, I drop the sword I used on the wooden dummy. I don't dare ask the guards to help me train right now, but I can't let myself get rusty. Who knows when I'll need my skills again. With the uncertainty of upcoming events, it's best to stay honed. The rebellion is moving forward. I never ask Ryn about plans because of the liability, but if they have the red dragon, I'm sure they're moving forward. For once, I'm no longer willing to fight against them.

"I'll head to his study as soon as I clean up here."

The human messenger bows, then walks away. As I clean up, I wonder what my father wants now. It can't be anything good. It seems like everything I do anymore is wrong and harmful to our family. I'm not sure why he thinks I need to try. They only care about me as far as the advantage I give them.

I return the dummy and my wooden sword to the armory. When I turn, a low growl rumbles in my chest. Sule stands by the door, adopting a sultry pose. She's been nothing but trouble since she came here, one of the many reasons my parents are less than happy with me. Rumors abound, and she's at the center of the more recent.

"Leave me alone," I say with a snarl.

"Don't be like that. The entire keep thinks we are a great couple."

"Only because of the rumors you caused. Nothing is going to happen between us, so get it out of your head. You are not my type."

The annoying woman takes a few steps into the armory. "It's that Tiera woman, isn't it? I'm not sure why your parents are pushing her, but I would make a much better mate. She's never even around, so it's obvious she doesn't care about you."

"And you do?"

"I'm pursuing you, aren't I? I ingratiated myself to your pushy sister to be here. That has to prove something."

"That you'll do whatever you have to if it helps your ambition?"

I try to walk around her, but she steps to block my path and put her hand on my chest. I slap it away, not wanting her touch anywhere on me. Sule is made of slime, and I want no part of her anywhere near me. If only she'd get that through her head.

"Don't be like that," she says, looking at me through my lashes. "We could be so much together, much more than you and that Tiera."

"Tiera has nothing to do with this. I don't want her either. Now, get out of my way."

I push past her, not bothering to be gentle. I'm tired of this woman and her ambitions. Even if I was still in the market for a mate, Sule would be nowhere near the top of the list. She's spoiled and cruel, snotty and overly ambitious. There's no way I'd ever agree to mate with someone like her.

"It's the red dragon, isn't it? I could tell she was reaching above herself the time you visited. Pity she's not here."

My muscles tense as my feet stop moving. I turn back to her. "Ryn is more than ten times the woman you'll ever be. She's sweet and puts others before her own selfish wants, unlike you."

Sule crosses her arms over her chest in a way that pushes her cleavage out further. "I deserve the best, and that's you. If she truly cares about you, where is she?"

"Safe away from the deadly hands that search for her."

"It's her you go flying for when you leave every night, isn't it? Find her? No? That's because she doesn't care. I, on the other hand, want nothing more than to warm your bed. I promise I'm worth it."

She steps toward me, but I push her back. "Stay away from me! It doesn't matter how many rumors you start or how you plan to soil my name; I don't care. Nothing will happen between us. We will never be anything. You are nothing but a spoiled brat to me. Nothing!"

I hurry from the armory, finding people stopped in the courtyard and looking my way with wide eyes. Sule appears behind me, and the whispers start. Growling, I push my way through the small group of onlookers. I don't care what they think. Her tactics won't work. My heart belongs to one woman, and she doesn't hold a candle to her. Ryn is worth a hundred of Sule and her sister put together.

Inside the keep, I slow my pace as befits the third son of a lord. Even here, I can't get away from the whispers. Between Sule and Ryn, I've become a popular point of conversation. None of it matters. I will do whatever I have to, ensuring I help keep my heart safe. At one point, Sule's words would have set me off and made me spiral. After spending some time with Ryn, I know the lies that those words hold. She wishes to be by my side, but it's not smart to.

Iara stops me in the hall. "Have you seen Sule?"

"Why would you ask me? She's your servant."

"And a terrible one that I don't want, but it is what it is. She seems to like to stalk you."

Grunting, I rub a hand down my face. "Last I saw that parasite, she was trying to convince me she's the woman for me in the armory."

"The exact opposite direction I sent her," Iara mumbles before walking away.

For once, I find myself wishing Iara would be stricter with her servants. Maybe Sule would leave me alone if my sister was stern. I can't blame her though. I wouldn't want her close to me any more than needed either. Avoiding that woman is a high priority.

Father is waiting for me when I knock. When I walk in, I see a strange rod with dragons carved all over it on his desk. It looks to be made of some kind of bone, intricately engraved decoration all over it. A leather strap is threaded through a hole in the top. Strange; I've never seen this before.

Lord Archon looks out of my father's green eyes. There's no love there. No joy at seeing his son. All I can see is a lord ready to reprimand his subject. I'm not even his son right now. Whatever this meeting is, I don't think I'm going to like it.

"You summoned me," I say into the tense silence.

Father sits back in his chair. "We have news of your red dragon, and I figured it would be better to hear it from me. Gossip can be quite cruel."

My heart stops beating momentarily. "What news?"

"King Darac has captured the dragon you're so defiant about. It's only a matter of time until she's executed."

Gasping, I turn to run from the room. I have to get to her. I have to save her, or I'll die trying. The king can't be allowed to kill her. My heart couldn't withstand the loss.

"Threysoryth!" my father calls behind me. "You will stand as you are."

When my feet freeze against my will, I feel a strong compulsion to obey. No amount of struggle allows me to move in the direction I wish to. Now I know what that object is. Turning, I see the lord of all Ildracan holding the ivory rod in his hand.

"You can't hold me back," I say through gritted teeth.

Father's smile is malicious. I'd take a step back if I could, but that's heading for the door, which is beyond my capabilities at this moment. He's using the name artifact on me.

"This object says I can," he spits out. "I will not have you making a fool of me or our family. You've done enough of that already. You will stand down!"

"She is my..." I stop, unable to utter the word that I need to. I won't give him the additional leverage against me.

"I'm sick and tired of you putting her above your family. You will obey, or you will be punished in ways that will make you regret being born."

"I already regret being born into a family like this. Disown me already. Free me from the obligations of being treated like I'm worthless and a failure."

"If it wouldn't sully our name further, I would. Sit down, Threysoryth!"

Unable to fight the pull of the magical item in my father's hand, I find myself walking to a chair and sitting down. "If I'm such a detriment to your reputation, you should just get me out of your hair. I don't see the point of this torture. Let me move on with my life."

"You will move on. Once this nuisance is behind us, you'll mate with Tiera and be the proper third son."

"I won't."

He holds up the rod. "You will, or I'll make you. Don't start your future out on a bad foot. Take Tiera, and be happy she's still willing to accept you."

I frown, staring at the man who is more than willing to force me to comply. They can't reason with me, so they decide the best thing to do is force me. This tool is supposed to be used to retrieve rogue dragons or dangerous enemies. Instead, he's using it to force his will upon his third son. My eyes narrow.

"You using such an important instrument on a wayward son seems like a waste," I say.

"I wouldn't have to if that son would listen to reason. This was me telling you before you found out the hard way. Be grateful."

Pressing my lips together, I try to think of an argument. Before I can utter anything, the door flies open to admit my mother. "Archon, we have a message from the king. An army is marching on the capital. We're commanded to report, ready to fight."

"I'll start issuing orders. Get the keep ready for our absence."

Mother nods, casting an annoyed look at me before leaving. So, the king has Ryn. The king is going to be attacked. What do the rebels hope to achieve by attacking without their main weapon? Is this a lie from my father to distract me from my pursuit? Anything is believable. I wouldn't put anything past him.

"Looks like you have your hands full," I say. "I'll get going."

"You will not rush out on a foolish quest to save what cannot be saved. Threysoryth, you'll not try to rescue her from the king at all. And you're coming with us. We need all claws in the battle."

I freeze. "I'm not fighting against the rebels."

"You will fight with the rest of Ildracan, and that's final. I'll make you if needed. You will not embarrass us any longer. King Darac already has reason to believe that we are traitors. I'm not giving him any more reason to consider using the Jeweled Dracon on the Ildracan clan. Get ready to fly."

Father shoos me out to avoid further argument. Resigned to being forced to do what I don't want to, I walk toward the courtyard. This is nothing new. I've never had a say in what happens.

Delto forced me to take a human servant that I specifically told him to leave be. My parents made me travel around Ildracan in search of the perfect dragon mate. I had to court Tiera because she was the best match available. I was expected to sit by while my parents executed Ryn.

I won't give in this time. Ryn is mine. While I can't go on a quest to save her, I can't stay here. Maybe going with them will give me a chance to help. I'll fight with them, but my true mission will be looking for a way around my father's order; a way to save Ryn and help the rebels. I'm entering the battle on one side. That doesn't mean I have to stay with them.

Knowing this is my best chance, I do everything I can to make sure it seems like I'm cooperating. No one needs to know why I'm really going.

Hang on, Ryn. I'm coming.

Chapter Thirty-Seven
Familiar Fear

RYN

My legs tire, so I let myself fall onto the rocky ground for a rest. This is the day I'm supposed to help take down the king. That won't happen if I'm not there for the attack, but I can't fly without bringing too much attention. Even walking as a red dragon would be too obvious. Therefore, I'm trudging along in my human form, trying to race against time to make it to the battle before anyone can be seriously hurt.

Groaning, I lift my face to the sky. At least this trek is outside. The caves have caused serious melancholy. Outside, I get to feel the wind blow in my face. The sun streams down, warming my skin. It feels so good that I can almost forget the final battle that is on the horizon. Either I kill the king or he kills me. One of us will die today, and I'm determined for it to not be me.

Reaching into the small satchel I tied to my pants, I pull out some dried meat I found in one of the men's pockets. They must have expected to stay there for a little while. To think of it, we spent at least a day leaving the caves. I have no idea how long I was knocked out either. All I know for sure is that time is running short.

I continue walking, eating the meat as we go. It has an unfamiliar flavor, but it's filling. At this point, that's all that matters. Rynmoriath needs her strength for the battle to come, which makes me wonder if I dare shift long enough to allow her to hunt. Maybe when we're closer.

That thought makes me laugh. I'm not even sure I'm going in the right direction. I can only hope that Trev's directions are still accurate when I have no way to tell how much we were moved while unconscious. Inside, I feel something pull me this way, so I follow. Not like I have a better idea.

After a little longer, I decide I've had enough of caution. Being careful will do no good if I don't make it in time. "So, Rynmoriath, ready to come out, hunt, and fly us the rest of the way?"

My dragon stirs within me. I can feel her eagerness to be free again, finally realizing how important her freedom is. Now, the only thing enslaving us is the prophecy, and it will soon be done. Regardless of how this ends, we will no longer be controlled by fate. Our destiny will be complete.

Determined to have a happy ending, I allow Rynmoriath to break free. I don't need to picture her or plead for an answer. She bursts free right away, as eager as me to get this over with. The wounds from the earlier fight are healed.

Once on four legs, I stretch my wings, stifling the roar that might bring attention to the red dragon alone in the hilly country that is the Wyvthin territory. Here, the grasses and trees are replaced by rock hills. I climb to the top of one of the hills and take off, finding out that flight is as exhilarating as I always imagined it to be.

The wind glides over my scales with ease. It feels almost like swimming in a calm river. The wind picks up, surprising me by triggering an instinct I never knew I possessed. I adjust my wings to even out the flight without being blown too far. The gleaming sun warms my body, and I bask in the radiance. Flying is freedom.

Rynmoriath rips control out of my grasp and dives. The rush of air as we pick up speed sends a thrill through me. She grabs a goat in her talons, biting down to end its life quickly. We land, and I learn what kind of dried meat has been giving me sustenance on my walk. Another two goats leaves us ready to move on. My dragon sets us to hover, smelling the air for a likely direction. We catch the scent of many dragons on the wind and turn into it.

It's time to show Darac exactly why he's right to fear me. Rynmoriath approves of that thought with a small chuff. The green and gray hills speed by far beneath us, nothing but a blur in our hurry. The more we fly, the greater the scent grows. I allow Rynmoriath to keep the lead, trusting her to know more when it comes to following instinct and sense than I do.

When it seems like we're getting close, she banks to the right. My mind turns to confusion because we no longer close in on the smells of the coming battle. Still, I let her do as she feels is best, riding along in the back of her mind like she's been doing with me. She trusts me. Now it's my turn to trust her. An overwhelming sense of affection overwhelms me. My dragon approves of my thoughts.

We turn again, swinging around to come back up north. As she stops to hover, I praise her for how smart she is. Ahead of us is the army. My heart skips a beat at the sight of how much smaller the rebel group is. A wyvern that I make out to be Darac hovers in front of the larger army. I know what he's about to do.

We can't let it end like that.

Rynmoriath roars agreement and propels us forward with frantic beats of our wings. It's time to show the enemy what the prophesied red dragon is capable of. Silver fire forms in front of the tyrant, ready to decimate his enemies. I roar again, throwing a magical shield in front of the flames. They blow back the way they come. While Darac frantically tries to stop the power that's now reflected back at him, I unleash a bellyful of flames onto the army still waiting on the ground. Those in the sky are consumed by sliver fire while those on the ground suffer from orange.

I pull into the sky and turn back to the rebels, flying low over them as they scream triumph at my appearance. I'm happy to spot Nova and Dyne in the chaos of shifting warriors and humans. The battle has started with me throwing the first strike. It's time to end this.

Wyverns and drakes take to the sky while wyrms scurry and slither over the hills. I let the others take on what they can, focusing on keeping the silver flames away from my people. I can smell the increased frustration from Darac with every block. A few flames get through, but my enchanted armor deflects most of the damage.

Triumph isn't possible with how badly we're outnumbered. Someone hits me from the side. I roar my fury as the most recent shield is cast wide. Darac is careful to only send small blasts at a time, or the entire world would be burning right now. The wyvern clinging to me pins a wing. The other does its best to slow our fall. My jaws snap back.

While I miss anything substantial, I do end up with a mouthful of small feathers from its wings.

My clingy adversary hisses in pain but doesn't let go. Despite the efforts of my free wing, the ground is coming too fast. Fire would move the annoying clinger, but I can't guarantee it won't hit someone else.

A black blur flies into us, ripping the wyvern off me. I catch Nova's scent and send her a thank you. I feel her approval as the claws of my enemy rake across my scales, thankfully missing my wings. As I correct my fall, I grab an enemy wyrm to drag back into the sky. The wingless dragon hisses and snaps at me, catching nothing but air. I fly a little over the enemy army and drop the long, serpentine dragon, turning away without watching it land on those still waiting for a chance to join the fray.

Silver fire comes for my face, making me quickly turn. It won't hurt me. It might make it hard to see where I'm going. Another ribbon of unnatural flames shoots my way. I throw up a shield at the last second. Darac screeches and flies up, his dark blue wyvern gaining height quickly. This is something I've been told over and over; wyverns are fast. Dyne told me that I will have a size advantage. Speed is where the enemy will prevail. Since they're mostly wings, it makes sense they'd be faster.

Not that I'm much bigger. Dyne would have known this if I could shift earlier, but what's done is done. I still can't compete with a dragon that's eighty percent wing. That doesn't stop me from pursuing the evil man gaining more distance between us. How am I supposed to beat someone I can't seem to catch?

Before I can think of an answer to that question, I get hit from both sides at the same time. All wind leaves my lungs, stunning me enough that I fall a little again. I recover just in time to swipe my claws across the face of the drake trying to bite my throat. He roars and pulls away. A wing covers my face.

I'm being hit by two at once. I need to break free. Feathers tickling my nose tell me the second attacker is a wyvern, less impervious to my flames than a drake. Hoping there are no allies in the path of my fire, I let flames burst free. The wyvern screeches and falls, unable to keep its flight with a hole in one wing.

The drake takes my momentary distraction to gain the advantage. He grabs me from behind, pinning my wings to my back and trying to dig his fangs into the back of my neck. He's larger, so breaking free feels like it's impossible. I let magic fill me and burst it outward. This time, my attacker doesn't let go, but he loses his grip enough for me to turn and free my wings.

Blood flows from wounds old and new. Knowing this opponent is strong, I waste no time in digging my claws into his vulnerable belly. He pulls away, sags, then drifts toward the ground. Desire to follow and finish him off is strong, but I have to take down the king. Only I can do that.

My eyes scan the skies, finding the dark blue wyvern again. I know it's him because I can see the shine of the Jeweled Dracon around his neck. It must have been hidden in his shirt while in human form, but there's no way to hide it as a dragon. It's clear that he doesn't take the thing off. His fear of losing is enough to make it make sense.

Darac readies to throw silver fire at a small group. I blast him first. Screeching, he rolls out of my flames and turns to see me. The fury in me propels me faster, and I throw more fire his way, giving him no time to recover. Looking around, Darac must feel the battle is won enough to flee. As the man turns toward the spire in the city of Wyvthin, I realize how little he cares about his people. Only his safety means anything.

This turns my thoughts about the man darker, not that they needed any help. He's a disease, one that weakens his people, and he needs to be eradicated. It's time to fulfill the prophecy and give the people peace. Darac will die today. When I am ready to chase after him, a chilling voice enters my head.

Little rabbit, there you are.

Freezing, I feel like every part of my body is paralyzed but my wings. The familiar fear takes over, making movement impossible. Even after all this time away, he can still do this to me. No matter how hard I fight against the terror halting all muscles, I can't win. I hunch to try to make myself look smaller.

I see you remember me, Delto says into my head as he comes into view. *I was afraid you forgot all the fun we had together.*

He launches himself at me, and I'm not sure if I can do anything to stop him. My tormentor has come to finish what he started.

Chapter Thirty-Eight
Rivalry

THREY

The flowing grasses are slowly overtaken by rocky hills, signaling our move into the Wyvthin region. Dread coils in my belly. I don't want to take part in this war, and if forced, would rather be on the other side. King Darac no longer holds any sort of loyalty from me, even the forced kind he used to. If it wasn't for my father carrying the name artifact with him, I'd be elsewhere right now or rescuing Ryn from the evil man's clutches.

My only hope is that there is some way I can circumvent the power holding me on this course. Right now, my love is probably suffering in the dungeon under the king's spire. Maybe the distraction of the war can give me a way to sneak in to save her. I need to play nice and look for a way to get around my unwilling desire to follow my father's orders.

Our wings carry us quickly, and others join us as we move. The call went out right before we flew, so other Ildracan cities are still catching up. Time is of the essence for all plans, including secret ones. If only my secret plan was formulated in a way to be possible.

It's about time you put your family first, as it should be. My uncle's voice in my head makes me cringe. *We can use your unique brand of immoral fighting.*

Despite my successful attempts to fly apart from my angry uncle, I can't escape his words. All we need to do is think at each other to speak in dragon form. He's not happy about the last 'battle.' My sneaky tactics were needed, but he sees them as a lack of honorable fighting. Honor would force me to lose to a general, so I'd much rather fight in a way that I can win. There's no way I was leading him to Ryn.

There's no honor in following a dragon in secret either, I say back, hoping he doesn't find some way to teach me a lesson in the chaos of battle.

When your actions go against what's good for your lord and family, covert is the only way to stop your stupidity.

And backhanded tactics were the only way to get you off my tail.

When my uncle grows quiet, I find myself happy he becomes bored torturing me. I should have known better. *Where did you meet her?*

I don't know what you're talking about.

I'm not stupid, Threy. I know you go out in search of her every night. That was the only night you tried to shake me. Might as well tell me. It's all over today, so there are no secrets left to hide.

Instead of rising to the bait, I keep quiet. There's no telling what the outcome of today will be, so I refuse to give him any information that may be harmful in the future. I'm sure that they wouldn't be able to find anything from our abandoned nest, but that doesn't mean I'm going to give him any sort of advantage whatsoever.

Maybe I should have your father make you tell us.

My muscles tense at the jab. I refuse to reply. He's trying to goad me into doing or saying something stupid. I know his plan and refuse to follow it. Pushing all threats out of my head, I force myself to focus on what I need to do.

Get to the battleground, find a way to get around the convulsive orders, find my way to the dungeons, and free Ryn. Just the thought of going on a rescue mission takes my breath away. I'm not sure how I'm going to accomplish what I need to if the mere thought of breaking Father's orders creates pain and makes it hard to breathe. There has to be a way.

We're almost there. Get ready to fight, Father says into my head and everyone else's.

My heart skips a beat. We're almost there, and I still have no idea what to do to achieve what I must. Ryn is depending on me. I'm failing her in so many ways. I'm a terrible mate. It's not like we were given a choice, since we didn't know red dragons don't need the ceremony to join together like that.

That's something that I still can't wrap my head around. I'm mated to the woman I love. I've wanted this for so long, and I have it. I've had it before I even knew about it. My chest swells at the thought, feeling the love that I know is there. Even though I can't locate her, I can still feel her. The fact that she's still alive is my only source of hope. I need to keep it that way.

As we crest the next hill, my jaw drops. The battle is already engaged, and the numbers are heart stopping. We pause and survey what's happening. The battlefield is already overcrowded. I wince at how outnumbered the rebels are. Without Ryn, they don't stand a chance.

Unnatural fire randomly spouts out in different directions, leaving streaks of silver in my vision. I'm in awe for a few moments since this is the first time I've seen the Jeweled Dracon used. It's terrifying.

The king is here. He has the power to end all this, so I find myself wondering how the battle started without him blasting the rebels with fire from the Jeweled Dracon. Maybe it began before he could finish stashing Ryn in the dungeon and get out to the fight. That's the only thing that makes sense to me.

How am I going to get to Ryn? The next burst of breathlessness brings a whole new question to the front of my mind. How am I going to break my father's hold over me?

No plan is going to work if my mind and body won't let me implement it. Not that I have a good one, but I'm not willing to give up. My mate needs me. I need to stop failing her. Ryn will be free again, as soon as I figure out all the particulars.

A flash of red grabs my attention in the midst of the chaos in the sky. I push the hope away. There's no way. I'm only seeing what I want to see. If I want to see my red dragon, I have to get to her first, and I'm determined to do so.

Father orders us to the side of the fray, where it's not as thick. Taking a deep breath, I follow his orders. I don't care what he says; I can follow his orders to fight, but I don't have to do it well. Rebel lives are safe from me. This is something I vow.

The dragons in our army hit with excitement. I hold back and look for where I'm least useful. I see a wyvern flying to join an attack where the rebel is already overwhelmed, so I make a point to fly in front of him. The wyvern tries to fly around me, but it's too late to avoid collision. We're thrown into the tangle of scales and wings, disrupting the killing blow about to happen. The distraction allows the rebel to take out one of her attackers and focus on the second.

The third wyvern growls and snaps at me. *Watch where you're going! Your lord should never let someone as incompetent as you come to such a crucial battle.*

I'm sorry. I was focused ahead and didn't see you.

He snarls and snaps again, turning to find someone else to attack. I look behind me to see that the fighting pair is missing. Hoping the rebel won that fight, I examine to see where I can hinder my side's efforts most.

A mass of black scales hits me from behind. I dodge to the side to avoid having my wing crushed. Uncle glances back but continues to the middle of the fray. He won't try to take me down directly. His plan is to distract me enough to weaken me. Who's lacking honor now?

I guess it's still me since I'm sabotaging our side's efforts. At least I have company on the side of trickery. Another flash of red grabs my attention, and I can't discount it this time. My uncle forgotten, I strain for where I swear I saw it. That's not right. He caught her, so there's no way she can be here.

None of my internal arguments work because I see the red again. All thoughts of battle gone, I fly in the direction that will give me answers to my questions. I need to know for sure. Maybe it's a dark orange dragon that my mind is telling me is red. How can she be here? She can't be—unless the king was lying.

Shocked at the possibility, I stop and hover to examine it. It wouldn't be the first falsehood the tyrant used against his own people. King Darac isn't known for fairness. Maybe it was a lie to dishearten the rebels. No, that's not right. Wouldn't they know whether she was caught or not? Maybe it was to discourage others from joining the rebels. That could be. It still doesn't make sense because he has the

Jeweled Dracon to keep everyone in line. Why would he need false information?

More determined than ever, I push forward in search of what my heart hopes to find, but my brain says isn't possible. I have to find out for sure. Is she here? If so, how? The how isn't as important.

I fly past fights, having no interest in engaging in any of them. There it is, the red. I push myself harder and feel my heart stutter, then beat stronger than it was before. There she is. Ryn is here, free and fighting with the rebels.

Right now, she hovers, staring at my brother. By the fear I smell, I know Delto taunts her. He's traumatized her, which is why I always do my best to get between them. She seems to be frozen while Delto grins at her.

When he lunges her way, I react. This isn't me going against Father's orders to fight on his side of the war. This is the culmination of a lifetime of sibling rivalry. This is revenge for all the pain my older brother has caused me and Ryn. It ends now.

I hit him, inches from him connecting with the red dragon. Claws dig into dark green scales deep enough to draw blood. Delto turns on me, lunging for my throat with a growl that can be heard over the noise around us. I push away, flying higher with him following.

This is the last straw, brother. You will die for your insolence against your future lord. My patience is at an end, Delto says, grabbing my tail in his jaws.

I'm pulled down by my tail. Delto lets go and attacks me from behind. His claws dig into my hindquarters, leaving snarls of pain and the scent of blood in the air. I kick out, catching his front legs with my back feet. My opponent jerks away from me, but it doesn't last long.

Hot flame hits me, blocking my view of the sky around us. The green drake slams into me from the side, and we roll through the air.

We fight hard, both landing bites and scratches. Delto gets his fangs around my throat, but I'm able to pull away before he can do deadly damage. My claws digging into his stomach afford me a little space to breathe.

He's bleeding from a bunch of wounds. I'm bleeding from more, and I'm beginning to tire. I barely have time to catch my breath before Delto is on me again. He wasn't lying; he's out for blood and won't stop until the life exits my body. I can't let that happen because I need to protect Ryn.

Agony sears through my wing as Delto tears through the webbing. I'm able to stay in the air, but I no longer have the agility or speed I did. My claws leave lines of blood on his face and scratch into his eye. Roaring, he increases his attacks through the pain, tearing into my other wing and breaking bones in the first.

Somehow, I manage to get him off me. When I realize I can't stay in the air as I am, I understand that he pulled away on purpose to let me fall. Unable to correct my descent, I tumble downward, rolling end over end. Each time I find myself face down, the ground is much closer. There's nothing I can do to even slow my fall.

Threy!

Ryn's scream in my head brings tears to my eyes. At least I get to hear her voice one last time. Delto readies to follow me down, probably to finish me off when I hit the ground. This was always my destiny, to push my oldest brother far enough to make him kill me. There was never any other end for me. Being a general under him was never in the cards because I don't respect him enough. This is the end that has always been meant for me. Darkness takes over when my body hits the ground.

Chapter Thirty-Nine
Body of Fire

RYN

Threy stumbles in the air, having trouble keeping flight with a giant tear in his wing. This is what it takes to shake me from my terrified stupor. Anger overwhelms me. At Delto for hurting Threy. At myself for freezing and getting the love of my life badly injured because of my weakness. When Threy falls, I scream his name.

The fury builds until I can take it no more. Delto readies to follow the falling dragon, and I unleash all the rage I hold for him and myself at the man who may have just killed my mate. The green dragon jerks out of the flames I hit him with before they can do any significant damage. Roaring my anger, I launch myself at the man who has done nothing but torment me since he laid eyes on me.

I channel all the pain and fear into an attack, adding in the emotions I throw at myself for being too weak to take this dragon down. Delto's eyes widen at the sudden change in my demeanor, one of them disadvantaged by a wound that cuts into it. He recovers in time to keep his throat from my jaws. Claws rake my sides, and I realize he's trying to reach my wings to do the same to me as he did to Threy.

Pulling back to keep his claws away from that important part of my new body, I swipe at his face. Delto dodges it, then comes for my throat. A blast of flames deters his strike. Pain sears through me as his jaws clamp down on my foot. He's strong. The strength of a future lord.

Dyne's words about wyverns being faster because of their size remind me that I'm smaller than Delto. It's an advantage I should be able to utilize to some extent, so I tear myself from his fangs and slip from his grasp. I fly higher, getting out of the chaos of the raging battle. The green drake follows me, keeping me in the sight of his good eye. I should be able to use that as well.

Once free, I gather magic and wait until he's close to release it in a pulse like the one that nearly crushed me and Prill at the ward. Delto hisses as he falls back, and I use this momentary distraction to dive for him. My claws dig into his stomach as my fangs pierce his neck. He fights back, but I have too strong of a grip on him. I clamp my jaws harder, ignoring his attempts to reach my vulnerable belly. His squirms do nothing as I bite until I taste a gush of blood.

Panicking, Delto tries to push me away. I hold on until his struggles weaken before I drop him. My enemy from that fateful day in the stable falls like the dead weight that he is. I'm bleeding from many small wounds but nothing deep enough to cause concern. The deepest wound is the fact that I may have gotten Threy killed.

I feel for our bond, finding it and unable to follow it because of Dyne's block. Frustrated, I search for the block within myself and throw all the power I have against it. Rynmoriath helps by strengthening my magic. I can feel her panic bolstering my own.

The block shatters under our frantic attempt to find Threy. He's alive, but he's weak. I follow the feeling that leads me to him. Dyne's voice enters my head. *You have to go for the king.*

I have to find Threy. He's gravely injured because I was too weak to confront Delto. He's on the ground somewhere.

I'll find Threy. The king fled and can't be left to recoup. You're the only one that can withstand him. If you don't, this will all have been for nothing.

Frustrated, I roar into the sky. Threy needs me. The rebellion needs me. Why does everyone have to need me?!

Get the king, Dyne continues. *I promise I will get to Threy and do what I can. You wouldn't be able to help him anyway. I'll take a small group to protect him and watch over his injuries.*

He's right, and my helplessness makes me growl. I send him the direction I feel Threy in. Anger continues to climb, so I turn it on Darac. The man who took everything from me and is trying to do it again. He will know pain like no other. Vengeance will be mine.

Heading toward the city, I'm deterred by a few wyverns that guard the path I need to take to reach the tyrant. I use magic, flames, and claws to knock them out of my path without thinking. My mind remains only on the last task I need to do. Nothing will stop me.

As I close in on the spire in the center of the city, I see Darac's dark blue clinging to the side. Three wyverns fly out to meet me while he clambers inside a small hole above him. I blast the three with fire, but they separate to avoid the flames. Furious, I use my magic to catch one on fire instead. It hisses and screeches, falling in a giant ball of flickering orange.

The other two hit me at the same time, causing me to lose altitude. Sharp beaks peck at my scales hard enough to draw blood. I knock them off of me and use my magic to push them away, hitting one of them before they can recover. He dies quickly, but the other hits me hard and wraps his wings around me. Roaring, I fight against the binds. The wings are too large, and I can't get free.

Looking down, I let a burst of fire out. Burnt feathers fall. Hissing, the wyvern lets go. I manage to stop my fall short of the ground, but he slams into it. I'm on his throat before he can recover.

After I'm sure no one else is going to attack, I fly up to the hole near the top of the moss-covered tower that Darac disappeared into. I may be almost as small as most wyverns, but I'm not as small as him. I find a large hole further down and enter that one. He's not getting away that easily.

Stairs; I need to find stairs. Of course, they're right in the center, spiraling upward. As I start up, I'm attacked again. This time, it's easy to direct my fire without missing because it fills the entire stairway. I keep on the heat, releasing it after a minute to see a crisp lump of scales and feathers lying on the stairs. Wyverns aren't impervious to fire like drakes, so I do this a few more times on the way up.

I feel tired, drained. I've been using my magic so much that if I don't watch how much I use it from now on, I'll be too weak to fight once I reach the top. I'll need to rely on my physical attributes and my fire to get the rest of the way.

Near the top, multiple dragons come my way. This time, drakes are in the mix. This fight might be harder, and I have to remind myself that I can't use my magic. That thought becomes unnecessary when a line of silver fire comes down the stairs. All dragons succumb immediately, and I shake my head at Darac's stupidity. The Jeweled Dracon flames can't hurt me. In his desperation, the coward is taking out any further chance to weaken me before our final confrontation.

Squinting, I continue forward. When I reach the top, I throw up a shield to push the flames back at him, so they stop. The dark blue wyvern stands on his legs, wings spread wide with the claws at the end of them clenching with anger. I can also smell fear, which increases when I throw my fire at him.

Darac dodges. I launch myself at him before he can recover. We tumble across the open room that holds a garish throne. No other furnishings are visible, showing that he wants himself to be the only draw for focus. That ego leaves it open enough to avoid hitting anything in our tumble.

Fangs bite into my shoulder, bringing more pain and blood. I dig my claws into the wings he tries to cover me with. The pain can't be much, but Darac still pulls away with a hiss. He wants to push strength on the people to control them. The only strength available to him is the power of the king and the Jeweled Dracon. He's weak underneath all that.

Darac is no warrior. Neither am I. This should be a decent fight.

One thing he has going for him, he protects his throat at all costs. It changes nothing. He dies today, no matter what I have to do to accomplish it. The idiot throws more silver fire at me, more an annoyance than anything else. I counter with orange flames in his direction.

The wyvern comes at me from the blindness of the heat. I roar and snap at him, getting a mouthful of feathers. His claws scramble over my scales. Darac clings to me like an annoying pest, so I roll. Bones in his wings crunch, causing him to let go and pull away. Webbing tears beneath the feathers. Moving will be a lot harder for him from now on.

He stands on his hind legs and tries to walk toward the stairs in an ill-conceived effort of escape. I stomp my front foot on his tail. Darac stumbles and falls, and I'm on him within seconds, taking the back of his neck in my jaws. My belly fills with fire.

Don't please. I concede, the cowardly king says into my head.

For all you've done against dragon and humankind, your fate is sealed.

Darac begs, but I clamp down harder to open the wounds further. I feel power growing from the amulet around his throat, so I don't hesitate any longer. The fire leaves my belly, entering his veins through the open wounds I still clench my teeth into. He struggles as hot flames enter his body to cook him from the inside out. Claws scratch across the stone floor in his attempt to get away.

Then the screeching starts. It's an ear-piercing shriek that makes me wish I could cover my ears. Still, I don't stop until Darac lies limp beneath me. I roll his body to make sure all life is gone. Smoke pours from his empty eye sockets, nose, and mouth.

My eyes fall to the instrument of destruction on his throat. It's a glass sphere with black smoke swirling within it. Two dragons circle the globe, looking like they're on fire. This is the artifact used to bring an entire kingdom to heel. It holds the power of the god Drakyth within it, one this man exploited. The gift misused by the coward who rules by fear and violence.

I slide a claw under the chain and lift, breaking the neck that's slowly turning to ash. I clasp the chain in my talons, feeling the anger growing. The fact that this small piece of jewelry brought down an entire species and held Sertran in the grip of fear enrages me. The sounds of fighting outside remind me that the battle is still raging, so I make my way down to the nearest entrance I can squeeze through.

Once in the air, I hover for a few moments to look at the fighting that continues. The rebels seem to be losing ground, so I don't waste any more time. I fly above the thickest fighting and roar until I grab the attention of most. Eyes focus on the object dangling from my claws, and the fighting slows until the air is almost quiet.

Darac is dead, I say into all of their minds. *He no longer holds sway over you. Leave now, and you will live. Keep fighting, and I will finish you all off myself.*

The dragons look around to see everyone has stopped fighting to stare. I wave the holy trinket through the air to remind them that I now hold it. A little at a time, dragons slowly leave at the commands of those leading them. The air clears until only the rebels and a few wyverns are left. It seems these ones are not willing to give up after their king died.

That's fine. The anger still courses through me, searching for an outlet. I'll teach them why they should listen to me. Careful to keep the Jeweled Dracon tight in my claws, I set to showing the leftover wyverns that they no longer rule.

Chapter Forty
The End and
the Beginning

RYN

Threy's chest rises and falls. He lives but still hasn't regained consciousness. Worry consumes my every breath, sitting here and waiting for change. Broken bones and cuts are healing as I sit. That doesn't do anything to stop the worry. I've lost so many people in my life that it's hard to hope for a happy ending. Do I deserve the happiness I long for?

Looking at my shaking hands, I continue to debate the answer to that question. All my life has been filled with pain and loss. My family. Friends I've come to care for. Trev. Now, Threy. A happy ending doesn't seem to be in my future, but maybe it's because I don't deserve it. I'm not sure why. It just seems to be a strong possibility. My life is one heart break after another.

I grip Threy's hand in mine. It's still big enough to engulf mine, but it lacks the strength I remember. "Don't be another heartbreak. I need you."

The lack of response almost kills me. I did this. My inability to get over my fear of Delto caused me to freeze. If I would have fought back, Threy wouldn't have had to interfere. I'm a despicable mate.

"He'll be fine," Dyne says from the other side of the curtain. His blue eyes are full of sadness and exhaustion as he peers around the cloth divider.

Straightening from my crouch over Threy, I lean back in my chair and wipe my eyes. "You can't know that for sure."

My father takes a seat on the other side. "He's a dragon. If he was going to die, he would have done it by now."

What Dyne says makes sense, but I can only nod. My fear won't dissipate. I've been through too much already. How can I believe he won't take a turn for the worse?

I glance up, flinching when I see the grief in his blue eyes. When I told him about Trev, he broke down. Guilt overwhelms me again. "I'm sorry."

"You have nothing to apologize for."

"If I would have shifted before Darac—"

"No. Don't complete that sentence. Trev isn't your fault. He was the last of my family before I met your mother, which is one of the reasons it hurts as it does. Even after, he was all I felt I had. Looking after you from a distance didn't help the feeling of loneliness. My grief shouldn't live in your conscience because you didn't cause it. Darac did it, just like he did to the rest of my family. You've avenged him."

More tears fall as I look at Threy. "It doesn't feel like it wasn't my fault."

Dyne sighs and gets up to walk over and wrap his arms around me. "Neither of them would blame you, so you shouldn't either because nothing you did caused any of it."

"Threy only had to fight Delto because I froze. He's here because of my weakness. Trev died when I failed repeatedly to shift. Of course, I could after."

"It was your love for him that enabled that first voluntary shift. I've been thinking about it, and I think it was your strong emotion that brought your dragon out. As for Threy, even if you would have attacked Delto, he would have joined in. Threy loves you and would do whatever necessary to keep you safe."

I want to argue more, but I know he won't hear any of it. No point in wasting my breath. Even if all blame doesn't rest on me, most of it does. My actions could have stopped both. I failed, and the guilt will live with me for the rest of my life.

My fingers brush the stray tears away, so I can change the subject. "Atan? Nova?"

"Your human friend lives. As for Nova, she's in a healing camp. Unfortunately, she was hit by silver fire."

I bite my lip. "How bad?"

"She'll live. Her left side is covered in burns, but she'll live. According to Nova, she'll still fight too, so don't count her out just yet. It's all she talks about."

My heart isn't in my chuckle. That sounds like Nova. I'll have to stop in to see how she is once things calm down. Atan is another matter. Will he be upset if I show up to check on him?

"Casualties?" I ask.

"Most of the rebel forces, but some still survive and many of the lords are asking when they'll need to swear to you."

I jerk up. "Me?"

Panic must show on my face because Dyne holds up his hands. "You defeated the previous king and hold the Jeweled Dracon. Dragon tradition dictates that you take the throne."

"What if I abdicate?"

"Then one of Darac's distant relatives will claim it, and we'll be right back where we started."

"Out of all the possible outcomes, this is the one I didn't think of." Although, I feel dumb for not considering this possibility. "I don't want to rule. I want to live in peace with Threy for the rest of my life. Why can't the prophecy leave me alone?"

"Ryn." The weak voice takes my breath away. I push Dyne and return to my vigil position. Threy's green eyes look at me with relief. I sob.

"I'll speak to you later," Dyne says before he exits.

"Threy, you're alive."

He lifts a weak arm to wipe the tears that don't seem to want to stop. "I'm not leaving without you. It's time for our happily ever after."

"I don't get one. I have to be queen."

"You'll be a great queen."

"I lived as a human for the vast majority of my life. Dragons are not something I understand well enough to command."

Threy kisses my knuckles. "You forget that you have me. I happen to have grown up as a dragon and know them quite well. I'll be by your side through it all. Nothing will separate us again."

Leaning down, I place a kiss on his lips. One strong hand reaches to wrap its fingers in my hair. The kiss is gentle and full of love; just what we both need after everything endured. Our tongues engage in a slow dance, savoring the taste of each other in this moment of peace. I have no doubt the calmness won't last long, so I'll savor it while I can.

Once our kiss ends, I climb into his bed with him to snuggle close. We remain silent, reveling in the simple presence of each other. This is all we need after so much distance and uncertainty. Our love is one thing we can count on. When my stomach grumbling overcomes the sound of his soft snoring, I slip from his arms in search of something to eat.

Outside the area designated for these wounded, I look around. We're inside the spire, near the bottom, and I have no idea which way to head. I grab the attention of a servant walking by. "Excuse me. Where can I find the kitchen?"

The woman stops, her eyes widening with awe. "The red dragon..."

"You don't need to—"

"I'm so sorry, my queen. We've been waiting for you for so long that I forget myself. It's a floor lower; second door on the right as you go down."

"I—"

She scurries away before I can tell her that she doesn't need to apologize. Others look at me, then quickly away. I grimace. This is going to take some getting used to. I'm not someone special. The prophecy doesn't get to dictate who I am. I'm still me.

Sighing, I follow the stairs down and turn into the door indicated. The scents of cooking food engulf me as soon as I enter the short hallway. The first door is the servants' dining area. I find the kitchen in the next one.

Once I'm noticed, the commotion finally stops. Everyone stares at me, and I feel like this may have been a huge mistake. "I am searching for a little snack," I say into the silence.

Panic ensues, causing me to shake my head. A tall man with gray hair walks over. "Your majesty, you should have sent your servant to fetch food for you."

"I don't have a servant."

"Oh, that's terrible. I'll send word that you need some."

"Some? I don't really—"

"Every monarch needs multiple servants. I'll send word. Until then, what would you like?"

For people who want to show me respect, they sure don't let me finish speaking. "I'm not sure. What's available?"

"Oh my. I'll make you something special."

"I don't need—"

"Come this way. There's a private dining area. Rest your feet while I prepare your food. I'll also send a reprimand to the head of staff for not having people to serve you yet."

I sit where he indicates. "It's quite alright. The battle only recently ended, and I was visiting the wounded."

"That's right, the consort mate king. It's understandable, but you still should have heard from a servant about placements. It's inconceivable. I'll send word."

"You know of Threy?"

"Master Dyne told us about your mate while briefing us on the new order. It's pertinent information."

I open my mouth to talk more, but he scurries from the room. My head spins. Is this how my life is going to be now? This is insane. I'm no one special, no matter what everyone else says.

After a short wait, a young woman scurries in. "I'm so sorry, my liege. Our manager got injured in the silver fire on the stairs and isn't expected to be able to return to duty. We are a mess right now.

Someone needs to be appointed in charge. Until then, I'll be more than happy to serve you."

"It's alright. It's pure chaos in here right now. What's your name?"

She blinks her brown eyes while standing straight and pushing her blonde hair behind her ear. "Um, Ranera, my queen."

"Pretty name. You don't need to fear me, Ranera. I will take your help, but I don't want you to scurry and jump around me."

"It's not proper."

I sigh again. "Who is in charge here?"

"You are."

"Then that is my requirement."

Ranera looks nervous, but she nods and mutters ascent as my food arrives. The cook scurries out before I can thank him. It smells divine. Lifting the lid on the tray reveals some sort of stuffed bird breast, potatoes, carrots, and fruit.

"This looks delicious. Do you know what kind of bird this is?" I ask Ranera.

"Rock grouse, my liege. It's a delicacy reserved for royalty because they're extremely hard to catch. That is most likely the cook's special stuffing inside."

"Would you like to try some of it?"

Her eyes go wide. "It's not proper."

I'm about to argue but decide against it. It's best to ease her in slowly. Instead of making her more uncomfortable, I devour an entire meal that melts in my mouth, surprised by exactly how hungry I am. Standing, I prepare to return to Threy as Ranera takes my dishes to the kitchen.

When she reappears, she says, "A messenger asked for me to show you to the council room."

So much for my plans. "Very well."

Dyne waits for me at the door. My newly appointed servant waits outside while we go in to be met with a bunch of people I don't recognize. I'm introduced to the royal general, who is very polite for being on the side I beat, and various vassals and council members. The remaining rebel leaders are also present. It's a quick meeting, where everyone present swears fealty. It happens so fast that I have to catch my breath as they file out after scheduling my crowning ceremony for five days from now. I barely caught all the planning; it happened so fast.

My father waits back while I stare at the door with wide eyes. "I'm not ready for all of this."

He reaches over and squeezes my hand. "The ceremony will take place at Mt. Firyad. There you will be crowned and the lords will swear fealty to you or be replaced. You'll also need to choose some advisors. You don't have to think about it now. It's been a long day and is getting late."

"That's an understatement. Will you be my advisor?"

"Always. If you want, I can let you meet the remaining fairy dragons who would be the best to lead my people over the next few days. The council will discuss everything in subsequent meetings as well. You'll have the final say in everything."

"I'm not qualified for this."

"You'll have me and the other advisors to lean on. We will help however we can."

I lay my head on the table and take a few deep breaths. "I'm not meant to be queen. I have no idea how to rule. The Jeweled Dracon scares me. What of the king's family?"

"The queen is imprisoned until you can decide what to do with her. They didn't have many children, and all the males died in the battle. As for the Jeweled Dracon, there's more to its power than destruction. It can do a lot of good as well. If you don't wish to use it, you can simply keep it as a talisman to announce your status. What you do with it is up to you. For now, go to your chambers to clean up and rest. You deserve it."

I want to go back to Threy, but I nod. I can at least bathe away the ending of the war. Exiting, I ask Ranera to lead me to a place to sleep. Upon entering the chambers, I grimace. Everything is opulent, shiny, and dark. Black and green are the dominant colors.

"Is this my only choice?" I ask.

"These were King Darac's chambers, my liege. They're yours now as befits your station. I can recruit others to change decor."

"We will need to because I don't want to live in the reminder of him. Not right now though. I need a bath, and there are more important things to attend to."

Ranera leads me to the bathing chamber, where my mouth drops open. This room is tiled in the same blacks and greens as everywhere else. It's lit brightly by light globes all over. The pool is huge, easily five times the size of Threy's.

"If it pleases my queen, I'll move my things into the servants' room while you clean up. Unless you need help, of course."

I shake my head. The last time someone 'helped' me in a room like this, I was almost drowned in scalding water. I'd rather be left alone. "I can take care of this myself. Go ahead and move in."

When she's gone, I take a long, hot soak. Grime darkens the water around me until it floats into the more distant parts of the steaming pool. I climb out, dry with the fluffiest towel I've ever seen, and throw on a silk robe. Threy waits for me on the black leather couch.

"Threy? You're better?" My heart skips a beat.

"Still worn out and sore, but I'm getting there. Your servant retreated to her room when I showed up. Went from being a servant to having one."

Tears blur my vision. "This is too much change too fast. I shouldn't have a servant."

Wincing, he jumps to his feet, which makes me feel guilty for hurting him. Threy rushes over and wraps me in his arms, stroking my hair. "You deserve every good thing you receive, Ryn. Things will die down soon. For now, how about we both get some rest?"

He leads me into a huge bedchamber, closing the door behind us and lifting the expensive black sheets. I slip in, and he climbs over to me from the other side to wrap my aching body in his strong arms. Everything hits me all at once, and I silently cry myself to sleep.

It's completely dark when I wake again. I move, disturbing my mate.

"How are you feeling?" he asks.

"Still tired, but a little better. You?"

"Good."

A strong thumb lifts my chin for a kiss. I slide up his body for better reach, and he groans. I stop. "Did I hurt you?"

Threy surprises me by rolling on top of me. "You did not. The feeling of your delicious body climbing me started something."

He thrusts his hips at me, rubbing his hardness along my inner thigh. Heat immediately courses through me. "Are you healed enough for this?"

"I've been told to take it easy, which I will. Nothing can stop me from taking what is mine right now."

His lips take mine again. We slowly peel our clothes off between kisses, and he moves to my throat. I gasp and press into his touch as his hands find my breasts. Threy nips and suckles his way down my collarbone and over my chest until he takes one of my nipples into his hot mouth.

Moaning, I dig my nails into his shoulders, earning a growl from him. The pressure builds in my core. The place between my legs grows wet.

Soft lips and tongue move down to my belly button, then back up until he can devour my mouth once more. When his tip touches my entrance, I wrap my legs around his hips. He enters me, and I suck in a sharp breath as I stretch around his hard cock.

As promised, Threy is gentle with each thrust, burying his face in my throat. The build up is slow, all the more pleasurable because of it. The heat in both of us rises to meet. Each soft thrust in brings me closer and closer to the edge. When I'm pushed over, I try to keep my cries from disturbing my servant. Threy grunts his release.

He rolls off of me and pulls me back into his arms. "I love you and look forward to showing the world how much."

I nuzzle my face into his chest. "I love you too and look forward to every day with you."

It isn't long until Threy is softly snoring again. What just happened was probably too much for him, which makes me feel a little bad—only a little. I'm not naive enough to think this is the end. The prophecy is fulfilled, but my new life is just beginning. I'm lucky to have the people in my life to help me meet all the challenges to come. No, this isn't the end. There's still more to come. The future is never certain.

Chapter One: Encroaching Destiny

R^{yn} Delicious abs twist as Threy buckles on his sword. I lick my lips, watching every line and hard curve. The flexing of all muscles creates warmth in the pit of my stomach. The fact that memories of me tracing my tongue over them all last night flash in my mind doesn't help. I don't think I'll ever have my fill of staring at the sexy man in front of me.

When he turns, I take the few steps separating us from the closeness I desire. My hands frame his face while his mouth opens beneath mine. Our tongues dance, neither leading, working in perfect partnership that comes from familiarity. His taste builds the fire inside me higher, and I feel his rise to meet it.

My hands move to his neck before falling onto his shoulders to give them a strong squeeze that makes him growl. I don't stop, moving along his collar bone until my fingers find the crease in the center of his chest. Threy doesn't stop me. His lips continue to move against mine. My touch moves lower until both hands find the ends of the V that leads south. I trace them. When I reach for the laces of Threy's pants, he grabs my hands.

I pull away and give him what I hope is an impressive pout. "Don't want me?"

Threy releases a breathless chuckle and leans his forehead against mine. He's so intoxicating. His taste. His touch. His scent. I can't get enough of him.

"I want you more than you can ever understand," he says, emphasizing it by poking my belly with his hard on. "We don't have time. We are going to need to fly to the ceremony soon."

"Something quick then?"

"Nothing ever stays quick with you. Even if we manage quick, we fall into slow right after. When we get home, I'll ravish my queen as much as she'd like."

"She'd like to be ravished now. Your queen commands."

"As your advisor, I have to disagree with your decision."

Scowling, I walk over and plop onto the leather monstrosity of a couch. Threy is my advisor, as is Dyne. I'm supposed to join the council after my coronation ceremony to choose members. My eyes look around. I hate this room, but they won't let me move elsewhere. What's proper and all that. I hate proper. I don't want to stay in this city at all.

"Isn't a queen supposed to get what she wants?" I ask with a sigh.

"It doesn't work like that. Is this only about unlacing my pants?"

"No. It's about everything. I have no idea what I'm doing and seem to have no choice about anything."

"Things will calm soon."

"So you say. Right now, I feel like a petulant child."

"You're acting like one too." Frowning, I pick up a pillow and throw it at him. He catches it and says, "You just proved my point."

"Proves nothing," I respond while ducking to avoid being hit in the face by the incoming fluffy square.

Threy drops down beside me, and I lay with my head in his lap. He strokes my hair, sending calm to me through his touch and our bond. I breathe deep. Rolling over, I turn so I can look up at the man I love more than anything in the world. Not long ago, I thought this was impossible. The future was uncertain, our love jeopardized. Now, he's mine for everyone to see.

If only this giant weight wouldn't be hanging over me.

"I'm not meant to be a queen," I say. "The center of attention makes me nervous. I'd rather hide away."

"That fact that you think that means you are meant for this position. You've shown me that there is so much wrong with my people and given me a new light to view the world in. Now you can show everyone else as well. You'll change the kingdom for the better. The mighty red dragon is meant to wear the crown."

I laugh. "Mighty? I don't think that's a word that fits me."

"You took down the tyrant king."

"Because I had to. Because he was weak. His fear undid him. That doesn't make me strong. It doesn't make me powerful."

Threy puts one of his hands on my stomach, and I reach over to twine my fingers in his. His other hand goes back to stroking my hair. I can see him thinking, probably speechless due to my obstinate denial of greatness. I'm not as special as he thinks I am. None of his arguments and adamant statements to the contrary will change it. This frustrates him.

"Doing what you did because you had to doesn't mean you're not strong," he says after a few moments of silence. "The fact that this isn't what you want, but you're still doing it... that's strength. It's doing what we need to do—fighting to make the world a better place—that makes you mighty. You took on an entire army to end the reign of a tyrant. You risked your life for those you love."

"But I couldn't save all of them," I argue, feeling my lower lip tremble.

My love leans over to bring my fingers to his lips. Planting a gentle kiss on my knuckles, he closes his eyes. This close, I'm engulfed by his scent and heat. I shut my eyelids as well to better enjoy the feel and smell of him. The world feels right when I'm with him. I can almost forget the fact that an entire kingdom depends on me. I can almost ignore the crushing sense of responsibility that weighs me down. I can almost block out the memories of a cousin killed by a psychotic king.

Almost.

"It was war," Threy says after straightening. He runs a strong hand over my hair and squeezes my fingers with the other. "War contains casualties. Many people died to realize the freedom we now have, the freedom you can give us more of. He wouldn't want you wallowing in grief and guilt. There was nothing you could have done to stop it."

Tears sting my eyes. He doesn't understand. No one does. And I don't blame him for it. How can he understand? He wasn't the one that had to watch his cousin killed before his eyes without being able to help. I shifted, but not until after life faded from his eyes. I could have stopped the king if I wasn't such a failure. Trev would still be alive. The final battle and all the death that comes with it wouldn't have been needed. I was too weak.

Threy brushes the tears from my eyes as a knock sounds on the door. My servant, Ranera, rushes to the door. Dyne's entrance makes me jerk upright. This is an embarrassing position to be found in by my father.

When Dyne sees me all flustered, he grins with amusement. Threy chuckles and pulls me close to him with a hand around my hip. I shoot him a look to let him know I don't feel this is appropriate. No matter how hard I try to pull away, I can't shimmy to the side. He only holds me tighter.

My father smirks. "You don't need to be embarrassed, Ryn. Dragons are open with their affections. I'm used to it."

"With your daughter?"

"It's seriously not that big of a deal. It's fine. I'm just glad you're finally happy."

I feel myself deflate. Being a dragon feels so foreign to me. All I'm doing is messing up and acting like a human. I'm a dragon, but I don't know how to be one properly. How am I supposed to rule those I only understand from a human standpoint?

"I can't do this," I mutter.

"Nonsense," Dyne says. "After everything I've seen, no one is more qualified than you. You took on a wyvern with the power of our god behind him, and you did it because you wanted to free everyone from his cruelty. That's pretty impressive."

"I don't know how to be a dragon, so how do I lead them?"

Threy squeezes me tighter. "You are a dragon. You just have to be yourself."

I bite my lip, which leads my love to pulling it from beneath my teeth. "But everyone will know I'm not fit because I don't know the first thing about being a dragon."

"We'll be here to help you as much as you need it."

"That's going to be a lot."

"How often doesn't matter."

"Threy's right," Dyne says. "At the moment though, it's time to leave. I came to fetch you. I'll lead the servants on the ground. You'll fly with the others."

Dyne can't fly because Darac scarred his back with the fire from the Jeweled Dracon, which rests against my chest beneath my shirt. It's not a large necklace, but it feels heavy against my skin, almost making it hard to breathe. Such power is dangerous, as the previous king showed everyone. I don't feel competent enough to wield it.

Threy stands and holds a hand out to me. I push the dark thoughts down, take his hand, and let him lead me out.

The spire of Wyvthin is bustling with activity. Hearing Threy grumble makes me feel better about not liking this place because I know I'm not the only one uncomfortable in a tall tower with stairs at the center.

Outside, I breathe a breath of fresh air. There are too many people crowded in there. It makes it feel stuffy and close. A full entourage awaits us, bowing at my appearance. I hold back my grimace and manage to smile well enough to have it returned.

Prill rushes over. I was happy to see that he made it through the final battle when so many perished. I'm less happy with his next words.

"My queen, it's a long trip, so I want to offer my services. I will guard you with my life."

My lips press into a thin line. Before I can answer, Threy jumps in. "I'll take all the help I can get. Prill, right? She's told me about you."

Prill bows low with his chest puffed out, and I send Threy an annoyed scowl that makes him grin. This man has made it into our conversations about everything that happened while apart. We speak at night until exhaustion pulls us into sleep, making up for all our time apart. Prill has come up multiple times. He knows how I feel.

"Thank you, my king," Prill says.

I turn away to roll my eyes, which makes Threy let out a chuckle. I'd elbow him if everyone wasn't watching. This is going to be a longer trip than I first thought.

The call comes to shift, reminding me that nudity is viewed differently to dragons. I grit my teeth, eternally grateful when Threy steps in front of me to cut off the view to those in front of me without seeming to. He doesn't mind being naked because he's used to it, but he knows it makes me uncomfortable.

Prill takes note of Threy's stance and hurries to stand behind me, facing away and greeting people still entering the area. Two large men give me the semblance of privacy. Yet, I wonder how many people find my discomfort as a weakness. There's no way no one knows what's really going on. To minimize the amount of time I need to spend hiding, I quickly strip and call Rynmoriath forward.

She's happy to comply, no longer content to stay in my head. Both men jump back as my body grows larger, red scales forming on my skin. As soon as I'm done, I get to watch Threy strip. Even in this form, it does things to me.

Rynmoriath rumbles low as we watch the clothes come off our mate. His entire body looks as if it was sculpted by Drakyth. I feel my tail thrash back and forth with a mind of its own. Threy shoots me a smirk before he begins his transformation.

I watch with fascination as copper-colored scales sprout all over his naked body. He grows larger than I am, being the full-blooded drake that he is. As he stretches his large wings, I watch the sunlight glisten off his scales, giving him a golden cast that shines brightly.

Prill is also a drake, a light blue beast of a male. When we launch into the sky, both males stay close to me. I try to ignore the destination and think only of the feeling of the wind blowing over my red scales. It's like the caress of a careful lover, but my mind keeps drifting.

The ground far below us grows rockier the further we fly southwest. I'm about to consider turning around, but that's when I see it. A massive mountain spears the blue sky above. Black rock covers the surface with some green growing through the cracks. The entire air smells of heat and sulfur.

The great mountain consumes the view. The closer we come, the larger it seems. Mt. Firyad. Drakyth's seat of power.

And where destiny plans to consume me.

Map of Sertran

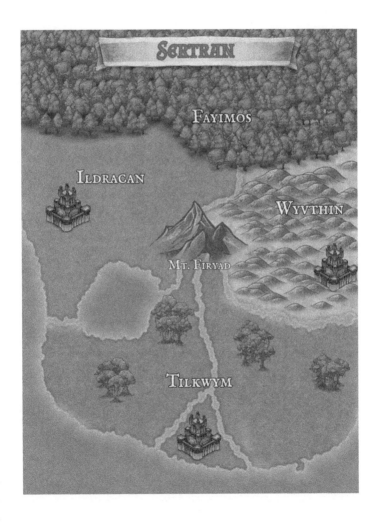

F or more information on Kiera A. Reynolds and upcoming titles, please visit:

Facebook: https://www.facebook.com/kieraareynolds

Instagram: https://instagram.com/kieraareynolds

TikTok: http://tiktok.com/@KieraAReynolds

Newsletter: https://subscribepage.io/IA2DJe

Kiera A. Reynolds can be contacted at kiera@kieraareynolds.com

Milton Keynes UK
Ingram Content Group UK Ltd.
UKHW010635290424
441924UK00005B/274

9 798224 165995